What people are saying about *The Harbinger of Change*:

Harbinger of Change is a real page turner that will keep you up late into the night with anticipation of what happens next. What more can you ask for??!! Timothy Jon Reynolds tells a great story. *Harbinger of Change* is action packed, has a vibrant energy, and is absorbing and complicated. The characters in the book are described with depth, detail and likeability.

—Heather McLaughlin Merath

Riveting, intriguing. Timothy Jon Reynolds immediately draws his readers in with the complexity of the characters and their dilemmas. *The Harbinger of Change* is an unpredictable, twisting tale that kept me on the edge of my seat, often torn between reading faster to see what would happen next, and slowing down to savor each delicious morsel of the story. A very timely, apt novel that leaves the reader wondering ... what if?

—Patricia Whitman

I thoroughly enjoyed reading *The Harbinger of Change*. I am still catching my breath after following this fast-paced adventure around the world. The story took me on a ride as I watched the various pieces fall into place and the story materialize in front of me. I know a good book when I sit there for a half hour after finishing the last page and consider everything that just took place. I am still thinking about this story and am excited to read the next book in the series.

—Ross Kurz

Other Novels from Timothy Jon Reynolds:

Harbinger of Change series

And the Meek Shall Inherit
Without Wrath
Chesed
And Thou Shalt Not

Others Novels

YOCTO

The Meth Chronicles

Rock

The Harbinger of Change

Timothy Jon Reynolds

AMERICAN PRIDE PRESS

Printed in the USA
ISBN 978-0-9909779-5-7

Front cover art and design: Andrei Bat
Editorial consultant: Roy Rasmussen
Editor: Patti Whitman
Interior design and layout: Marian Hartsough

American Pride Press
1344 Disc Drive #372
Sparks, NV 89436

Visit us at www.timothyjonreynolds.com

ONE

Assignment

Dr. Daniel Cooper was making his way out his condominium's parking lot at a very unsafe speed. He was running behind schedule thanks to his damn garrulous neighbor. Cooper's BMW 350i turned the corner off of California onto Mary Avenue at such a high speed that the tires squealed their disapproval. Very uncharacteristic for someone who'd never even had a nosebleed.

Fighting to beat the train, he jammed his accelerator hard like he was trying to merge onto a busy freeway (something he almost never did). Danny loathed taking any chances in his life, which is why he almost always avoided the freeway. He hadn't purchased the car because of its performance, although that was formidable; he had bought it for its high safety rating, as well as the prestige.

Out of fear of earthquakes, Danny lived in a new steel-framed condominium, not even two miles from work. He knew that if he didn't leave by 7:50, he'd catch the train delay. If that happened, he would get to work two minutes late and he would miss her. She was never late. Of the list of a million things he loved about her, her punctuality was as big of a turn-on as her looks. But all were trumped by her essence—there was not one thing on earth that compared to her smell. He bolted up Mary Avenue just as the railway-crossing arm came down in his path.

Slamming the steering wheel, he cursed old Miss Dumont for having snagged him as he was leaving. She lived alone and always tried to lure him over for dinner, dessert, or some other banal encounter that was bound to bore him nearly to death. Daniel always flew by her in the mornings though, with the perfect excuse that he had to go to work. She normally allotted him that space, and it was a good thing because he had a tight schedule to maintain in the mornings.

He looked up and down the tracks. He knew that if he moved now, he could make it. He'd been late three other times and in all instances, he had counted the time the train took to actually get to the crossing. It took thirty-two seconds. The first two times it happened, the impulse was there but the thought of actually driving around the flashing train signal was only a fantasy. The third time, though, the impulse almost turned into action as his obsession to interact with her prior to work was becoming compulsive.

This time, before he could stop himself, Dr. Daniel Cooper stepped on the gas and drove around the crossing arm. He was doing something he had never done in his entire life: He was risking his life in pursuit of a personal passion. Not only that, he wasn't controlling the experiment—another first.

He started around the crossing gates without knowing exactly how much time had elapsed. Albeit the train took thirty-two seconds to reach the intersection, it only took ten for it to come into sight. Dr. Daniel Cooper of Conceptual Laboratories discovered what having a train bearing down on him sounded and felt like. His heart was racing like mad as he skirted out of the situation, swearing to himself that he would never be so foolish again.

Seeing as his foolhardy move had enabled him to gain back some lost time, Daniel thought he might now get lucky and catch her just as she entered the building. On really fortunate days, she'd be wearing boots or some other garment that Security made her remove. That was currently the favorite moment of his day. He carried the thought of those precious moments all the way to bed each night.

It was so unbelievably sensual to watch her slowly remove her garments. His mind drifted to the possibilities as she removed them and placed them into the scanner. Her bare or stocking feet were even more amazing as he got to watch her pad through the detector and then replace her clothes on the other side.

Dr. Daniel Cooper had become an expert on stalking Nancy Chavez, even though she appeared to be totally unaware he had any interest in her at all. She actually worked for him, and lately she had seemed very vulnerable; she'd even opened up to him. Daniel would have to get there in time to make sure he went through security with her, to make sure he started this day exactly as he was envisioning it to go.

Daniel had learned to act nonchalantly whilst the woman that was consuming his every thought partially undressed right next to him every morning. Being next to her in that intimate moment was as close as he'd ever dreamed of, until now . . .

He looked in the rear-view mirror and told himself, "Today's the day." His face was flush with excitement as he pulled up to the security building. The building was squarish and gray with tinted windows. In front of the building was a gigantic black marble boulder and flower garden that encircled it. On either side of the edifice were the gated entrance and exit points.

Daniel pulled up in a hurry, and of course, the car in front of his had some issue, which brought his heightening anxiety to an all-time high. He never had a good day when he didn't get to walk in the door with her, and today of all days, he must!

Finally the fool in front of him found his identification and moved from his path. Within seconds Daniel was through and headed for his parking spot. His spot was a lot closer to the employee entrance than Nancy's, so he still had a chance. Much to his chagrin, he was pulling in just as Nancy was entering the building. Unless he ran on a dead sprint, she would be through security by the time he got there. Not only that, she wasn't alone. She was talking to a brunette Daniel recognized but did not know. *Great, just great. . .*

Daniel meandered through security forlorn, his plan having already gone afoul. He decided to drop the whole thing right there. *Who am I kidding?* They all had tight schedules and he found scant minutes to be around her during the day anyway, but that was the least of his worries. If he didn't figure out how to replicate his predecessor's success in the EMP Net and get things going, then they were either going to get rid of him or cut funding—that meant layoffs in his department.

Nancy was the last person he had hired, so he had to figure this project out and get the funding renewed or she would be the first to go. He would have to abide, as the owner Bill Westinghouse would be watching. The thought of not having his current access to Nancy was not a prospect Daniel wanted to face. Of course, until recently, these crumbs were all he could hope to obtain. *But that's all changed now, hasn't it? Why else would she tell me about the breakup with her boyfriend?*

Daniel got into his office and dove into the work pile on his desk, including his email inbox. By the time he popped his head out to check on his staff, it was lunchtime. In hopes of seeing more of her body, Daniel had tried to loosen things up in his lab by relaxing the dress code, but true to form, Nancy was wearing her lab coat.

She was always covering up her looks, and Daniel loved that and hated it all at the same time. On one hand, no one knew she was a diamond in the rough and one could take one's time worming one's way into her life. On the other hand, he was short on fantasies to live by, and "Hottie in a lab coat" was just plain worn out.

Daniel decided this would be the day; this would be the day he asks her to go to a movie with him. "Just as friends." He was throwing that in there in case his impressions were horribly wrong. It would leave her an avenue to get out of the situation and would not preclude him from her future friendship. If it went wrong he would just put twice the effort into building a platonic relationship with her, to convince her he was no cad.

But if it went right, he could get to spend real time with her, to be able to sit next to her for a whole movie and secretly smell her the whole time. Daniel suddenly worried that she would want to talk about the movie afterward, so he decided to watch it alone first—that way he would be sure to have lots of intellectual insight to spout about the film of choice.

The absolute thrill of this prospect almost made him drop his salad on the floor as he glanced at Nancy eating her lunch. She was perfect. *How could every man not see it?*

Returning to his desk, Daniel was once more drawn into the mundane tasks of running a department. Although the necessity of such tasks were not lost on him, Daniel also knew that if he could just focus on being a scientist, maybe more actual scientific things would get done here at Conceptual. He was waiting for test results from the B group and was pretty excited to see them come through when his stomach rumbled and he looked at the clock. It was time for his constitutional. *Right on time.*

This was one of times during his day that he got a chance to walk past Nancy's office for a quick peek, except today after he got his peek at Nancy, Angela Peterson called him just as he was about to make his right turn to the bathroom. Daniel decided that the intrusion was not all that bad, seeing that after he signed Angela's requisition forms, he could walk back by Nancy's office again.

Dr. Cooper did just that, and even in that brief one-second encounter, his heart swelled and he imagined more—so much more.

As Daniel reached the bathroom, he realized that Angela had kept his pen and that one cannot do the jumble without a pen. Of course, Angela had forgotten a form that he needed to sign, and then had begun blathering some inane small talk that Daniel had no interest in.

Clenching, he headed back to the bathroom. This time he took his eyes off Nancy's area as he passed. He intentionally did this, as he never liked to leave an obvious trail. In one of the rare instances in his life, his gastric need subsided over the delay. After looking in the mirror of the bathroom at his complexion, Daniel washed his hands out of compulsion and headed back to work.

He was now going to cross back over her path again and he surely would avert his eyes to appear preoccupied. He often tried to act like Nancy Chavez was the furthest thing from his mind, as it helped him keep some semblance of control.

As Daniel made his way by, Nancy's office was empty; his trepidation had all been for naught. He made his way past Angela more than a little disgruntled. Daniel had not broken up that routine in years now, yet somehow because of this annoying woman he was left hanging.

He brought his screen back up, and the email he was about to read earlier held some staggering information. He had to read it twice to be sure. This was a major win, and combined with the data in his safe, they were not only going to get their funding renewed, but they were going to be one big step closer to creating an intercontinental ballistic missile shield to protect America. What would surprise most people was, it wasn't going to be done using lasers.

Dr. Daniel Cooper swelled with pride viewing this new data, as it was a fact now. *Imagine that.* He was barking up the wrong tree the whole time, as he was trying to get the power to do this with a Non-Nuclear Electro Magnetic Pulse, which complied with parameters set forth.

Of course a NNEMP has a power output one million times less than the EMP caused by a nuclear detonation, but even so, getting the power to make their desired burst takes energy, a lot of energy. The Russian

"K" project showed the way. Detonate an atomic bomb thirty-five kilometers up and one can short out an entire continent. Daniel was looking to target a much smaller area, but with the same "shorting effect."

Daniel walked across the lab to the hallway that housed his safe room. The hallway was not locked in itself, just an unlocked door, but the two rooms that lay therein surely were. The hallway was off limits to anyone but him. The locked room inside held his project's safe and the laboratory's video storage files. As Daniel was approaching his door he looked up to the left and observed with curiosity that his predecessor's door was slightly ajar.

He'd heard that the man had a breakdown and that was why he left; but Daniel had also heard rumors that people had seen James Haberman after hours. Now he knew that rumor was true. His instinct was to hit the alarm and let security work it out, just to teach everyone involved in this charade that he was not one to trifle with. But with the results he held in his hand, he had to rub it in the face of "The Great James Haberman."

Dr. Daniel Cooper approached the door cautiously, assuming the confrontation would be tempestuous. What lay inside, he had a hard time grasping.

First, Haberman's vault was a monstrosity. It reminded Daniel of a metal version of the monster from *Little Shop of Horrors*.

Second, Nancy was in the room and she was retrieving something from one of the smaller safes that looked like an odd metal flower sticking out of the side of the weirdest master safe mankind had ever seen. What drug James Haberman was on when he thought of this design, Daniel could only guess. Daniel wasn't even aware he had shouted Nancy's name or that he asked how she'd gotten in there.

Under normal conditions, he never would have spoken to her that way, but he was absolutely overloaded with emotion. First his adrenaline had been driven up at finding a way to save her job and then he had found Haberman's door open. He was just on edge.

She didn't even flinch as he yelled, so he assumed he had mostly yelled in his head. He didn't know how she figured out how to get in here, but he knew she was going to be highly thought of, as getting into this room was a quagmire the top brass had been trying to solve for the past year.

Dr. Daniel Cooper reached out to touch Nancy's shoulder for what he hoped would be the first in a lifetime of touching. He was going to marry this woman and he was going to spend a lifetime making her happy.

That's when he saw her turn and plunge the white blade of the ceramic knife she was concealing straight into his chest.

* * *

Bill Westinghouse sat in his chair listening to the two idiots before him and he so badly wanted to pull open his top drawer and plug both these sycophants with the Colt 45 he kept in there. *Hell, I have a permit.* He looked at the two bureaucrats sent here to rattle his cage with disdain. *Jesus, how did I get here?*

He was just a bright boy from Texas, with some family money to spend and a patriotic heart. His initial idea had been simple: he would start Conceptual by accumulating the greatest minds in the science and math world to come and work for him, and then he could spin his family connections to get Department of Defense contracts. After a while though, they had gotten so good, they started fixing other people's bugs too—well, not they; him, James Haberman. James Haberman was the greatest mind of the time and Bill was lucky enough to get him right out of MIT.

Cooper was one of the great minds to come out of the next generation, but Haberman was the best he can remember, and everything was great as the two of them started something that took on a whole other life, with everyone wanting to go after its footprints. Conceptual had been at the top of the world. Then came the breakdown. James Haberman's letter was succinct, and it ended with "I'll be back, all my work is in my safe." Of course it contained a few other pieces of information that they were not happy about. *Oh yeah, that's how I got here.*

"Are you even listening to me, Westinghouse?" Kirk Rogers, Assistant Director of Homeland Security was looking at Bill as if he were something stuck to his shoe. Rogers was a spitting image for Charlton Heston and it was hard to talk to him without daydreaming a little.

"I hear you, Kirk, but what am I to do? We can't take the whole building down for Christ's sake, and he said he'll be back, but it might be a while. I guess we'll just have to have some patience. He was pretty clear that attempting to get into the safe would be questioning his patriotism and would not only be punishable by losing its contents, but probably half the block as well."

"That's asking too much, Westinghouse!"

Bill absorbed Kirk Rogers' last emotionally packed sentence admirably, given his temptation to draw the shiny pistol in his desk and end him. He retorted calmly, "Haberman's final words were, 'best to trust me and wait until I get back,' and Gentlemen, I concur."

Kenneth Beck was a short man compared to Rogers, only five-nine and weighing about a hundred and sixty pounds wet out of the shower. But there was an air about him that suggested he could take men many times his size, and to reach his current position as Assistant Director of the CIA, he had had to do just that more than once.

"Bill, we understand the issues here, but Cooper isn't making the needed progress, and Conceptual must take the next step or our funding for this project is over. Our Field Agents have scoured the planet ten times, and we still have nothing on Haberman's whereabouts. That safe holds the only research we have to resurrect a very vital program, a program that has wide-impacting National interests at its heart. So we're going to give you and your team a month to come up with a solution to resolve this."

Bill Westinghouse replied to Ken Beck in as condescending a voice as he could muster. "A month to undo a safeguard that the greatest mind I've ever known has set, huh, Kenneth? I'll tell you what, we'll open her up to you and your team and see if you can figure it out."

Beck chided, "Didn't you people ever stop to think what would happen to the vaults if one of these people died or disappeared?"

Bill stared, then started. "Gentleman, as you know, safeguards were in place to make sure the doctors didn't really have control of their vaults the way they thought they did. Our problem is Mr. 'Off-the-charts' outsmarted us all and reprogrammed his vault so we have no control, so now we'll have to wait to see what happens. I guess we can put it to the staff once more to see if anyone can come up with an idea, but the reality is, as stated in his letter, any attempt to enter that room or access that safe will be met with dire consequences. Gentlemen, when a man like James Haberman tells you that you are going to have 'dire consequences,' you better be upping your insurance; you're going to need it."

Bill knew that Ken Beck never liked him, mostly because he came from privilege, something he'd heard Beck did not have the pleasure of doing. As a result, there was an animosity that made Beck's composure slip a little. With too much personal inflection he shot out, "For all we know he's working for the Ruskies, Westinghouse! And if he is, you and this whole place are going down, Bill, and no one is going to give a shit that your daddy is a State Senator."

Beck got up abruptly and Rogers followed as he retorted, "You've had a good run, Bill, but we need to get that satellite into its Beta mode, and if that means tying some heavy duty cables around Haberman's safe and lifting it out of here with some Chinook Helicopters, then that's what we'll do. Then we will simply fly that fucker down to Moffett and laser it open. It's up to you Bill, you have one month to produce him or the plan, and then it's our turn."

They both left with an air of haughtiness that they really didn't deserve to have. *Especially Beck, that guy was dumpster sludge.*

Bill's office overlooked the fountains. As he watched them and their entourages get into their respective limos and leave, he couldn't help but think about Haberman. *James sure screwed me up.* He knew he was pushing James too hard. Although James would never admit it, Bill knew that he was putting too much pressure on him and the Satellite Project was James's most aggressive new idea ever.

He just expected James could handle it, that he thrived in that high-pressure world, but apparently that wasn't the case. Now he was being thrown to the lions and he was really wondering, *what in the world is in that safe that could blow up half a block?*

Bill only hoped these guys thought about it long and hard. Even if they breached the vault, the files had security, too. It was a losing bet; and worse, they would be "insulting a great patriot." There was also the human element. It was in his personnel file. James Haberman did not like to lose at anything—ever. His chess playing was legendary when he was growing up, and many had him slated as the next Bobby Fisher. He was always a ferocious competitor, and it didn't surprise Bill that James didn't want anyone touching his work.

Actually, it kind of showed that he was serious about coming back. *Jesus Christ, I hope these idiots come to their senses before a lot of great work is lost.* As he looked at the last of the Government Boys leave, he realized that the good old days were gone, and he was one step away from being unemployed, or worse, **under indictment.** He needed a break. His stomach rumbled and he had a thought about where to head for lunch and who he would call to join him.

* * *

As Dr. Cooper stared at her, transfixed in a stare of death, his eyes sought answers. Although the blade went directly into his heart, his brain had a brief amount of time to compute one last thought, to formulate a theory, and come to a conclusion. Danny looked at the woman he knew as Nancy Chavez one last time in total confusion. By the look on his face, it was obvious he did not reach resolution to his query before he slid off the end of her knife blade, and made his final descent to the floor.

As his body was in mid-descent, Vera Maldonado had already begun to flash back to the start of her day. Just a few short hours ago, she never would have imagined she could be where she just put herself by killing this man. For two years she had lived and worked in Sunnyvale. Infiltrated as a mole under an alias inside Conceptual Labs, she had been placed there to do one thing: steal the contents of a safe. So for two years she had distracted her mind with exercise or nature in her free time. She could literally be in a Redwood Forest within minutes of her apartment. She found that cathartic these many lonely months. As she closed her door one last time earlier today, she knew she was never coming back.

Vera had sacrificed two years of her life for Pablo and would happily do ten more, for he had saved her. He had shown her that love is not cruel or hard, that love had a soft, caring hand that would always be there for her, and finally, that love didn't want anything in return. That's why it had to be her to do this. She was the only one who loved him enough to do this, the only one with the fortitude to see it through. Vera looked at the felled doctor as emphasis on that proclamation.

Her heart was racing because they were about to make history. Moreover, they were about to change the balance of power in the world in a way no one could see coming. There were going to be so many firsts in what they were doing. The U.S. had been attacked before, but by other world powers, never by two people. This time they were going to be attacked by old Pablo and Vera. Two more common names there never could be. Of course, Pablo was anything but common, and this was the old blindside.

America had endured a lot of tragedy and war in the last couple of hundred years, but this was going to be something different. This was something no one had expected in their worst nightmares, let alone their waking reality.

All she had to do was pull off the front part of a perfectly-made plan. A plan made by the smartest man in the world. Then, Pablo promised the rest would come quickly and the U.S. would never know who or what hit them. While they were shaking down the usual suspects with Russia, China, and half the Arab World, she would simply slip back into South America unnoticed. It was such a beautiful plan, but it took time and connections to get her into Conceptual Labs.

Conceptual Labs was a think tank that employed some of the smartest people in the world. Originally Conceptual stood on their own and just invented new weapons, but after their reputation took hold, they started taking on existing ideas and fine-tuning them; oftentimes increasing payloads, distance, accuracy, and other variables. Conceptual had the highest clearance level among civilian contractors. They were responsible for the Neutron Bomb concept as well as some of the most top-secret germ warfare enhancements known to man. Ones that terrified even the most seasoned warmongers.

Pablo spent two years getting her trained as a technician in his own private school. He fabricated a family history for her. According to the legend he created, she was the sole survivor of a horrific car crash and was raised as a ward of the State. Her dossier came complete with phony school records, teacher reports, friends, neighbors, and even church records from Baptism to First Communion.

Who knows how much money or effort went into this plan? she wondered sometimes. Vera could only guess it to be in the millions, which to Pablo, was nothing. Vera knew that once she closed her door this morning, there was no going back. She had no life in America anyway, as this was a fictitious existence. Her life was with Pablo. She had no remorse for her actions, no feeling of longing to stay in the land of opportunity, keep her job and simply mold into her alias of Nancy Chavez, American Citizen.

America, a place where an orphan could climb to any title she was willing to work for. That thought was the least appealing thing Vera could think of. She missed her Pablito. She was nervous, but more about failing Pablo than anything else. She was determined not to fail him. The day before, she packed her things very carefully and loaded them into her car. Inside her case she packed a new outfit, a blonde wig, glasses, a new passport based on her escape identity, and finally, her running shoes. Using the identity in the bag, Vera was quickly going to become Michelle Fernandez, Sales Rep in the wine industry, traveling to Chile.

Every time Vera had self-doubt, she steadied herself with the thought that the man who had made this all happen had freed her from the shackles of one of the most brutal gangs in all of Brazil. The fact that it happened without a shot being fired or a bomb exploding was troubling enough, but even more bizarre was how the gang actually looked in awe upon this average-looking young man who had just walked in and freed her.

She saw the sadistic way these people lived because she was one of their victims, forced to live among them. They feared little. Her liberation from them was the closest thing to a miracle as she had ever seen in her enslaved lifetime, one where there was absolutely no hope of happiness or a future. Orphaned on the streets of Rio, she was an easy target. Property from the time she was ten years old, and somehow Pablo freed her.

After her rescue, Pablo had showered her in kindness and love, and she learned how to both give and receive love, something that did not come easily to her as she was always waiting for "the catch." Although her nature was to never trust anyone, Pablo had broken down that wall. She learned to love him deeply, and as she did, she learned of his pain, and of his tortured past.

Vera saw the reason for her rescue now. She was not the only victim that would be rescued by this kind and wonderful man as he continued on his path of righteousness. Only now he was looking to save the whole planet at once, not just one soul at a time.

Vera looked around the room. It was just as Pablo described, with even an accurate description of James's safe. James let Pablo in on the secret. When he was in his prime, he would request outlandish things from Bill Westinghouse just to see how far he could get him to jump. The safe, with a style reminiscent of Modern Art, was just one example that Vera knew of. The secret James gave to Pablo was that only one vault of the safe contained anything at all. The whole monstrosity was just pointless subterfuge.

Vera was racking her mind as how to extricate herself from this dilemma. She knew her last thoughts were just serving to distract herself from the unthinkable. Vera's mind drifted to her Pablo. Just thinking about how he would approach this scenario helped her, immensely. Unfortunately, thinking about Pablo also led her mind to wander.

After Pablo saved her, it took a lot of patience on his part to make her anywhere near right in the head. Once Pablo programmed her to be able to live life free of the memories of daily torture, he had created a situation that was designed to set her free. She remembered awakening alone one morning and immediately becoming scared and confused by Pablo's absence. Vera knew right away that she was somewhere unfamiliar, but when she pulled back the curtain she could never have guessed just how far she had traveled the night before.

They had been to Paris three months earlier, so she immediately knew what the tower meant. *Why am I here though?* That's mostly what was swimming through her foggy head. *How much wine did I have last night anyway? Where was Pablo?* She scanned the room and spotted something on a table. It was a briefcase and an envelope. On the envelope was written "Vera."

Shaking, she opened the envelope first, not the briefcase. What it contained, rocked her to her foundation. Pablo had truly set her free. In the briefcase were fifty thousand U.S. dollars. In the envelope there was a bank account number and a statement from the Dexia bank in Zurich. The amount of three million dollars was listed as the last deposit. She was a millionaire! The letter read that if he truly loved her, then he would do this for her. He knew his life is going to be complicated and it would not be fair to her. He wanted her to truly live, enjoy life to the fullest and owe to no one. The letters last words were, "Go out and live life and forget about Pablo Manuel."

Looking at the letter she thought of her Pablo at the time, *oh what a foolish man he was, but his heart was in the right place.* Of course, when she immediately returned to him, he knew that as far as she was concerned, it wasn't about money. It was about loyalty, love, and God's will.

When she volunteered to do this for him, Pablo quickly came around to the realization that she was completely loyal to her man, and he had trusted her unconditionally ever since. Her loyalty was as unquestionable and solid as that of any zealot. Pablo now understood that she found salvation in him, the man who had brought her the two things she never dared to hope for: kindness and love.

Pablo reluctantly accepted the fact that she would die for him, which was a realistically possible outcome of what she had to do now. Vera made Pablo face the fact she was not exactly the jail type, so if it went bad, it was going bad "all the way."

Looking down on the shell that had once housed the life of Dr. Daniel Cooper, Vera remembered her mindset as she backed out of her parking stall earlier that morning. Her mindset was that she intended to do whatever it took to get this done for her savior, and Dr. Cooper dead on the floor was just one more example of how much she loved her Pablo. Switching channels in her mind, she went over the layout of Conceptual Labs' compound one last time.

Conceptual Labs was a futuristic four-story glass building locked in the heart of the Silicon Valley. Although the building was made of glass, it had no opening exterior windows and had only the main entrance, fire exits, and roof exits as its points of entry and exit. It was a beautiful complex though, with an innovative pool as its centerpiece. Inside the pool were several ceramic fountains of dolphins and other aquatic life. It also had spherical objects that hung on bent metal poles over the water. The poles put on a beautiful light show at night and were placed in no order around the fountain plaza, giving the fountain a completely different look than it had in the daytime.

The building facade was a montage of twisted stainless and glass designed to give the effect that one was in the future, but a disjointed future with no symmetry as far as Vera was concerned. The complex itself had a very high razor-wire fence surrounding it and a trench that was fifteen feet deep on the inside of the wire. So driving a car in or out through the fence line was not going to happen.

The fence line looked like a Demilitarized Zone, but it was covered nicely with a large tree line of Eucalyptus, managed to perfection. Just past the outer trench, a huge row of Oleander was planted to camouflage the final outer fence. The front of the complex was controlled by a guard shack and had some special terrorist prevention enhancements.

Any person driving by and not knowing what Conceptual did would never guess some of the world's most hideous weapons and enhancements came from this place, including some of the foremost in laser and EMP technology. That's where Vera worked, in the EMP lab.

Dr. Cooper had spotted her around Conceptual. He was obviously one of the men that Pablo's pheromones had affected, and he happened to be the very man that Vera needed to get inside of James's vault. Vera loathed the man, especially the way he made her call him "Danny" and always undressed her with his eyes. But he was everything she could have hoped for in every other respect. As brilliant as he was, he was no match for her incredible Latin beauty and Pablo's sensory enhancements.

Dr. Cooper had been nerdy, of average height and weight, with unkempt, jet-black hair and black horn-rimmed glasses, straight from the Sixties. He always wore the obligatory short-sleeved, white shirt with a pen in the front pocket, black dress pants, and black dress shoes, every single day.

She, on the other hand, was so gorgeous that she would catch men staring at her wherever she went. At five foot nine and measurements of 36-26-36 to go with her hourglass frame and beautiful straight black hair, she had the keys to the castle. Given all the free time she had, she was always driving out to remote places and running up to ten miles at a time. As a result, she was really in shape. Vera was careful not to be too revealing, though. She covered up her figure a lot, even finding some really non-cute, non-prescription glasses, just to nerd herself up, as she had perfect vision.

At the Christmas party though, she dressed in a very tight dress that molded to her body. Even then she kept it covered up with a coat. That was until she spotted Danny alone at the snack table. She casually strode over and got some celery and carrots and started a light conversation. During that conversation she flapped her full-length coat like a bat's wings while asking him, "Is it hot in here?"

After that night, he was dumb around her. She would use tactics like inadvertently touching him at work or letting her hair fall on him "accidentally." A touch here, a scent there, and Dr. Daniel Cooper was madly in love with Vera almost immediately, but lately, more than ever, as they worked in close proximity on a daily basis. She had been rejecting him for almost a year now, but recently, she came in forlorn. When he asked her why she was upset, she divulged a fake boyfriend breakup story and softened her stance against him. Dr. Cooper was not suspicious at all, but almost surely if she would have allowed his advances to happen early on in their working relationship, it would have raised a red flag.

Relationships with Lab Assistants were not permitted at Conceptual. In fact, there was a laundry list of things employees weren't allowed to do. They weren't allowed to have foreign national friends, or especially lovers. They weren't allowed to have gambling debts, or any debts at all, outside what was considered normal living expenditures. Credit checks were run every six months. Employees weren't allowed to have any kind of convictions, either, not even a DUI.

The security staff controlled the cameras throughout the building, except in the actual labs. There, the doctor in charge controlled the cameras and recordings. Security was so tight in Daniel's sector that even

Conceptual Labs' own security personnel did not have clearance to see what was going on.

Each doctor was in charge of their own lab and also had a room containing a private vault to store their work in at the end of each workday. All hard drives from the tabulation computers and lab cameras were kept in the safe rooms, monitored by numerous security controls. The camera drives were not housed in the project safe, but rather in a separate-locking storage cabinet. Conceptual was a company that took no chances in the espionage field, so the doctors in charge were vetted harder than the President. If one masturbated in seventh grade camp, then they were going to find out about it, if one wanted to become a Project Manager at Conceptual that is. Being an assistant was only slightly less intrusive, and Vera knew that it must have cost Pablo a fortune.

The EMP lab was on the first basement floor. Vera had no idea of how many basement floors there were, because all information at Conceptual was on a "need to know" basis. Workers weren't allowed to talk about their respective projects, but that did not preclude them from talking about each other. That was how Vera had heard that the previous Project Manager was a genius named James Haberman. Apparently the man had cracked under the pressure a couple of years ago. He left and was still on sabbatical. The gossiping workers said that James Haberman was so important that Bill Westinghouse maintained his vault just in case Haberman returned.

Of course Vera knew this information already. It was the reason Pablo had placed her at Conceptual: to steal the contents of James Haberman's safe. The lab workers believed that Dr. Cooper had been unable to get out from Haberman's shadow, and that was why he was such an asshole. Vera knew that one by one, Cooper had changed his staff for one reason or another (the real reason was that they had previously worked for James Haberman), until Vera got an interview for what would prove to be the last position.

She had entered Conceptual at an entry-level position in the Laser Research Division. Pablo had special knowledge of lasers, and it was there he was sure he could get her into Conceptual. The fact their plan had progressed this far, on this track, only a mind like his could have achieved. If everything had gone right today, she would have been in Pablo's arms by tomorrow.

Vera looked at the dead man on the floor and started her own recalculation and tabulation. Management stopped the merry-go-round soon after she was hired. She knew she had him at the interview. She knew she had him up until the moment she plunged the knife into his heart. *That look of betrayal on Danny's face is something I will never forget*, she thought to herself.

The work on Dr. Cooper's last three experiments was hardly a misfire by any means, and a man with less of an ego would have been very proud of himself. Instead, Dr. Cooper was constantly working in the shadow of his predecessor—not in real life because the man was gone, but in his very shallow mind, a competition was going on, and he was losing.

Unbeknown to Conceptual Labs at this time, the design of their office was a veritable fishbowl. Vera was sure that one day they would come to the understanding that making their employees live in a glass house was what afforded her the ability to easily learn about everyone's habits and traits.

The two work shifts were supposed to be slightly staggered, but often that line was blurred when work ran over. Sometimes, they had everyone working all at once, depending on the deadline; but typically, there were four people working at any given time. Most days Dr. Cooper had locked his safe at seven, but sometimes they were there until as late as ten o'clock. Most of those days, Vera saw her coworkers very little, even though they were all housed in glass.

Work schedules were grueling and their department took on the task of trying to restart a project left by none other than the "Great James Haberman." Haberman was the one who perfected the laser that shot down the satellite from the Nevada desert many years ago.

Everyone at Conceptual with the right clearance level knew Haberman's sector was working on the next laser and a special EMP project when he snapped. His absence secretly put the employees at Conceptual into a funk, as everyone was sure they were watching history in the making. Haberman was that good.

Cooper understood the concept, but the project required involving other departments, and he didn't work well with the other project managers. Vera had overheard him mumbling once, "It's bad enough they have to leave Haberman's vault here, but now I have to take input he never had to deal with." Most people learn to shut others out when they were functioning at a high speed, but Pablo had taught her that life was like chess. If a person focuses one-dimensionally, then one will overlook two thirds of the board.

Vera had gathered the information about Dr. Cooper's life and frequently relayed all of his idiosyncrasies to Pablo. Pablo formulated a plan, especially loving Dr. Cooper's predictable, obsessive-compulsive behavior. Pablo taught Vera that all great minds are egocentric and typically display OCD-like behavior. He even brought her to the knowledge that Einstein was a high-functioning autistic. But it didn't take a genius to observe that every day at two-thirty, Dr. Danny Cooper (as he liked to be called) went for a thirteen minute constitutional, a habit that had not been broken in the last year.

As is the norm with most companies, the lunchroom at Conceptual was the epicenter of gossip, and Dr. Cooper was a frequent conversation piece. Vera, a good listener who never gossiped and never said anything negative, was like a sponge. She had absorbed many things, like how Dr. Cooper prided himself on his vegan diet and the regularity it gave him. So he would never have broken his constitutional or he would have had to admit he wasn't perfect.

His regularity was just the thing Pablo needed for his plan. The timing was so thin, but fortunately Danny took exactly thirteen minutes, which was the time Vera needed to do what she needed to do. It did seem a bit strange to have such monumental things come down to one small thing, but Dr. Cooper's precise bathroom routine was what had led to their original plan.

Now she had to have a new one.

TWO

Escape

Pablo sat back and looked out at the noonday sun's oppressive effects on the land. Although he was in an air-conditioned office, he could sense the heat outside just wilting the foliage. He was staying in Guayaquil temporarily, but soon he would move back to the compound near Ibarra. It was really a hacienda like no other, built in the backcountry of Ecuador. He had systematically purchased every other property in a ten-mile radius, under different aliases and blinds of course.

He was neighborless, which was good because the construction never stopped—construction that required dump truck after dump truck of dirt to be hauled away. At last count, they had dug out all four levels and were using their imported workforce to set the facility up. Pablo knew it wouldn't be long before they were operational. His team in Brazil had already started producing key components inside one of his software companies.

Pablo was sitting like "The Thinker" without realizing it, lost deep in thought. *I wonder how it went? How is she?* He had lived with the guilt of this moment for two years now—two years and now it was here, the day of reckoning. The immoral would suffer greatly if she were success-ful. Of course, if she failed, then things will take quite a while longer, as one part of the plan would be altogether useless because the information

19

lay only in James's safe. How far had he come since the simple days?—the days in Otavalo, speaking their native Quichua at the table with his family.

Pablo had six brothers and sisters, with four boys and two girls. He was the seventh child born to José and Delores Manuel. He was not born by some common story, though, as his was exquisite in its uniqueness and destiny.

José had been a Master Roofer. Delores had worked at the market, weaving textiles for the tourists and locals. Their life was uncomplicated, filled with children and laughter and love after many hard hours of work. That was until a carnival came to town and José talked Delores into seeing the *Adivina*. It was a move that his father wished he could take back a thousand times.

The woman was very, very old and she was hunched over the table when they walked in. She wore a full-length wool coat and an old blue scarf over her shockingly-white hair. Her eyes bulged as if someone were choking her, and the lines on her face were like the driest desert on the planet, looking so dry it appeared as if they would crumble and break if she moved her mouth to speak.

Delores was immediately terrified and mesmerized by this woman. The old woman had grabbed her hands and looked at her deeply in the eyes, as if in shock. Then she had let go and stared at her for a long time. Finally she had said, speaking in a semi-trance, "You have six children." Delores could only nod, so she did. "But what you don't know is there is going to be a seventh. Not just any child, I know this is hard to believe, but this child will change the earth. He will move mountains, but be warned, he must be guided carefully. Left to his own devices, he could become very dangerous and misguided."

When they started, the old woman had an air of pomposity that could be called hubris, for she had the inside deal, she knew the cards, she was in control. Delores noticed a new look on her face after the hand grab. It wasn't necessarily fear, it was more like she was overwhelmed at what she'd seen, like it was too much for God to hand her.

His mother had heard what she had wanted to hear, though, and soon she forgot the look of true foreboding from the old woman. For many months after that she was the happiest person in the world; but then she miscarried, and miscarried again. Finally, at the doctor's office, she got the news that her uterus was too weak to support a baby. The depression Delores suffered at that news lasted weeks; she couldn't accept that the prophecy would not be fulfilled. There was no way to tell her that there was no prophecy, and that the lady was just an actor of sorts, who guessed about people's lives for money. The aftermath of the news was affecting their marriage and testing their love.

One day José came home to hear something he had not heard in a long time. His wife was singing the lullaby, "Dormite mi Niño." She was doing the dishes and she was singing. He had asked what the occasion was. She announced that she was three months pregnant!

"But the doctors?!" he had said.

She had put her fingers over his lips and said, "Stop getting in the way of destiny with questions and doctors, José, and hand me that towel."

Six months later, on October 10, 1990, he was born and named Pablo Jairo Manuel by two very appreciative parents. It had never been lost on him that even his birthday was unique, as he would soon enjoy 10-10-10 as his twentieth birthday. His first years were spent as any child's should be, filled with love, joy, and bonding time with his Mama.

Delores noticed the special things about her child early. Like when he was three, she and her husband were talking about money worries in a way that a child should not have known. But he did and took worry on too. At first they thought he was just parroting them, but when he went to his piggy bank and handed it to his Mama, they began to see that he was not just another child in the line of the Manuel family.

They tried to explain it away by thinking that he must have heard the word "money" or something, but they both knew it was more than a little odd. He was done with picture books by the time he was three and a half and started sounding out words with his sister Jasmine as she was soon starting kindergarten. Soon he surpassed her and was reading at the age of four.

A lot of children develop at different paces, though, and they couldn't point to any specific behavior and say, "That old woman was right." That is, until Pablo was five.

There were different languages spoken at the market: German, French, Portuguese, English, and Spanish. Delores knew the people in different places that spoke these languages. One was a baker, butcher, and so on. By the time he was five, Pablo spoke to all of them in their native tongues and understood what was being said back—not just parroting. Not just words, either, but light conversations, even inflections. The women would always ask her who she knew that spoke their language and Delores would answer, "Only you," and they would laugh and never quite believe her.

At home, Pablo would have to be stopped from doing all his siblings' homework, even before he started school. Delores always had that sentence dancing in her head, "He'll move mountains." He was so far ahead in school that the Principal taught him directly, and by seventh grade he was smarter than the Principal. He had read every book in the school—twice, albeit he memorized them the first time, he was just bored.

One day his uncle showed up, and the two brothers talked for a long time. It was a day that would change his life forever and it was the second part to his amazing story, one that led to him sending Vera to America to extract his mentor's things out of a safe at Conceptual Labs.

Pablo went to leaning back again in the chair. He watched the river flow by outside, waiting the wait that tortures. The kind of wait that one has to endure as the doctors wheel a loved one off for surgery, it's a world that the family members have no control over. One where they have no choices left, where their loved one's immediate future is out of their control. At this point, Pablo could only pray Vera made it out of the San Francisco Bay Area, so that later he might be able to help her.

* * *

Vera's training taught her to be cool in a crisis, but who can really be cool after just ending someone's life? *Jesus, did I really just end someone's life? A shallow turd of a man, but a life nonetheless.* Pablo taught her about nerves and about breathing. If one hyperventilates then the hands shake even more, and it can lead to blackout. She stopped what she was doing and took thirty seconds to get her breathing right. Her hands steadied a little.

Okay, time for Plan B. Her first problem was that she was just supposed to stroll out after work, a hidden compartment in her briefcase as her means of concealment. So just walking out the front door two hours early would be impossible. *Or would it?*

Vera remembered the plans for the room she was standing in. It had laser light sensors, pressure sensors, and heat sensors. The heat sensor was the key, but once she set the alarm, she would have scant minutes until it triggered a lockdown. She remembered from her training that the heat sensor was set at sixty-eight degrees, the same as room temperature. His body would still be higher than that for a while.

She already knew that it was one and a half minutes from her desk to the door via the staircase. Once the security door came down, only Homeland Security could open it again. She had no more time to waste, this was the plan, and there was no time to grab anything other than her keys. She made the sign of the cross over her chest and forehead out of superstition and set the alarm.

For a year they had planned. In the daytime she would study with him—physics, philosophy, art, literature, martial arts. Pablo was a masterful teacher, and his use of many languages when he was teaching made it hard to concentrate, especially when he used Italian. *God, I love him.* At night they practiced her being Nancy Chavez, and although they practiced English whenever possible, they honed it at night. It was amazing how he got her accent to fall away whenever she wanted now, just like he could.

They practiced a myriad of things, including using Google Earth to plan exit routes, last minute ditch routes, and just general memorization. They went over police and Federal Investigation tactics as well as the location and strategies of their safe houses. During her daily runs she found many places that she ran to the highway from, so she knew where to stop her car on the highway and run to safety in a worst-case scenario situation.

Basically, the last four years were done for this moment and it would be this moment that differentiates a champion from second place. She was off the script as of right now, so it would have to be done the hard way.

* * *

Pablo remembered observing his father and uncle talking that day. It had turned out to be a very emotional day, as he was not the only one eavesdropping on this conversation. He had been at the window and he had heard his uncle tell a tale that Pablo would later unravel all the way, almost to its actuality (which was ironic because it was all a lie).

His Uncle Julio was a slick man, and like his brother, he was tall for a Hispanic. He stood five-foot-ten and weighed a good hundred and sixty pounds. Their Papa, Jairo Juan Manuel, had raised the two of them after their mother had died when Julio was very young—victim of the true king of the jungle, the mosquito.

His trade was roofing, so he taught the boys how to roof. We'll, first he had taught his José, as José was his first son by a long shot. José was eighteen and going to work when Julio was just in grade school, so Julio saw the effects of this type of work from the outside.

At fifteen, they started working him when school was on break, and by the time he was seventeen he'd had enough and ran away to Quito. Julio wanted nothing to do with the laborious life of roofing. There was no way to even let him know when his own father died, until he had called months later. Julio believed that there must be an easier way to make money, and he was right yet wrong, both at the same time. Nearly a decade younger than his brother, he had a lot to learn about the evil that lies in men's hearts, the world, and coca.

* * *

Nearly two thirds of the world's cocaine is grown in Peru and most of that is grown in the Upper Huallaga Valley. There it is processed into a cocaine base, where it is flown to Colombia for processing and distribution to the U.S. and Europe. At the epicenter of this trade is the Communist Party of Peru, or as the rest of the world knows them, the Shimmering Way terrorist group.

In the 1920s, José Carlos Montoya started Peru's first Communist movement. His belief was that if one put Marxism-Leninism into action then one would open a "Shimmering Way" to true Communism.

In 1980, Adian Gomez thought that would be a good name for a political organization, and thus the Shimmering Way was born. Their objective was simple: to run out the bourgeois democracy running Peru and replace it with "true Communism." The greater idea was to not stop with Peru. True to that agenda, their philosophy spread to other places in the world.

Like people anywhere on the earth, the Peruvian Communists work with what they have. What they have is the best soil and conditions to grow cocaine in the world, and cocaine equals money.

In 1992, the Peruvian Government captured Gomez, kneecapping the organization. But Luis Santiago Calderón decided to change that fate. He became the leader, and he knew that cocaine was the way to get the money for the work he wanted to get done. Calderón's grandfather had worked for Montoya, and was killed outside a bar in Lima by someone who didn't agree with his ideology.

Luis knew the legend in their neighborhood, as his Padre was left fatherless and was the subject of much cruelty as a result. That was the reason his Padre was so against any kind of life where one stood out. He would roll in his grave if he saw his son go from Private to General in the course of fifteen years. Most parents would have been proud, but not his Padre. He would have been sure this was a sign he was about to die.

His Papa had taught him to keep his head down and stay out of trouble, so Luis was never allowed to fight. His nickname from the other children was *gallina*, but he was no chicken, he was just handcuffed. Luis could still see his father's peaceful face in his casket, a victim of a bad heart, taken when he was just over fifty.

His legend really grew from there, and it revolved around him being so angry, so hostile toward the world. His first day back at school, he had gotten into his first fistfight. A kid that had been bullying him his whole life bullied him no more. The rest of his youth was spent going from one fight to the next until he met Octavio.

Octavio had announced himself as an independent contractor when they had met in a bar in Lima. Luis had been going to this bar for a year, as it was the same bar where his grandfather's life had ended. He had been standing his "angry ground," looking for something he could not define. He couldn't count how many fights, but it was always the same. He would profess his love for the concept of the Shimmering Way and someone would object. Then he would fight that person.

But not that night, that night he met someone who agreed with him and actually did some work for the group. Luis was floored when the man said he could introduce him to some of them. His path was finally set.

In his sixth year, Luis got his moment to rise. They had taken several setbacks from the Army, as the U.S. was coercing the Peruvian Government to go after the growers in the Huallaga Valley. The Americans had also coerced the Ecuadorians into letting them use their air base at Manta for anti-drug operations. The pressure had really been on, and he had been thinking he might soon be joining Gomez in prison.

Then he got the news: he had to go back home to Lima because his mother was having surgery. It was there that his sister told him that his cousin Ignacio had been promoted to Sergeant in a special drug enforcement unit. Sometimes life just happened that way.

He had gone to Ignacio, and thus the arrangement had started. It had started with a few men in the know. It had soon stretched to practically everyone.

The U.S. had placed the Shimmering Way on the list of known terrorist organizations, and had pledged to help the Peruvian Government fight the cocaine trade. The only problem for the U.S. was that most of the Peruvian Military was on Luis' payroll. Planes loaded with cocaine left for Colombia even though the army base was just a few miles away. Nothing was done. The Shimmering Way did not decrease their production: they just got smarter about how they did business.

Not all the cocaine was sent by plane. Some of it was sent by car, some was sent as cargo, and some smugglers employed things as diverse as submarines to move their cargo. Some was simply sent by mules to one of Ecuador's many border cities. With all the heat coming from other countries, sometimes a good old pack mule line got the job done just fine, and was nearly impossible to intercept.

* * *

Julio had made friends after some time in Quito, but they were the type of friends that could either get one killed or make one rich—flip a coin. One thing was for sure: he was one of them now.

He was told they were going to the City of Gualaquiza. He was still processing this information when Francisco handed him a machine gun and asked him if he knew how to use it. All he knew about weapons was that a machine gun was "pretty darn heavy." So he was taken to the basement of the warehouse and shown the range. After a small instruction period, he was allowed to shoot. It took several clips, but soon he was hitting the target with some accuracy. This pleased Francisco. Julio was allowed to go armed, but he didn't dare ask why.

* * *

The walk down the corridor and back into the lab felt like an eternity, mostly because Vera realized that the exterior exit and guard shack would still have to be negotiated *if* she made it out of the building. *Damn, how the hell did it happen? What variable took place that caused this? It must have been some god-awful blown tire situation that just fucking happens. Damn it!* Then she was in the lab; no more time for grousing.

She ducked in and grabbed her keys. But instead of placing them in her ninja-like satchel (which was now was placed across her shoulder for rapid movement), she instead opted to keep them in her nervous hands. There was no need to try to put everything in the briefcase, because according to the new plan, she wouldn't need it.

Her watch told her that thirty seconds had passed, and by now, the alarm in James's vault room was resetting. She exited the lab at a hurried pace. The lab rats she worked with were all in their own underground cubed worlds, oblivious to the changing face of the wider world happening right in front of them. She breached the stairwell door into the main lobby after a spirited stair sprint, which reminded her of something: her work shoes were useless for running.

Immediately in front of her was the bank of glass doors; the security counter was slightly to the left; and the employee exit was still left of that. Employees were required to only use the designated employee door as a means of entering and exiting the building. All employees were inspected every day, both coming and going. Employees were not allowed to exit via the main doors.

* * *

Brian Franklin had seen her a thousand times, and a thousand times he could not believe what a beautiful woman she was. It was so hard to remain professional around her, as she was not only completely intoxicating; she was also so damn nice. *God, I love her.* He wasn't always on the front desk, sometimes he did her security check, and every time he loved it, because he got to soak in her aroma as he inspected her things. Her smell absolutely melted him.

Brian desired her essence and sought it out, but could never quite pinpoint it. The closest he could come was *Ciara.* He seriously thought something was wrong with himself the day he bought that perfume even though he didn't have a woman to put it on. Little did he know that her perfume was invented by the man who masterminded this whole thing, right down to the security guard falling in love with her.

Once Pablo had obtained a unique scent from his greenhouse (some of his orchids could be found nowhere else), he had added the pheromones, and had instructed her how and when to apply this love spell. So every day, whether Brian knew it or not, he was being programmed to want her, to know her every movement, to never stop thinking about her. He had her life timed to the tee. So it was quite mystifying to see her come out of the stairwell and start heading for his desk with what appeared to be a satchel of some kind swung over her shoulder.

His normal defenses were down, of course, or he might have spotted the small trail of blood that she hadn't noticed on her dress. That might have led him to being suspicious when the time was right for suspicion.

* * *

Vera came out of the stairwell with her heart in her throat. Then she saw Brian was at the desk and she drew a breath of relief, because she knew this guard Brian was under her spell. Her charms didn't work on all the guards. She figured some were gay, because even the married ones hit on her, but those few didn't. Some were women too, of course, although one of them was under her spell as well. So she locked eyes with Brian and right away he was tractor-beamed in, and came around the desk to greet her. As she got within five feet from him, he started saying with incredulity, "What are you doing here?"

Then, the hammer fell.

Immediately, the building's alarms started going off, and the seal process began. The steel door slowly shut, as a loud alarm blared and red lights flashed. *Just like in the goddamned movies!* She had one chance. As she approached him, she feigned a look of shock and bewilderment about what was happening. Without warning, her right hand shot out in a backhand chop, hitting Brian in the throat and instantly giving him something more to worry about than the alarm or her presence at a weird time.

Martial arts and self-defense moves were also something Pablo helped her to master. She kept up with her training via video and self-training. The chop was brutal and exact, partially crushing Brian's wind-pipe. As she ran past, she saw the look of absolute shock on his face. He wasn't a stupid man, and she bet that he had it figured out by the time he hit the floor. She wasn't sure he was going to live, though, having felt a sickening crunch with the chop.

* * *

Brian believed this to be his luckiest day ever. He had no idea what she wanted, but this meant he got to see her three times today! He didn't know why, but aside from the satchel, she looked different. As they approached each other, he went to ask her what she was doing here.

Then simultaneously, the Homeland Security Alarm went off and he saw her chop his throat, lightning-quick.

At first he thought it was a joke, because she had the same pleasant smile she always had on. But when the blow struck and it had the immediate impact of a trained martial artist, he knew it was no joke. He went down, and went down quickly. His immediate need was to get air, which suddenly wasn't a given anymore.

Flaying, clutching, scared out of his mind, Brian was completely befuddled by the cacophony of sound and movement of the terribly loud alarm and the rushing personnel. To call his last thirty seconds surreal would have been the understatement of the year. It was the second time in one day that strange phenomena had occurred in the same building. Right before he passed out, he got the most beautiful beaver shot ever, as she deftly penguin-slid right under the steel door like she was in some *Indiana Jones* movie.

Plus she was barefoot, *that's why she looked different,* he was thinking as a choking, terrifying, blackness came. He noticed one last thing before he lost consciousness: a set of keys was lying inside the door—keys that didn't make it out with her.

* * *

As Vera looked into his face, she could see the confusion. Why did Nancy just throat-chop me? Why was the alarm going off? Then she was past him, and the door was halfway down with twenty feet to go. She had already stowed her shoes in the stairwell, realizing that women's work shoes were worthless. Her running shoes were in the car.

She wasn't going to make it at her current pace, so she kicked it into high-gear, and when the timing was right, she slid head first through the opening that was now two feet, at the most. By the time she got to her feet, the door had closed and she was now between the steel door and the bank of glass doors. From her training, she knew that the glass doors were also now locked down and reinforced.

She immediately went to work on the last glass door to the right. Taking off her necklace, Vera opened the locket and removed the tiny foam earplugs inside. The inside lid was a timer and it was counting down from thirty. In the locket was the compound called Octanitrocubana. Pablo said that using it was a calling card. *Whatever that meant?*

He didn't always explain what he meant. Blind faith was what it took to get her here and to get the job done, and she had no problem with blind faith to a man like her Pablo. He warned her that once she activated this locket and stuck it to the doorframe, she should get to the other side quickly, place her earplugs in, and duck and cover. "This is not the Movies," Pablo had told her. "Anyone in proximity of this blast will lose their eardrums, or at the very minimum, their hearing will be obscured by unbearable ringing."

She already knew what to expect because Pablo had decided that she needed to feel the blast too, beforehand. "It's like shooting a gun," he had said. "Once you get past the shock that a contained explosion has gone off in your hand, you learn to harness it. No one masters weapons," he taught her. "We harness them, they're in control, and we must play by their rules or we die. Never forget that."

He had taken her to a quarry that he had purchased. It was the perfect way to test the many weapons he was working on without detection. *God, he was so brilliant.* Vera loved how Pablo saw things that no one else could see, how he really was different.

Then he had shown her how three ounces of something James had taught him to make sounded and felt like when it exploded. The effect of the blast was deafening. It shook her bones. It literally moved her flesh in a sonic wave that was absolutely terrifying and it destroyed a solid block of granite!

When planning the explosion, Pablo had told her that she would be wearing this destructive compound around her neck on her last day of work, and she needed to know what she was dealing with. The explosion the locket created was exactly as she had remembered at the quarry. It blasted a massive hole in what used to be the door frame and glass door.

The debris field was blasted out like a shotgun discharge all the way to the fountain. The facade of the steel security door was blackened, but not breached. She immediately removed the small foam protectors from her ears. Then she bolted along the inside entryway and exited the ruined doorframe of the glass entrance door, being careful not to step on any debris. *That would ruin everything,* she thought.

And then it hit her. *My keys!*

Vera knew she'd had them in her hand when she came up out of the stairwell. *What did I do with them?* Then she remembered. She had placed them in the open pocket of her dress as she was walking up to Brian. She had done it unconsciously when she decided she was going to chop him. So she had stowed them, and now they were gone, probably on the other side of a door a tank couldn't penetrate! *Fuck! Way off the Grid now!*

* * *

Bill Westinghouse was heading to lunch at one of his favorite digs. The place was called Buck's, and it was nestled in the foothills just over Highway 280 above San Carlos. He liked it so much because of its contrast to the area in which it resided. A few miles of rolling hills away, there were houses that were more palatial than residential, and yet there Buck's sat.

With its nondescript roadside building look, it would have almost seemed a cheesy place if one had just walked in off the street and weren't really paying attention. But its theme was anything goes in Americana, as long as it's interesting and fun. There were toys from Cracker Jacks dating all the way back to early 1900s, each stuck and adorned to the walls. There was the scale model sub used in the movie *Das Boot*, sleds that NASA had used to test monkeys, and of course, the Star Wars figures abounded. So there was this odd place that served great food, nestled in one of the richest areas in the world. While eating a hamburger, one could have very well been sitting next to the two gentlemen who scrawled out the idea for Google on a napkin.

Buck's also had this blonde waitress who made Bill feel twenty years younger when she hit on him. Of course he tipped her a twenty for lunch once a week, which might have had something to do with it, but she always had something kind to say. Today, Bill needed it.

She dropped his food, asked how his day was going, and then showed him what the perfect ass walking away looks like.

Halfway through his half Reuben and salad, Sandy Burroughs appeared and sat down, uninvited. Actually, he had been invited. It was the reason Bill had left for lunch today. But nonetheless, Burroughs just sat down without the customary mannerisms.

Sandy was a San Francisco tax-attorney who had been hired by James Haberman to act as an intermediary in case an emergency came up. He was a squat man, in his early sixties with strikingly, gray hair, coke-bottle glasses, and a dull gray suit that should have been retired

in the Sixties. Bill knew that he was also *the* tax lawyer for many a millionaire over on Russian Hill, although his reputation was not supported
by his looks. What Bill didn't know was that Sandy and James's father
had gone to Harvard together.

"Bill, how are you?"

"Not so great, Sandy. I'm afraid I need you to pass a message on to
our friend. It will be short and sweet."

He handed the lawyer a letter. It read, "Sabbatical over. STOP. Time
to click the heels three times. STOP. Wolves are at the door. STOP." He
told Burroughs that aside from its obvious connotations, James would
get the meaning, as it held an inside message for them both. As the man
contemplated the note, Bill could see his little wheels turning.

"I'm under no obligation to deliver this note," Sandy finally retorted.
"I was hired by James for one reason, and one reason alone. He's only
to be contacted if it's a matter of national security. That is the only reason
I am ever to leave a message by our designated method. This is not a
matter of national security. Do you want to elaborate a little more?"

"We worked together for many years. He knows me as well as any
human on earth. Trust me when I say there doesn't have to be any more
words." Bill, like Sandy, was not able to discuss his work, or the fact
that it could become a national security matter rapidly. "Do you really
think I would waste my time bothering to talk to a puke lawyer like
you if it wasn't a matter of national security? Now get your J.C. Penney
suit-buying-ass going and do your job." Bill rose to his full height of
six feet to tower over Burroughs for emphasis. He dropped his lunch
money on the table, not forgetting the usual tip.

Burroughs watched him leave, looked at the bills, and removed ten
dollars from the tip pile. *Over-tipping was an annoying habit.* As he picked
up Bill's leftover sandwich and took a bite, he wondered, *what the hell is
going on?*

Bill left the restaurant more than annoyed at the arrogance of that
little bastard. He felt like delivering a backhanded slap when he rose,
just to make sure that puke got moving expeditiously. He loved the new
sound system he had put in his Hummer and was currently playing
"Runnin' Down a Dream" by Tom Petty at a pretty high volume. He
was listening way too loudly when he cleared security and headed for
his prime parking spot adjacent to the fountain plaza.

As Bill cleared the guard shack, he looked to make sure his parking spot was open. Some wise guy had parked there last week, and when he got back from lunch, he had to park in the handicapped spot. Of course, that should never happen again, as Bill had had what could be referred to as a "bitch fit" on his staff.

It was maybe two football fields to his spot, and he saw it was open, as it should be. He sat and finished the song on volume eight. As Petty was singing the last chorus, Bill felt a major explosion. Simultaneously, he observed a shower of debris blast the zone immediately in front of the fountain plaza. Anyone standing there would have been killed!

He turned his car off quickly and immediately heard what the blaring Tom Petty song had been drowning out: the Homeland Security alarm was sounding. Leaving his keys in the ignition with his car door open, he ran toward the front of the building, gun drawn. It was a job requirement that he always carry his gun. Having all the defense secrets he did, he could become an easy target for a foreign or domestic enemy. Bill always took the approach that he never knew when he might need it, so why not have it?

As he approached the blown-out entrance, he looked at the front and saw an employee he recognized stumble out the mutilated glass doorframe. It was Nancy Chavez, and she was barefoot? *What in God's name is going on?*

Chavez staggered out, obviously stunned by the explosion. She looked around, terrified. She seemed to have a thin purse strapped over her shoulder, but other than that, she was displaying only confused behavior. She saw Bill and called his name: "Bill, help me. I'm hurt!"

He holstered his weapon and immediately ran to her aid, grabbing her, just as she seemed to collapse once he made it there. Bill was holding her close to him, trying to make it to the ornate pool where there were some benches. He started asking, "What happened?" when suddenly, she spun away. She was holding his gun, which was now pointed at him.

* * *

Pablo's office was so huge that it literally took up the whole corner of the second floor. By preference, his office was all glass. Literally everything in his office except the chairs was glass, and his view of the Guaya

River was perfect. He loved to watch the moving water of a river, as it took him back to times where his life still held a thread of family, where they were all playing together, ignorant of the vicious world.

This particular company he owned made ball bearings, and even though he had this office, it was only the second time he had ever been here. The employees were looking terrified upon his arrival, all except his secretary, who really ran the place and was paid handsomely for it. *Well, this will certainly remind them that the owner does have a face.*

He looked in the corner at the suitcase he had purchased earlier. They called it a suitcase in the description, anyway, but it looked more like some cocaine-processing equipment than what it was advertised as.

Pablo's mind wandered, and his thoughts were soon on the past again. Although he never could have known exactly what transpired with Julio, he recreated his uncle's life as much as he could in order to get a better understanding of the truth, and through that knowledge, get some kind of closure.

He let his mind become his uncle's and he relived that day, a day in which a Manuel was involved in a wholesale slaughter—one that triggered this whole madness. His mind was now completely in the past, fused with all the information he had. He created a matrix in his mind about how that day and the following months went for his uncle. With all the information available to him and his ability to never forget facts, Pablo was able to mentally become Julio and try to sort things out.

In one of those scenarios, he pictured Julio sitting back and drinking a *cerveza* (he loved *cerveza*), while watching Francisco's men pack. As predicted by his brother, Julio found himself almost immediately in the company of all the wrong people. But he was not a thief or a drug addict, so one day while performing menial work at the local Mercado, a man he had come to know asked if he wanted to make some real money. The job was to take a package to this guy and bring a package back, no questions asked. So he did it. His compadre paid him a month's salary, and that was it: he was hooked. He suspected that the package was coca, but he really didn't care.

One day he was delivering a package, and the customer took the package without making payment. Julio told his employers what had happened, and was afraid they would take it out on him, as he didn't even fight for it. This particular thief was not the type to tangle with unarmed. They calmly got the story out of him, and he made it to the part he didn't want to tell. He let them know what the man said, although the words crept out of his mouth with much fear, "You know where to find me, if you have the nerve to try."

Amazingly, that was the end of it. Francisco actually apologized to him before he was allowed to leave.

The next day the news was everywhere he went: some gang in Quito had been wiped out in a military-style raid the night before—all of them! Authorities say the raid looked to be carried out in military fashion, but they could not speculate on suspects. He had heard the name of the gang that ripped him off mentioned as the victims of the attack.

Julio knew right then that his employers were not just some street thugs who sold coca. They were some very dangerous people. His conviction of this was reinforced when they armed him with a machine gun and trained him how to use it.

As far as he could tell, their core group was nine people strong. They had many underlings coming and going, but there were nine leaders. And now, all the underlings came to Julio, who they had reassigned. The gang was odd in that they didn't want a street name or notoriety. All they truly seemed to desire was autonomy.

They were wise in ways that street gangs usually weren't. Julio suspected they were all in the military together at one point, especially with the way they saluted their leader occasionally, seemingly without realizing it. It was like a habit one has performed for so long that occasionally, no matter how hard one tries to the contrary, it comes out.

Francisco Zeledon was a majestic-looking man, and he often had a pipe in his mouth, which made him look a lot like a puppet dictator in some banana republic, complete with a Castro beard. But that's where the similarity ended, as he had no designs to run other people's lives. His dreams simply involved a beach, girls, and an unending stream of money and rum. The only problem was, they couldn't get a direct buy with the Shimmering Way and therefore, he could not advance in the ranks to obtain that beach dream.

Quito was becoming more violent, and the government had been under scrutiny to control it. Some of their recent exploits had people talking about a secret army unit. That didn't help, but Francisco insisted there was no way those little Shimmering Way cockroaches were going to get away with blocking their path to riches.

The break they were looking for finally came. They got word of a mule-team (both kinds, man and beast) heading to Gualaquiza. With that, Francisco decided they were going to put themselves on the map. He announced to the group, "If the Shimmering Way Zealots won't sell to us, then we'll take it from them!"

Francisco gave the word to pack up for a trip. They were going to start making their futures, rather than waiting for it to happen. Hell, if they're lucky, maybe they could even blame some of this on their enemies.

* * *

"Give me your car keys, Bill!"

"I don't know where they are," he lied. Her reaction was a bullet that ripped Bill Westinghouse's left knee apart. Not only that, Bill had a.45 caliber weapon, so the impact also threw him to the ground like a linebacker just laid a heavy tackle on him. Lying on the ground, writhing in pain, screaming, he yelled, "What the fuck, Nancy!?"

Vera yelled, "I will ask you again. Where are your car keys, Bill?"

His reply was not immediate, but it was truthful, for he could tell another bullet was coming right away for a wrong answer. He yelled over the alarm, "They're still in my car."

Bill's Hummer was like his ego: overinflated. But right now, she was glad that it was the closest available civilian equivalent to a tank. The person who had designed the guard shack had taken a lot of precautions. As soon as the Homeland Security alarm was triggered, steel poles three feet in diameter shot up out of the exits like the middle blockers on a pinball game. No vehicle of any kind could penetrate it.

The only thing they had forgotten (and Vera was sure they would be fixing this in future) was that the back side of the guard shack had only the standard steel poles that were used in parking lots everywhere to protect things. That was all that was guarding it, and the engineers had only put four of them in, all toward the center. The front of the shack had no poles, but it did have a massive black marble rock that weighed several tons in front, on the ornate lawn.

Vera had assessed long ago that a vehicle on a slightly angled trajectory could circumvent the poles and blast right through the shack itself. On the other side there was an angled gap between the steel bumper and the side rampart of the rock. The only difference now was she had worked it out using her SUV as the model, not this tank.

Plus, in her vehicle, she had her air bags disabled so she could take the impact facing forward. Now she was going to have to do it in reverse in a strange car. *Why not? I can't even see the Grid anymore I'm so far off it!*

She was pretty sure that there was still enough room, even driving this monument to excess. She backed it out and swung it hard toward the entrance, giving it enough gas to get the job done, but not so much as to be out of control, unfortunately for the two guards inside. She lined it up and at the last second shifted her posture correctly to take the impact with her spine straight. There was no time for those inside to react. The Hummer hit the shack at forty miles per hour and vaporized the entire building in an instant. The Hummer swayed and wobbled, but Vera soon righted it. She power-braked and was free after scraping the sides of the known barriers. She left a trail of broken humans and debris as she disappeared into the day.

Two side air bags went off, and the back window shattered. But the bigger problem currently was that her wig, clothes, and ID's were all in her car. She didn't even have shoes!

* * *

Gualaquiza was a typical remote South American village. The inhabitants were mostly what Julio called "Indians." They were simple indigenous people who had learned how to scratch out an existence with what the jungle provided. One of the mules Francisco employed was from this village, and he said that the Shimmering Way used this place as a major hub. No one in this town would speak a word about them though—not only from fear, but also out of respect, for they gave money to schools and orphans.

The news was that the Shimmering Way's mule team would be coming in on April 7, 2003. As Julio suspected, the members of his unit were exceptionally trained. They had arrived on the 5th, but not together. They all had different identities and different reasons for being in town. Julio and Francisco were there to buy gold, as Francisco was a jewelry maker in Quito. Once they had made their first purchase of gold from a local vendor, no one had given them a second look.

Meanwhile, Francisco's trained recon-men were figuring out the trade routes both in and out of Gualaquiza. Once they found the spot, it was a matter of organizing the rendezvous. Julio studied the map, and Francisco's men were very systematic. There were dots on the map indicating where each of his men were to be positioned, selected to maximize destruction and take away any possible cover the enemy might try to obtain. There was also an "X" on the map. It was right in middle of the ravine they chose, and it marked the planned spot of attack. Once the mules reached that spot, all hell was going to break loose.

Francisco's men found the perfect ravine for the job. It had high jungle on both sides and ran deep from the jungle floor, stopping at a tributary. Anyone coming from Peru to Gualaquiza would have no choice but to take this route. It left little in the way of cover for people who became trapped just inside its maw.

Once the water was crossed, the Shimmering Way would enter the bottom of the ravine where it was two hundred yards wide, quickly narrowing to two hundred feet wide at the top. That is where Francisco's unit would attack, some three hundred yards in.

Julio had never killed anyone before, and the thought weighed on him. Sure, he'd been in fights, but carrying tiles up and down ladders all day gave one a certain strength that others might not possess. So all of his fights were short with him ending as the winner, but with fists, not bullets. This was happening way too fast, and he knew this type of behavior wasn't him. He was not a killer.

Sure enough, on April 7, just as their intelligence report indicated, the mule team approached with ten mules and ten men, all with AK-47s slung over their shoulders. They were hard men, as Julio could detect through his field glasses. They were men for hire, mercenaries, and soldiers of fortune. They certainly meant business by the looks of them, but so did Francisco's men. The fight was to be short and sweet, just as anticipated.

Once their enemy entered the bottleneck and arrived at the attack point, Francisco's men attacked with everything they had and wiped them out quickly, allowing no reaction time. It wasn't like the movies at all. From their ten vantage points (nine really as Julio refused to kill), they opened-fire simultaneously. The traffickers never knew what hit them. The men were all dead along with half the mules, in a matter of twenty-five seconds. The other were animals unable to flee, for lack of ability to drag off their dead and tethered brethren, and just belted out a sickening sound that Julio never knew such beasts could make. He found it creepy.

He never fired a shot from his position, and he stayed put when it was time to get down to the bottom of the ravine to reap the rewards. It was better than they could have ever hoped for. The street value of the haul was over "ten million U.S.," he heard Francisco yell.

The mules' bags were emptied and a Hummer was brought in to haul it all away. As they were nearly done loading it, one of the men dropped a bag a little too hard. Francisco called out to "be careful!" He was in the middle of saying that the bags could rupture when half of his head disappeared. A sniper's bullet had ended his sentence, causing an explosion of head mass that drenched the four people in Francisco's immediate vicinity.

After a moment of shock, they all drew their weapons and started to fire into the tree line where they believed the shot came from.

Suddenly, there was another shot, and another head exploded. Actually, not in that order Julio realized, but it just seemed that way, as everything was happening so quickly. Yet, when his mind broke it down, the head actually went first, before the sound.

"Sniper!" yelled a man known as Hector before he made a break for it, up and out of the bottleneck. Another shot rang out, and another red explosion erupted. It appeared that Francisco's men were caught in their own trap. None of them knew where Julio was or that he was even missing. He just had a perfect catbird's seat to the slaughter—twice in one day.

One round after another, there was a shot, a red explosion, and retaliatory fire where the suspected shot came from. Their unit was down to three men. They had been taking cover around the Hummer, but Julio could see that the sniper was moving, simply by the angle of the shots, which meant they were sitting ducks, regardless. Julio wanted to remain a live duck, so he stayed out of the fray.

He could see a plan forming as he observed all three men were talking together. Suddenly, two men ran in different directions. The third man aimed his rifle into the tree line on the ridge. There was a shot, and for the first time, Julio saw someone fall from a non-head shot. It was a kill shot nonetheless, blowing a sickening red spray out the target's chest, leaving a hole that was visible from the back.

The second shot caught the other runner at the top of the bottleneck, a good fifty yards from where he had started, the red splash of the headshot punctuating the kill. The third man had seen the shots. After the second one, he had taken careful aim and smoked out the area of the sniper shot with military expertise, tearing the jungle to pieces with a fusillade of hot metal.

Julio was fairly sure Francisco's man had succeeded in killing the sniper. For five tense minutes, time passed without a shot. The last surviving member of his team appeared to be weighing his options. Julio didn't know who the man was trapped in the ravine, since he was wearing camouflaged face-mesh. But the man had apparently had enough of waiting, and he started to make a crouched move around the front of the Hummer. Then unbelievably, smoke shot out of the bush right in front of Julio. The last man's head exploded.

Out of pure survival instinct, Julio raised his rifle and blew the shit out of the bush with the entire clip on his AKS-762 Chinese assault rifle. The bush fell over the ridge crest and into the ravine. Julio had undoubtedly killed the insurance policy the Shimmering Way put on their shipment. *I guess that never occurred to Francisco,* thought Julio. *Pretty costly oversight,* he thought as he wretched uncontrollably.

THREE

Repercussions

Vera careened out of the remains of the guard shack with a purpose and made her way east. That was just a scent to throw off pursuers though. Her true path was north. She got on Central Expressway and headed toward San Francisco, a place full of mass transit and mass people. It was easier to hide in a place like San Francisco where even the most outrageous disguise would not draw a second look. They also had a drop car there.

There were four "drop cars" stored in different locations. Each was either in a twenty-four hour storage unit or a rent-a-shed. All of them had special safe boxes welded in that contained $50,000 in cash, a credit card, a fake passport, a fake ID, and a gun.

One was in San Francisco, one was in Stockton, one was in San Jose, and the last one was in Santa Cruz. That one was her idea, and it was a crazy, last-chance kind of deal that involved her going through some heavily wooded areas, and then hiking through the backcountry to get to Santa Cruz.

That thought loosened an idea, with the thought of jogging reminding her she needed shoes, desperately. There was a good chance she was going to get discovered driving this obvious-looking tank, and she needed to be able to move on foot if the situation demanded. It was a strength she needed right now, and did not have. She also needed a new car.

She made a left at Oregon and a right turn onto El Camino. Before she knew it, she was pulling into the Stanford Shopping Center.

* * *

Ken Beck and Kirk Rogers were still on the ground at Moffett Airfield in Sunnyvale when the news broke. They took the call together. As soon as they hung up, they burst into individual action. They roused all the troops and sounded all the alarms, concealing their knowledge that this was the worst possible news. Some probable Foreign National had gotten their hands on top-secret, weapons technology of the highest classified level. The very reason they were visiting Westinghouse today wasn't to fret over things they didn't know anything about, but to fret over what they did know about!

Unbeknownst to Westinghouse, they had James Haberman working on some projects that might have been worth losing a block over, if they ever thought there was a real chance of those files being compromised. Now they were fucked. One thing was for sure: they'd rather be anyone in the world other than this Nancy Chavez. There was no rock she was ever going to be able to hide under again. She was going to be the most hunted person in the world.

* * *

Matt Hurst was working another closing shift, and he was tired. Since Jan had been prescribed bed rest for the duration of her pregnancy, his life had been a non-stop, pile of shit. Matt had left Macy's as a Loss Prevention Agent to become the Loss Prevention Manager of a new, posh women's clothing store called *Stor*.

He had been promised the world, as far as what security devices he would be allowed to implement, because the store management had wanted a strong security department. For the most part, they had been true to their word. Matt had a lot of say-so in where certain high-end items were placed, and nothing of any real value was displayed near the exits. He set the price guidelines for sensor tagging and most importantly, he decided where the surveillance cameras would be placed.

They had also been kind with the electronic surveillance tools (his toys), and that made his job so much more fun. The drawback was that they expected the long hours, and didn't much care about his problems at home.

Most people believe that shoplifters account for the majority of a store's losses. However, that isn't actually true. As a matter of fact, at least seventy-five percent of any store's losses are attributed to employee theft. Although he missed catching shoplifters at times (he had people for that now), Matt worked hard and took to working employee cases like a duck to water.

But not tonight, though. Tonight he was doing it all. His closing agent had called off the only night he had low coverage, *of course.*

He had already received two voice messages from Jan. The first was "angry Jan" the other was "whiney Jan." *Augh, if this is what parenthood is really going to be like, then my new mantra needs to be "just shoot me now."* Matt remembered it wasn't always like this. They used to laugh, have fun, and fuck like animals. But ever since she had discovered that she was pregnant, she'd had this kind of blame thing going on, all because the timing wasn't perfect and neither was the protection they used. *What the hell, I'll face the music after my pastrami sandwich from Togo's.*

At six-two, two hundred and twenty pounds, he wasn't much of a salad eater. Despite his big frame, he was quite the accomplished tennis player and was used to hearing the quote, "How the hell do you move that fast?" He unwrapped his sandwich and turned to the monitors. He wasn't always going to do this gig. He had plans to be a homicide detective, and he truly believed that the things he learned at this stage could only help him later.

God, I love Togo's, but the douche bag put freaking mustard on my sandwich. He looked at the message light on his phone and shoved it into his pocket so that he couldn't see it. *Damn it, does it ever get any better?*

When he turned back, he saw her right away—but not as a potential shoplifter. Matt Hurst was looking at a woman who might have been the most beautiful he'd ever seen. She was absolutely stunning.

* * *

Agents Joe Raley and Max Lozida of DHS got the high-priority alerts on their phones simultaneously while they were sitting in the same car pulling out of their Sunnyvale subdivision. The alert had the location of the initial crime reported as the address of a company called Conceptual Laboratories in Sunnyvale. The suspect had now moved off their premises, and was last seen heading south on Central Expressway. Next, their phones buzzed with their orders. They both noted that Rogers himself was in charge of this, and they were to head north via El Camino Real.

Their instructions were to be on the lookout for a Nancy Chavez, who was driving a stolen Hummer owned by Bill Westinghouse, Owner and CEO of Conceptual Labs. Chavez was wanted in the murder of three people and the attempted murder of at least two others. The main story had been suppressed from the mainstream media for now, but that was only a temporary situation.

The word from Rogers was, "we have to find this girl fast!" They were now headed up El Camino Real toward San Francisco, as they were instructed to do in their scenario, eyes peeled.

* * *

Matt found her to be literally breathtaking. He could watch her shop all day. Yet she did seem to be in a bit of a hurry, so he feared that this treat would end all too soon. She also seemed to be hiding something. It was a little voyeuristic he was sure, *but damn, this girl and a pastrami sandwich (even with the horrid mustard) are as good as it gets.*

As she wove her way through the clothing rounders, he saw something that troubled him: she was barefoot. *Now that's interesting,* he thought as he swallowed. *Barefoot huh? Why barefoot?*

Matt considered that perhaps she was one of those "earthy" girls; but he soon concluded she was too clean cut, too well groomed. Maybe her feet hurt, so she took off her shoes? Matt had known many women to do that on occasion. In an effort to remain unbiased, he allowed that she had probably given them to the register girl to hold. The camera followed her silently as she went into the shoe department. *Maybe her shoes were damaged?* Matt kept spinning positive as she made a quick selection of some running shoes and went into the fitting room. The attendant was on break, as usual, whenever Matt needed help.

* * *

Joe was small-talking like he did whenever he got nervous and needed to think. Max was just the opposite, and it made for some tense partner moments at times. This was one of them.

"Joe, pipe it," Max said. "I'm trying to think. You're doing it again."

"Sorry," was Joe's only response. He wasn't. He just moved to mumbling his thoughts and looking out the window. Then he looked down at his smart phone and came up with something new to say, "Looks like Westinghouse was able to show our team on site her car before the ambulance sped him off to emergency surgery. They found an escape identity and her clothes in the car, including her running shoes."

"Okay, Joe, why do you have that look?"

"They also said they found her work shoes in the stairwell."

"Yeah," said Max, annoyed again at the way Joe was dragging out his thought.

"Well, what if she wanted to get to San Fran, like our scenario has it, but she wants to get some shoes first?"

"Joe, she has no money, no shoes, she's scared shitless and you're telling me she's going to break off to go shopping?"

Joe smiled, "Well technically, she would probably be shoplifting. Maybe she saw that movie with the guy in the tower, he sure wished he had shoes."

"You mean *Die Hard?* You're nuts!"

"Well, the next corner is the Stanford Shopping Center, it will take ten minutes to tour the parking lot and then I will be free for you to ridicule at will."

Max knew better than to fight this guy's hunches. Not that many of them turn out to be shit, but Joe was a person that could not be deterred once he was on a path he believed to be righteous. Plus, it was fun to push his buttons when he was wrong.

Both of them being early in their careers, and both being single, they often hung out together after work, much like brothers. A lot of people said they looked like brothers, both being around six feet, with similar weights and both having brown hair. Tonight they had plans to go to the Giants baseball game, which was why they were in civilian clothes. Max turned his left blinker on and merged into the turn lane.

* * *

Matt was getting impatient. Although he knew that the subjects were in there, sometimes it seemingly took years for them to exit the fitting rooms. *There she was.* She was out and wearing a new outfit, but she wasn't carrying her old clothes. *Really? There is no way this girl is stealing, no way!*

If the attendant were there, this would be a no brainer. He would call and have her check the stalls. But with her gone, he would not have time to check because he was working the suspect alone.

She worked her way through some racks of clothing and got into the line, which was about four people long. Once there, she started to wait. Matt was very relieved. Oftentimes, people's odd shopping behavior was just that, odd to the average person or random agent watching. He relaxed and resumed his voyeuristic lunch break, really mesmerized by this woman. *She is so exotic.*

Then he saw it, that quick furtive movement of the eyes that every shoplifter does out of compulsion. They just can't help themselves, and it usually happens right before an action. He just couldn't believe it as she broke off the line and headed for the door not a minute later. The clerk was over-engaged and calling for help.

* * *

Joe just about punched Max's arm right out of the socket when they turned the corner and spotted the Hummer parked in the number one spot at a place called *Stor.*

"No fucking way!" exclaimed Max. "Let's call it in and get the troops here, so we can bring this bitch down!"

Joe slapped his hand off the mic. "Are you kidding me dude? We have a chance to become household names and you're going to call for backup? Really?"

"I hadn't thought of that," Max said.

Joe chastised, "Listen, if we can't take this one chick ourselves, then we should turn in our badges and our man cards right now. Now let's go take this bitch down before she gets some shoes."

* * *

Matt waited to make his move until he saw her just about to exit the east side door, which he noted was the furthest from his office. His stomach growled, and he realized this was not the best time to have just wolfed down half a pastrami sandwich. *Damn, there she goes, so now it's the hundred-yard pastrami dash to get her. Thank you, Agent Charles, for getting a cold.*

In such instances where he was pursuing a shoplifter, Matt had found it faster to exit the door closest to his office and do his sprinting outside the building rather than running through the store, which was often rife with obstacles. It seemed to take forever; but when he rounded the corner of the building, what he encountered in the parking lot was not what he had expected. His perpetrator had now become an apparent victim of an armed robbery at the very least, and probably a kidnapping to boot.

* * *

After the initial elation of being the last man standing, Julio Manuel realized that maybe he wasn't, and he went back into hiding for another ten minutes. Nothing. Not a sound.

Julio decided that nothing risked was nothing gained. He decided to go for the truck, which also happened to be loaded with most of the coca. He moved swiftly, but not in a panic, for nothing good came from panic, although he was suppressing it with all his might as he came down the embankment into the mid-neck area of the bottle. The jungle man lay sprawled, a scoped rifle by his side. *Jesus, that guy moved right in front of me and I never even saw him. I am so lucky to be alive.*

The next scene was straight out of Hell. It was terrifying, with so many headless bodies, and this horrid brain spray everywhere. Coupled with the riddled bodies of the mules everywhere (both the animal and human variety), it was so overwhelming. Julio began to retch uncontrollably again.

Still dry heaving, he got into the Hummer. Unbelievably, it had the keys in it and it started. He thought he saw a shot to disable the engine, but as it turned out, one of the sniper's headshots was through the hood of the jeep.

Before he knew it, Julio was out of the trap that had killed twenty men. *But now what?* Then another thought occurred to him: *Now I'm a killer of men, and my mother and father will never forgive me for sacrificing my place in heaven with them for drug money.* That was a troubling thought. Then he had an idea. *Yes, a good idea at that!* He headed back to Quito, *if I'm going to Hell then I'm going to do it in style.*

* * *

Matt came in hard and fast on the blindside, and nailed assailant number one, who was holding a gun on his female suspect at four feet. The other had a hold of her from behind. Matt hit the man very hard, and they went down, yet the man didn't drop his gun, to Matt's surprise. Now he was in a life-or-death struggle to get control, and his opponent was very strong.

As they quarreled on the ground, Matt observed the other male perpetrator. He had the girl in a choke hold now, with one arm around her neck. His free hand was aiming a gun at Matt's head, trying to get a clear shot.

When Matt saw the gun aimed at him, he had a massive adrenaline surge and rolled over, forcing the suspect he was grappling with to raise his gun up. Then with all his might, Matt forced a shot out by squeezing the culprit's hand with the trigger finger trapped inside the guard.

Joe Raley never knew what hit him. He was dead before he hit the ground.

Max saw the shot erupt from his gun. He grappled with Matt for a second more; then Max Lozida seized control and did what he was trained to do. With a series of deft moves, he disabled Matt to the point where he was able to spin and shoot, which he did without hesitation.

Matt heard and felt the concussion of the shot, but he was still alive. He saw Agent Max Lozida of Homeland Security drop to his knees, his arms moving spasmodically in a way that told Matt he was not alive anymore. Matt confirmed this with one look at his opponent's face, which was missing the right eye.

When the body fell, it revealed his female shoplift suspect. She was holding the second assailant's gun and was lying on her back on the ground. *She saved my life! The only problem is, why is she pointing the gun at me now?*

* * *

Julio got back to base, pulled into their electronically-controlled private yard, and parked the Hummer in the warehouse. He realized that before his group embarked on this grab for power, his brethren had left a calling card in Quito with the impact of a "death squad." The people were terrified of them now. Since he was the organization's face on the streets, no one was going to know that he was not protected anymore.

All he had to do was act the part and he should be able to sell the coca without fear of being ripped off. After all, no one wanted to end up like *Los Pequeños Locos*. He'd heard some of them were even scalped.

True to form, the people bought it hook, line, and sinker. Julio sold the coca in just six months. Then he disappeared, just like that.

He moved to Guayaquil and started a new life a very rich man, a rich man who kept to himself and his concubines. He settled on three.

Pablo came out of his dream-state and wished he could go back and impart one thought into his uncle's head at that time: *Leave the coca and run.*

* * *

Matt didn't have long to shake off the cobwebs before he found out why she was pointing the gun at him. She was now addressing him sternly.

"Where's your car? You're driving me out of here!"

"The fuck I am lady!" The bullet's ricochet was five inches from his right hand on the ground. People had come out of the neighboring stores, but now ran back inside terrified. Matt picked up his hand. It burned from the minute pebbles left from the bullet hitting the asphalt.

"The next shot is through your head and I dig the fucking keys out of your pocket myself!"

"Look lady, what you did here was self-defense. As far as the shoplifting goes, that never happened. You saved my life!"

Vera looked at him as harshly as possible, trying to impart the seriousness of his situation.

"Listen to me: you are my prisoner. If you open your mouth one more time when I didn't ask you to, I will kill you immediately! Do you understand me?"

Matt shook his head in agreement.

"Are you married?"

"Yes," he said, "I never wear my ring at work."

"Good. If you ever want to see your wife again, get up, get your keys out, and get us out of here right now!"

Matt could barely hear her over the ringing in his head. *Damn, guns were loud.* He had heard enough to know he was temporarily screwed though, so he got to his feet and broke for his car, undoing the alarm as they approached. The last two minutes of his life had been so intense and surreal that he could swear this could only happen in a movie.

Vera was making a habit out of suddenly changing lives in ways that could never be undone. She decided on Stockton, since she knew that the international airports were dead. Even with a disguise, things would be so heavily scrutinized that she would stand little chance. Who knew how much footage of her they would choose to release. She commanded him to get to the San Mateo Bridge, warning him that if he tried to pretend that he didn't know where things were, she was going to end him.

Matt thought he detected a Spanish accent just then. *This is getting interesting, once you get past the terror.* He transitioned from Highway 101 to Highway 92 East. Soon he could see the mass of people that was the East Bay from the top span of the bridge. He could also see the road ahead all the way across the Bay. As luck would have it, the normal traffic was nonexistent. They were soon past the Oakland Hills and heading out of immediate Bay Area.

Matt could still not understand the lack of traffic that he was counting on—other than the fact that he was cursed; there was always that...

* * *

Ken Beck and Kirk Rogers arrived at the scene not knowing what to expect. They had heard the initial reports: two dead agents, suspect vehicle recovered. But the suspect got away, possibly with an accomplice, who witnesses say murdered the first agent. All available personnel were in the field now, and the President was going to have to be briefed very soon on exactly what was in that vault. The Palo Alto Police were initially in charge, but soon they were put into supporting roles when the Federal Investigation Units showed up.

Rogers commented, "This is unbelievable, Ken. It really is. Who the hell are they? China? The Russians?"

Beck retorted, "This was certainly too brazen for a superpower, too overt, too much an act of war."

Rogers wanted to believe that. He wanted to believe that the Russians wouldn't get their hands on what was in that vault. As of one hour ago, he was the only person outside of CIA personnel who knew what was inside. Rogers suspected that something was bringing the two of them together, a suspicion reinforced when Beck asked if he wanted to go visit Westinghouse with him.

Even he was shocked to learn the extent of what was in the vault, and what the ramifications would be if America weren't the one to build this electronic space net. The club possessing that information was a small one, and it looked like he had finally joined, which wasn't a good thing at all.

Kirk Rogers approached his agent in charge, "Did we talk to Security here yet?" he asked. "Do we have a video of the parking lot?" His questions were being shot to Jordan Satain, one of Lozida and Raley's after hours drinking mates. "Sorry, Jordan, not trying to be insensitive. You okay?"

"I'm okay, Boss. I'll take time to process this all later. Right now, I just want to get that bitch."

"Okay, good. So what gives on Security?"

"Well, this is a new store, so parking lot cameras weren't going in until next week. The Store Manager says her Loss Prevention Manager was here and he was closing tonight. So maybe he's at lunch."

Rogers looked at Satain and said, "Take me to the Store Manager."

A few minutes later they were in the Loss Prevention Office. There was a half-eaten Togo's sandwich and a drink on the monitor station. The main camera was on the door that she probably would have used to exit. After some trial and error, they were able to play the DVR back and see what they were looking for.

They watched the entire footage twice, and they both came to the same conclusion. When Nancy Chavez walked out that door, Lozida and Raley must have been waiting. Then Hurst must have come upon that situation, misunderstood it as a robbery, and somehow killed one or both of the agents. Hurst, then either left with her, or was taken by her against his will. Incredible!

Rogers asked, "Was this guy possibly part of it?"

Beck thought about that and replied, "Preliminarily, the evidence says no, he's a victim. But with stakes as high as this, we can't make absolutes about anything." He had reached the part that he loathed. It was time to dial in his boss.

Rogers was in his car talking to his boss. Ken Beck had just hung up with his. It was so unjust that in this world he chose to live in, a whole career could be derailed by one bad day or one bad decision, or hell, even one bad phone call. He just had such a phone call and he was sure Rogers was getting the same. He had never heard Bob Thompson so put out with him. Although Thompson would never show his cards to the point of losing composure, Rogers knew the man, and he knew that he was not happy with him. That much he gathered.

Ken Beck vowed at that moment that he was going to kill that traitor bitch, if it was the last thing he ever did. He didn't give a damn about any of the normal rules or what exonerating thing they found out about her in the process of hunting her. He was still going to kill her.

Her defense would just be some lame lawyer jargon like, "She was coerced" or some legal shit like that anyway. Beck knew that she was not coerced and decided that he was going to serve as her judge, jury, and executioner. He would never believe that she was any kind of innocent. That murdering bitch was going to talk before he killed her. *No one fucks with my Country or my career!*

FOUR

Proposals

In the seventh grade, Pablo had a discovery of the mind when he found chess. Chess was an ancient game that had been played for centuries by many, yet only a few had ever reached its highest echelons. One could play the same opponent for a hundred years and never play the exact same game twice.

It was just what Pablo needed—that and access to the Internet. His Principal, Mr. Garcia, was able to give him about two hours a day on the school's office computer, once they had nothing else to teach him. It was a good salve.

Pablo quickly found Yahoo Chess, and his streak was on. He soon reached a rating of over 2,000, which put him in elite company. That elite company, he would soon find out, was mostly people running chess programs against their Yahoo games. Pablo figured this out because on games where he was black and moved second, he dismantled people. But on games where he was white and moved first, they put up a much better fight.

One night, after a hard fought battle, his opponent asked what program he was running and he said, "None." This infuriated his opponent, who refused to let it die, insisting that "everyone here" was a cheater. That was when he figured out he had been beating some of the best chess programs in the world.

Chess drew him in, and he became fascinated with how life often unfolds like a "well-played" game, with the unpredictable unfolding in the face of the predictable. At times a game appeared to be headed in one direction; where it ended up could be an entirely different place.

Like now, for example. Here he sat in this office, waiting to hear what had happened to a plan that he said could not fail based on the facts. Oh sure, there were always variables, but the calculable facts had been very solid.

Now he knew how James felt that day against him. One minute one is confident and in control. The next, one realizes that he has been side-swiped and is powerless to move.

He looked out at the river; the very river his uncle was living on when he met his fate that day. That fate was the reason the ominous object was sitting in his corner. It would be a tool for revenge.

He watched the river and drifted back into his uncle's head, placing the facts together in chronological order. He had compiled the order from his many real-life expeditions into his uncle's past behavior.

* * *

Life was good in Ecuador's capital. Julio was enjoying the good life, even if he had to drink a pint of rum every night just to get to sleep. Even if he still awoke every night with the jungle man in his room, waiting, watching. He could see the man's eyes just as they had looked the day he saw him sprawled out on the jungle floor; looking out of his jungle suit, staring blankly, never knowing what or who just killed him. Just like the jungle man's first victim, Francisco: one second he was there and the next microsecond, he wasn't. Living, then dead; fate decided with the snap of a finger. *What gives men such power?*

According to the concubines, Julio would open the windows and listen to the river when he needed calming, which was every night. He had moved right on the Guaya River in Guayaquil, into the hacienda of his dreams. The house had six bedrooms, a billiard room, an indoor garden, and a maid's quarters. Yet he employed no maid. The three women who lived there did clean, but they all slept in his bed, and cleaning wasn't their specialty. It had the patio Julio always wanted, too, with a pool and hot tub. The pool actually fed right into the indoor garden, but one had to swim under a glass partition to make that happen.

He had all the *panocha* he could ever want and enough rum, weed, and coca for a lifetime. He tried to stay away from the coca, though, it made him loco. So why was he not happy? Wasn't this the life he had chosen? He had wanted to be as far from that backwards-ass place as he could get from the time he was ten. So why was he yearning for something that he hated? *Familia* was the answer, of course, and he knew it.

Then it hit him: the idea that would save his soul and maybe stop the nightmares. He had to make a plan. Then he would get to Otavalo and put something wonderful into motion, something that would benefit the whole world. He sat at his desk and began writing. There was much to do to save his soul.

* * *

The storage unit was in Stockton. Matt saw that it offered twenty-four hour service. He pulled up and punched in a code, and the next second, they were in. The unit was the largest in the complex, and once they arrived, Matt got out and unlocked the padlock with the combination she provided.

He pulled open the roll-up door and couldn't believe what he saw. Inside the unit was a luxury BMW sport utility vehicle. It was silver, with darkly tinted windows. It appeared to be brand new. There was also a workbench, a giant standing toolbox, and a steel locker cabinet, with four lockers and a mirror, as well as the common steel mesh bench seat in front. *What the hell is all this?*

That's when he felt the gun in his back. She took him in and had him pull zip-ties off a shelf on the workbench. Within seconds, he was bound and secured to the bench seat leg, which he noticed was bolted to the floor. *So there goes the plan of picking this up and knocking her out with the whole bench seat.* She quickly swapped cars, taking the BMW out to the street, and parking his Mustang in the shed. When she came back, she went to work immediately.

First, she brought out a radio and got the local news, and she was all over it. For the next thirty minutes she assessed the news. Meanwhile, she altered her looks to the point that even Matt began having a hard time recognizing her. She expertly tucked and clipped her beautiful straight black hair into a crop. Right before his eyes, with one placement of the wig, she was now a blonde. Some eye contacts, and she now had green eyes.

She changed out of the stolen clothes she had obtained from *Stor*, and got into an outfit from one of the lockers. She was even more amazing in underwear. Then she got into her clothes. It was a pantsuit. As she bent over to get into it, she made a stripper-like wiggle move that transfixed Matt in a way he did not expect. He was fully attracted to his abductor. It was an attraction that went beyond fear, not a healthy thing for a man tied to a bench.

The other thing was her smell. *What the hell was up with that intoxicating smell? I really need to get my head screwed on straight. What the hell is wrong with me?* Suddenly he focused on the news, as it was covering their story. "The employees at Conceptual were killed prior to the incident at the Stanford Mall. Police are reporting that the two incidents are definitely related. Police are still looking for *Stor* employee Matt Hurst, who may have been abducted from the scene by Chavez and possible unknown accomplices. His vehicle is currently the point of an intense manhunt, as Chavez is considered armed and extremely dangerous. Anyone with information on Matt Hurst's black 2005 Mustang, with a white racing stripe down the middle, license number…" Matt had heard enough. The jig was up here, as this girl was not getting away. Then he looked at the blonde girl with glasses who was approaching him and he barely recognized her. She had a rag in her hand. Matt resisted, but it was no use, as she covered his face and his world went black.

* * *

The comm light came on, and Homeland Security Director Stan LaRue was live with the President. President Lawrence Caulfield was a patient and gentle man, even though his stature would indicate otherwise. He and Lincoln were now recorded as the two tallest Presidents to date. They would be linked in many other ways too, from geography to demeanor. He had won the election because the good people of Kentucky were sick of Wall Street types and others who would change the structure of capitalism if allowed to do so.

He was a good-old-boy Senator from Kentucky, who had kept his nose clean because he was a good man, not because he thought that one day he might be vetted for the Presidency. He had been raised right, and had also turned out right by nature. Those two don't always go together, much to the chagrin of many a diligent parent.

Lawrence had worked as a Public Defender, and afterward, in private practice he would take on any case pro bono; all anyone had to do was ask. Whatever he had in this life was good enough, and he didn't need more. His college sweetheart and their three kids were all he really needed. That, and some food on the table. He was really that simple.

Thus, special interest folks had little to do with him, and he made few friends on Capitol Hill. Billed as a Democrat, he rarely considered himself partisan, and was often heard saying, "If a person sticks to partisanship to a fault, then they've turned a blind eye to the bigger picture." That bigger picture was what they were supposed to be doing here. They had been hired to see the job got done to the best of their abilities, for the American people, not themselves. Consequently, he was occasionally known to vote outside the party lines if someone else had a good idea, not a popular habit amongst his peers.

The people of Kentucky sure loved him though, mostly because they knew what they had. Word had spread that this man cared, and this man had honor and more than anything, this man loved Kentucky and America. So waste disposal projects were sent away, even though they would have created jobs, because who wants to be known as the guy who allowed toxic dumping? And the list went on of projects that had been rejected by him because they "were not in the best interest of the State." That was not to say Lawrence hadn't been creating jobs, because he had been able to turn stimulus money into a growing Green Economy for his state. Kentucky had become the current leader in solar panel manufacturing in the U.S.

One day, as he was leaving the Hill to go home for winter recess, Lawrence had been approached by a man with a purpose. The man was representing a conglomerate that wanted to talk to him. The man had just started his spiel when Lawrence put his hand up.

"If you know anything about me at all, you will stop right now. I have no interest in hearing your special interest jargon, and I have no interest in entertaining you another second, Sirrah."

As he said this, he brought himself to his full height and used his authoritative, intimidating voice.

Yes, the man being browbeaten had thought, *he will do quite nicely*.

Lawrence Caulfield had looked at the man he would later think of as a mentor, and had asked him, "Why are you smiling?"

The rest was history. He had found a group of people like himself (more like they had found him)—patriots through and through. Together they would make history.

Now he was facing the first crisis of his Presidency.

He addressed his Homeland Security Director. "What's the word, Stan?"

LaRue cleared his throat. "As you know, the incident in California today was more than just a high-tech robbery. It was most likely an act of aggression from a foreign country."

"That's sobering," President Caulfield responded.

"The worst is yet to come, I'm afraid. It looks like we lost Dr. Daniel Cooper of Conceptual Labs in the process of this crime. The other stinger is this: what was stolen out of that safe could not only set the EMP Net Project back for years, it could also be used against us at a later date."

"I see," was the reply. "Continue."

"Well, as you know, Haberman was working on our EMP net, and he was also working on cold fusion lasers. Remember Nevada? He was also the foremost mind in the field of power sources for drones. His work with new battery concepts was as good as it gets. All his data was in that safe."

"So potentially, what they stole could be a serious national threat is what you're saying."

It was a rhetorical question. Stan waited a long time for the President to speak. "What about the kidnap victim, Matt Hurst?"

"Okay, here's the thing. It looks like it could be a legit abduction, but we did find a thread. They both go to the same gym, which is the '24 Hour Fitness' in Mountain View. Logs show they were there at the same times on multiple occasions over the past year.

"That's a pretty big thread, Stan, and too much of a coincidence for my liking. Matter of fact, based on my instincts, there are no coincidences in these types of situations. No, we'll sort it out later, but for now, they're both wanted fugitives."

* * *

Vera brought the BMW back and parked it outside the shed. She had already done her inventory, which included her new identification, money, and, of course, her weapon. *But what about this hombre?* The plan was never to kidnap anyone. She could let him be, and eventually some-one would find him, but most likely he would die in here, as this place was hot.

So what to do? She couldn't trust to take him, as he seemed too capable, especially the way he had handled the guy on the ground and had taken care of her problem in the parking lot. *No, he was too dangerous to take.*

She found his badge, so she knew that he was the Store Detective, and that he had planned to arrest her for shoplifting. His identification read "Matthew Hurst." She found his California Driver's License in his wallet, which had his address and some personal info, but it would have been nice to have his phone. Alas, that was not an option, because she had thrown his phone out over the bridge. Pablo had taught her about cell phone relay towers.

She decided that she would bind him frontward in the back of the SUV. She planned to head out to her destination and call Pablo from one of her disposable phones. There were three phones in the shed, and she was going to burn one to call Pablo. *He'll know what to do, and if it's kill this pendejo and dump his ass in the woods, then that's what I'll do. Too bad though, he's not too bad-looking,* she thought. He looked like one of the 49ers she'd seen on posters everywhere, with his mane of chestnut hair parted down the middle. She broke off her little sexual fantasy and loaded him into the backseat.

Even though she was in shape, she had to use her wits and leverage to get him into the SUV without killing her back. They then started out toward Sacramento.

After about an hour of traveling at a steady 65 miles per hour, the radio stopped playing news and broadcasted something unexpected. The announcer said that there was a message from the President of the United States. That snapped her out of her thoughts, and she focused on what came next.

"Ladies and Gentlemen of the United States of America, I come to you now as the Commander-in-Chief of the Armed Forces, as well as your President and fellow American. I have thought long and hard about the best way to handle this situa-tion, and I have decided not to box out the very people that elected me, the people that can help the most, and that is you.

What I'm calling for is simply for America to turn into an episode of *America's Most Wanted* for the next forty-eight hours. The incident in Sunnyvale, California was more than just a robbery and string of murders. It was an act of high treason at the very least, or an act of war at the most.

"Unfortunately, like 9/11, we don't know who attacked us yet. But we do know that they stole some very important pieces of research and microchips that will not only set us back years in our defense industry, but could be used against us later as well.

"We already know the woman known as Nancy Chavez, was a hostile agent placed into Conceptual Labs for the purpose of espionage. It is not known if she is a foreign or domestic agent, but we now believe that alleged kidnap victim, Matt Hurst, was an accomplice in the crime as well, not a victim. The two have already killed five people and seriously wounded a sixth, so it is imperative that we apprehend these two individuals immediately.

"I'm calling for the largest manhunt in the history of this Great Nation, and I'm using every means available to me as Commander-in-Chief to accomplish it, including the military, all law enforcement branches, and you, the citizens of this country. By and large, someone, somewhere, will see these two fugitives, because they couldn't have just vanished. TSA and Homeland Security are certain they did not exit the country via public or private transit. So that means that they're still in the Northwest, possibly driving a new vehicle.

"Now please, this is a serious situation. Reports need to be accurate, and we don't want any citizen engaging them. Most of us have cell phones, so let's put them to work. Like after 9/11, let's all put aside our petty issues, and focus on the continued survival of our nation.

"Now I'm not saying that if someone got this technology, it would lead to an immediate attack on us, but your children and grandchildren may not be able to make that statement. So please, let's all come together to stop this and prove to the world that no matter our differences, we always come together as a people when we have to.

"I also have a message for any country that is thinking about harming us. You don't need to attack us to get our attention. If you have a voice, then we'll listen, but if you have a sword, then we'll fight. If you threaten our freedom, then you've woken the sleeping giant, and whoever has perpetrated this has certainly woken us up. As this investigation proceeds, I will be honest and forthright with you, the American Citizens. There will be many questions asked in the coming months, as well as many answers given. Now let's work together to resolve this, and prove once again why we are truly the Greatest Nation on Earth. God bless us all, and God bless America. Goodnight."

Holy shit! That was the most terrifying thing she'd ever heard. Vera knew some people were going to be mad, but she didn't know how mad. Well, maybe she did, but she was hoping to be sipping wine and loving her man as she heard it all unfold, so they could laugh together at the fools while clinking glasses.

She was seemingly trapped, feeling vulnerable and confused, when she caught the back seat on a glance. *He was awake and heard the radio — interesting.* She knew the dose used to sedate him was low, and he would be coming around soon, but he had recovered more quickly than she expected.

As she passed Sacramento, she thought, *this really is a big place with a lot of people, so just calm down and hide in plain sight, be cool.* She made the call with more than a little trepidation.

"My Love," was the answer on the other end. "Well, as you can see and hear, I made a mess of things." (Pablo taught her about trigger words that are picked up by the government. They used to study a list of hundreds, so she was trained not to say gun or bomb).

"That's not true. You're still around and able to call from one of the phones, which means you're resourceful. Which safe house did you choose?"

"Number Three," she said.

His reply was, "Oh." But his disappointment was evident. Stockton had been the third choice for a reason. San Francisco was the first choice because it had more possible escape routes.

"Pablo, I tried," she said with her voice weak and breaking, "but I was sure they would look there first, or catch me trying to get there even, especially after the Palo Alto thing."

Silence. "Where's your *paquete*?"

With Pablo, Vera had learned it was pointless to act incredulous when he said things that he shouldn't or couldn't know. In this case, it was common knowledge, but regardless, she had learned long ago that she should just answer the questions succinctly and sort out the whys later.

"Secured in the back seat."

"That's not expected. Why did you bother with that?"

"I wasn't sure what to do and decided not to make this call near the shed, in case they got lucky and tracked us. Also, I don't want any more death on my hands, and he would have died in there."

"Where are you?"

"I'm on Highway 50 just outside of Sacramento, on my way to Tahoe."

"That wasn't in our plan anymore, we never even had time to finalize things."

"Neither was the President coming on and bringing down the whole country on us, Pablo! The plan has changed!" Her voice was building to a more confident level.

Pablo smiled on the other end of the phone. She didn't know it, but he had trained her right out of the KGB handbook he had acquired easily from a third party in North Africa, a trip that had yielded a very interesting encounter with an ex-KGB agent named Vlad Korzinin.

Pablo had instilled all the necessary traits into her, including skill at threat assessment and reconfiguring game plans when needed. Her decisiveness proved that she was an amazing woman, capable of learning, capable of change, but most importantly, capable of making hard decisions when the time came. That was a trait that couldn't be taught, and it was the only true way of knowing who one's partner was under fire. Just like there was no way of truly knowing someone until one has lived with them. Therefore, Pablo adjusted his stern attitude and addressed her in a more loving manner. "Tell me about your plan," he said.

* * *

Jan Hurst was sitting and watching the TV with her jaw wide open. *There's no way!* She was under house arrest in a safe location. Because she was on bed rest, they had had to make some accommodations, so they had gotten her one of those really comfy recliners— one that was as good as a bed, according to the doctor who checked her out when she arrived. They moved her here because "there was obvious concern for her safety," was their tag line. The daughter of a

Teamsters boss, she was not ignorant on how evil the government could be, and now this?

Jan felt like she was snared in something out of a movie. Her big worry was that neither she nor her baby would ever see true freedom again, at least based on the information she had heard. Of course, she had no knowledge of anything going on, but they would never believe that. If they couldn't find it, they'd create it, Jan was sure. Thanks to the Patriot Act, she was never getting out of here. *Why Matt though? Was he the next Oswald, some unlikely patsy in someone else's game?*

She didn't know for sure what was going on, but she was sure that Matt had nothing to do with it. Sure, they had drifted apart a little, but only because she blamed him for her unplanned pregnancy and for putting her career path on hold. She had been one summer away from starting grad school, and getting into Arizona State was not easy. So she was angry, but he knew that she loved him, she was sure of it. She also knew the man and he hated lying. He would have just left her if he was so unhappy.

Matt was a very confident man, not codependent in the slightest. No, this was something else, something unplanned, and now they were wrapped up in it. She was sure that it wasn't going to be just him who suffered. Well, she hoped that whoever took him had underestimated him. That would be their mistake because Matt Hurst, lowly underachiever, was the smartest man she knew. All he ever did was watch the History Channel, read Tom Clancy, and quote his favorite book, *The Art of War*. Whoever had him most certainly didn't know who they had.

Just then, a small man with ice-blue eyes came in. Ken Beck's eyes were so piercing that Jan could barely hold their gaze. When she looked at him, she had the feeling that she had done something wrong, even though she hadn't. To her, there was no worse feeling in the world than being accused of something that she hadn't done. She could sense that this man was no lower-level bureaucrat. One look at his malevolent scowl told Jan that this was serious enough to bring in a man who would try to kill her Matt. Jan inherently knew that she was not only looking at her husband's hunter, she could very well be looking at his executioner. She had never felt the kind of impending doom she felt when she looked into this man's eyes.

"Hello Jan, my name is Kenneth Beck. I work for the Central Intelligence Agency."

* * *

Matt's eyes were as big as quarters. *Did I just hear the President of the United States use my name? Did I just hear the President of the United States say I am part of this? Whatever this is? Am I wanted as some sort of terrorist? How could that be possible? They had to have seen the recording in my office. What is the meaning of this?*

It was very confusing, but he suspected he was being set up as a patsy. He sure snapped out of his little infatuation quickly. Full of rage, he would snap her neck like a chicken bone the first chance he got. Vera ended her call. She immediately broke the phone and threw it out the window. *She was a smart girl, or well trained at least.*

She looked back at him again, "I know you heard, and probably figured some of it out. So we need not pretend."

He took a moment. "What is this all about?"

Her reply was thought out, "You will never know what this is all about, as it's way over your head. You entered into it when you foolishly attacked a man with a gun."

"Then why not just let me go?"

"We're way past that. Don't ask again. The way I see it, one way or another, you're in this very deep and I doubt that you will be explaining your way out of it anytime soon. We've seen to that."

"Why would you do that?" Matt inquired, both hurt and angry in his response.

"Because you're going to help me get out of the country. Once we do and you get me safely to where I'm to be, then my associates will create a story that will allow you to return home."

"You're full of shit, lady, there is no way I'm helping you screw my country over!"

"Yes, you will. If you ever want to see your wife again, and ensure her future safety, you will do exactly as I say."

She pulled the car over, reached back and cut his restraints free with her knife, which she just noticed still had Dr. Cooper's blood on it. Vera wondered if that factored into her captor not making an immediate move.

* * *

Looking back to when he was twelve, Pablo had known that Otavalo wasn't going to be his home much longer. He had been walking home from school one day, after staying an extra two hours to grade papers for Mr. Garcia. He had seen one of his classmates and his sister selling tortillas on the corner. Every day they'd had to get home in time to get the tortillas, and then get out to work. Homework was for later. Fortunately Pablo's parents made enough money that he didn't have to work, but money was often tight. One pair of glasses or a toothache could cost José a week's pay.

Pablo didn't know how he knew it, but even then, he was sure that he was going to be swept away from Otavalo. He had taken his time that day getting home from school, feeling stagnated and lethargic; meandering was the best he could muster. As is often the case with special people, his life was frequently lonely. He had no contemporaries, and adults were awkward around him, so his days were sometimes a little odd and solitary.

At recess, Pablo would spend his time reading, although there was nothing physically wrong with him. In fact, he played rough with his brothers all the time, just not with anyone outside of his family. The Principal brought the newspaper in for him every day, and he would read instead of play. He was different, and when one is different, kids can be brutal. He endured the names and taunts, but his older brothers protected his interests whenever other children went beyond that. Still, his brothers couldn't be there all the time, and he was not immune to feelings of insecurity brought on by the honesty and cruelty of small children.

He had gone home that day, and went to look for the one thing that always brightened his world, his mama. He was a mama's boy through and through. When he went into the kitchen and smelled his favorite *chorizo*, his heart sailed and his mood improved instantly.

There had been a plate on the table with his food on it. His mama was out in the backyard hanging clothes. He could see her through the screen, and he went out to thank her before he ate. Just the touch of her swelled his heart and lifted him out of his melancholy as he ran back to eat his food.

Halfway through his plate, destiny had called, and he had gone to peek at it through the window. He hadn't seen his uncle in a while, and his *tio* looked different, with better clothing, jewelry, and a nice jeep. His papa was listening intently, and then Pablo heard him answer, "No, I won't have my child live away. Delores could never bear to have her Pablito be away from her for even one night, Julio, you know this!"

"I know José, but opportunities don't come up like this very often here. No, I take that back. They never come up here, ever! Why do you think I had to leave, José? This place, it's a place where you just exist, nothing is gained, and nothing is lost. It's just a circle of poverty. It is not fair that he is to be stagnated here, stagnated because you two are too scared to accept that this is bigger than you, that he needs to be given the chance to grow into whatever it is he's supposed to be."

They had stood and looked at each other for a long time. José missed his brother. He hated the fact that Julio had moved to Guayaquil and gotten a job as an exporter. But without that, they never would have been given this offer from Julio's gracious boss. According to Julio, his boss had heard the stories about Pablo and offered to pay an unheard of amount of money to send him to France for a year to attend a private international school, a school that was considered the very best private school in all of France.

"This school will allow Pablo to be accelerated," Julio stated as he showed his brother the brochure.

"No, my brother. I'm sorry. I will not ask her to do this. His path will happen with or without our help. And just like you, he will rebel against this place and move away. But at least for now, she has her time with him. Tell your boss thank you, but no thank you."

Then they all heard the sobbing. Delores had been listening around the corner while Pablo had been listening through the curtains. It was the uncontrolled, horrible sobbing that only mothers are entitled to when it involves their children. José was on his knees. "No, Mama, you heard wrong. I'm not letting him go. He's staying right here with us."

That only made her cry more. Finally, she spoke through the tears and stutters. "Do you think I want that? Do you think I want him to be like Julio, and hate this place so much that he leaves and never comes back?!" Her uncontrollable sobbing continued. "Let him go, José. Let him go or we will lose him forever. Just like this one," she said, pointing and staring at Julio.

* * *

In that same moment in time that a teenaged Pablo Manuel was practicing for *Le Mis*, another play was unfolding in Peru, only this one would be played out on the world stage. Nearly two years had passed since the sniper's bullet ripped open Felix's back and chest. The doctors had fought off four different infections and performed several surgeries to get him into a stable coma. Every day a therapist massaged and moved him to prevent the bedsores from happening. Keeping him alive was no easy task.

It was with no understanding of time and place that Felix Ortiz opened his eyes to. *Where was he?* His mouth was so dry that he couldn't call out, so dry that there wasn't any moisture in it at all. He looked around to see if there was water. He was in a hospital room of some kind, not a normal one for sure, and there was no water visible. He did have an IV line coming off a bag that was hanging on a pole. It went into his right arm.

His arms seemed to look okay, and he flexed his fingers. His right fingers were very hard to move, and there was some shoulder pain. His legs were under the covers, and although he couldn't see them, he could move and feel them. *That's good. But what happened?* Then it came back to him. *The ambush. Oh yeah.* He pulled back the open hospital shirt to reveal an exit wound that was hard to believe. *How am I still alive?*

He saw movement out of the corner of his eye and turned to find himself face-to-face with a man standing in his doorway. The man had a full beard and was holding a plate of food. He was dressed in fatigues, and when he saw Felix awake, he dropped his plate on the ground and ran off screaming for someone named Octavio. Felix was drifting out again. *Damn, I'm thirsty. I wonder why he ran away?*

* * *

Matt stared at her for a long second. "I could kill you now and take my chances."

"You could try," was Vera's response. "I guess you forgot that your wife Jan and your unborn baby are counting on you."

"What?!"

"I see you're confused and you're wondering how I could know that. We know everything Matt, never forget that, or that the people in charge are very powerful. But you actually had an OB-GYN appointment card in your wallet." Matt's face became less confused after hearing that, so he listened carefully as she finished her spiel.

"So what you are saying," Matt said sardonically, "is I have no choice."

"I'm saying that you better just get on board with the fact that, like it or not, you're in this waist-deep. And no matter what you do, there will be serious repercussions. We're the best bet you have, and the word from my employer is that if you sincerely help me escape, then he will give you his word to set you right again."

"Lady, when the President of the United States has the whole country looking for you, there will never be right again."

"Then do it for Jan, because there's no reason to let her suffer for your predicament, and trust me Matt, the people that have us both ensnared are more powerful than you can ever imagine."

He sat back thinking of her words, "The people that have us ensnared." That means she wants him to believe she's an unwilling participant in this too. Maybe he can use that to his advantage.

"Okay, tell me the plan and your real name."

FIVE

Revelations

Pablo was staring in a trance-like state at his phone, waiting to hear the worst. He couldn't stop his mind from rolling down memory lane though, to a time where his life was almost normal for a while.

At least in his last school there had been other gifted children, so he was never teased. The kids there were on a different path than those where he grew up in Otavalo. This school was a place of enlightenment, and the teachers were so dedicated, so caring. If he had one wish, it would be that he had his life back again, forget the millions, and forget the destiny to fulfill. He knew that he didn't have much of a life back then, but it was a simple and happy one.

His favorite teacher, Jeremy Lebuff, had been getting him to realize why they were doing things outside the normal lines with him. He had been gradually becoming aware of the Industrial Military Machine that was running the world. He then knew why they protected him so.

As his adult mind realized now, he would have been in great peril had he been exposed; but back then he had thought it overkill to hide all his incredible achievements. He hadn't wanted to blend in; he'd wanted to lead. *How naive of me.* He was just a kid then, and children shouldn't have to know the machinations of evil men.

Pablo looked at his phone and willed it to ring. He should have just been left alone back then, to be allowed to become whatever it was he was supposed to have become. *But it was too late for that now. Wasn't it?* His enemies would soon have other opportunities to interfere or not with his life, and this time there would be serious repercussions for not leaving him alone. Back then he was just a kid.

He reflected back upon his life again, back to when he'd had that brief moment of wonderment at all the world's secrets, when anything was still possible. He thought back to his second year at L'École des Roches International School, thinking back to the day he was most fond of. He remembered sitting back and taking a break after his part in the play was finished for the time being. He had watched his acting class working on their parts in *Le Mis* for the upcoming school play. He remembered he had been taking a moment to reflect on what he had accomplished in the past year. He was often able to do that; he could reflect back on any time and remember what he was thinking at that moment. Just like no matter what song he heard, he could recall the last place he heard that song, and the time before, and the time before that. The thought strings never stopped, and there was no apparent ceiling.

The school had been established in 1899, and Pablo had rewritten all the record books during his first six months there. He had already completed their pre-college agenda, which was a four-year agenda of History, Geography, Physics, and Chemistry. He had passed the Baccalaureate Option Internationale at the end of his first year, at the age of fifteen.

He had also become fluent in French, Russian, German, Italian, and English by the end of that first year. Although he was fluent enough to get A's throughout his testing, he imagined there were tons of slang words that he had no clue about, especially in English.

The teachers and the administrators hadn't had charts for him, so they decided not to create any. Instead, he would lead the way. They hadn't made fanfare for him, either. They had just allowed him to be whatever he wanted to be. It was said by his teachers that he appeared to have nearly one hundred percent retention of information. It was almost unheard of, but he had done it, right in front of their faces.

But of all the places he excelled, they had been just fodder to him compared to his true love, just something to do when he wasn't focused on the computer lab.

His lab teacher Mr. Lebuff had been ill prepared for what the upcoming months held for him. He had thought he was just getting another advanced student to wow him for a year, only to move on to another mentor. Little did Jeremy know, his life would never again be the same, for he had met "the student of a lifetime…"

He admitted he was not inspired when they met, but that soon changed, as no one who ever met Pablo and spent time with him was ever the same. That, in and of itself, had to be some kind of sign that Pablo was anointed, as he had an impact on people wherever he went, whether they knew it or not.

By the second week Pablo was at the school, the teachers had held a meeting where they had all agreed that his talents had to be kept under wraps. All of his tests results, and all his schoolwork needed to be kept private, because if big industry or government ever got wind of him, he would never have a chance to even grow up properly. He'd become a "lab rat" for sure.

The incident Jeremy Lebuff witnessed that had prompted the meeting was when Pablo wrote a chess program the first week he was shown the concept of programming. The program had been of the highest caliber, and Lebuff had actually launched it as a free website.

Pablo was able to recreate all these memories but Jeremy's life was not the only one that was never the same after their meeting. Jeremy was one of the few people who understood his need for assimilation, and even though there had been times Lebuff was sure the information he was providing was not necessary, he provided it to feed the compulsion of the boy who knew everything.

Jeremy had not only been a teacher. He had become Pablo's first friend and mentor. Jeremy had soon learned how much Pablo excelled at chess, just as he did at all subjects. He had watched Pablo decimate a visiting school, a school that had several high-level players on its chess team. In fact, the same school had decimated them the year before. The fact was, Pablo had never lost a game, and that was something else he had accomplished that no one before him had ever done.

Sitting in his office in the now, his eyes misted a little thinking of Jeremy. He wished he could reach out to him now, but he would never risk hurting the only family he had left.

In the nearly two years he had been at L'École des Roches, he had begun to understand the world outside of Otavalo. He had developed a great grasp of what he wanted to do with his life, and he was probably the happiest person who had ever walked the planet.

His memory returned to his favorite day again. The rehearsal had finished and he had thought he would head to the computer lab to wait for Jeremy. This was his free period and Jeremy had a classroom period with no lab. That meant that Pablo could play chess online. If he were lucky, his mentor would have the class reading and would be able to come next door to hang out for a while.

* * *

On that same day, U.S. weapons scientist James Haberman had sat and stared at his computer screen. He had been "patiently" waiting for his cell phone to ring. He'd taken a walk, cleaned the chateau twice, made breakfast and lunch, and was now playing chess online while he "patiently" waited. On the plus side, he had found a new site that he loved. It even had speed chess. It was quite well done and free to boot. He was undefeated and quickly moving up the ranks.

He had been currently playing *"La Oveja,"* who oddly seemed to be running the Perenyi attack, considered a Grandmaster level type of attack. *Hmm, I've seen this before; this person is running a program. Hah, he's in for a rude awakening.* James had moved when the phone rang, both on the chess game and literally, in person, as the ringer startled him out of being deeply buried in thought.

It had been his doctor Jean Lamont, and he could tell it wasn't good news. "James, the stem cells didn't work. Worse, it's metastasized."

"I see," was all James could muster. He didn't need the prognosis, as he knew it was "dead man walking."

Well that was it now, wasn't it? Time to go back and take care of some business before he checked out. Both his parents were still alive, and that wouldn't be easy. Even at eighty, most people expected to die before their kids. It wouldn't be easy telling Bill the truth either, that he had pancreatic cancer instead of the breakdown he had convinced everyone he was having.

Well, maybe he could finish his satellite project before he passed. He might have one more lasting legacy if he could finish it. He had been nearly done with the project, and it all came down to a question of the battery, which he had accidentally solved before he left. *All this bad shit was not going to be fun.*

He had looked down at the screen. *The Sheep, huh?* Well, after La Oveja's last move, he was sure of two things. The first was, "The Sheep" was a cheater, and the second was, he was going to lose his first game of chess in a very long time. *Shit, this is not my day.*

* * *

Whoever the cheater had been on the other side, he and his computer had not been expecting Pablo's variation on a tried and true master's attack. True to his instincts, the program had bought it hook, line, and sinker. Then he had slammed his enhancement on the attack, and it was just a matter of time. The poor sucker just didn't know it . . . yet.

His message light had lit up. Apparently, his opponent, "Dr. Sparks" wasn't happy with the last play. It appeared he had seen the program's error, too. *No, he was actually accusing ME of running a program.*

Even though he was the world's next great mind, he was also a teenager, so Pablo had replied, "HA HA," in caps for emphasis. "Sorry I beat your program. There goes your perfect record—too bad, so sad," and he had added a frowny face. *It was sophomoric, but, oh so fun.*

Pablo had endured the next few minutes, which were filled with a written diatribe about people like him, how they were ruining the Internet, and how they were only hurting themselves. When the guy was done, Pablo had asked him if he felt better, and his answer was, "No."

Pablo had told him, "If it makes you feel any better, it wasn't a program that beat you, it was me."

Sparks had doubted that and had said, "If we were playing face to face, you wouldn't be so cocky, as your lie would soon be exposed."

Pablo had laughed out loud and put an, "lol" on the screen. Then he had replied, "You do just that, my name is Pablo Manuel, and I'm a student at L'École des Roches in Normandy, France." Just then, Lebuff had come in, so he had closed the chess program, leaving the disgruntled loser to his sour grapes.

* * *

At that same time, in a compound in Peru, Felix's eyes had opened a second time, and this time, his mouth hadn't been dry: it had actually tasted good. *That's nice.* He had cleared his throat and croaked, "*¿Quién anda allí?*"

"I am, my brother," was the reply that had come from nearby. He had turned and seen a middle-aged man in a khaki outfit sitting in a nearby chair. The man wore round glasses and possessed a dignified but intense look about him. He wore no facial hair, on his head was a fedora that looked like it was covering up a bald head.

"Who are you?" Felix had croaked, still very weak.

"I'm the man who holds your life in his hands right now. I'm also the cousin of one of the men you gunned down."

Felix had gulped hard and said, "What do you want with me?"

"That, my friend, is a good question. The answer will set your future path, so choose your words wisely when I ask how many men were with you that day?"

* * *

Jan stared at the man before her with trepidation. His demeanor seemed to be kind and understanding, but the eyes said something else entirely. She was brought to a different part of the expansive house, quite literally, as they moved her in a special wheelchair to where she was to remain for the questioning, where a doctor stood on hand. The room had two chairs, a table, and a lot of glass walls.

Uh oh, she thought, *just like on the cop shows.* Apparently her face exposed her emotion. "Don't be alarmed Mrs. Hurst. This room has all the latest electronic devices, but it's hardly a torture chamber. The devices here help us determine if you are being truthful or not, that's all. So now I'm going to ask you some questions and we're going to see where we're at, okay, Jan?"

Jan nodded, but she didn't believe a word he said. *This is where they waterboard people, I'm sure of it.*

The questioning was constant, the pressure intense, and Jan never seemed to have the right answer to make this asshole stop. She was beginning to feel disoriented. She started to believe that she would say anything to get out of there. Then she realized that he kept repeating the last question because she didn't respond. *What was he saying?*

"Jan, are you focused? I asked you a simple question: did you know Matt was having an affair?" He leaned in and put his face right into hers.

Did he just say Matt was having an affair? It was all too much, the mixture of the lights, the pressure, this guy's horrible cologne, and now this information that Matt was cheating on her? It all became too much, and before she could warn him, or do anything, the vomit was launching.

She'd heard of projectile vomiting before, but until now, she didn't believe that barf could shoot that far.

Poor Agent whatever-the-fuck-his-name was was going to have to buy a new suit and take a bath in something other than barf. Apparently, she needed to start chewing better, because there were some sizable chunks of something in there.

The interrogation was over for now, and they had the medic check her out and take her back to her room. Agent Barf made sure he gave her the "I'll get you look" before she left, with a slight inward smile on her face.

* * *

As at his previous school, Pablo had been so far ahead of the curriculum that he really wasn't in his history class. He had really been working on his Master's thesis, as he had a special binder that housed his real work. Lebuff had convinced the school that even the students must not know the true Pablo yet, so he was rarely called upon in class. They had wanted him to have time to mature, time to prepare him, especially for the onslaught of attention and offers the world was going to make him.

The teachers really hadn't had anything left to teach him at their level, but they could mold him. They could make sure that his character was able to maintain in the world he would surely be thrown into, sooner rather than later.

Late in the day, the school intercom had buzzed and the voice had said Pablo was needed in the computer lab. That had gotten his curiosity up. He had wondered if old Lebuff had encountered a problem he needed help with.

Pablo had walked into the lab, where Lebuff had been talking to a white guy. The stranger had looked to be around sixty, but maybe a bit younger. There had been something about his looks that seemed labored though, making him look older. *Maybe he was a heavy smoker.* He had been around six feet tall, brown hair parted to the side, medium build. He had been wearing jeans, a t-shirt, and loafers. He had looked like he had been a lady killer in his younger days, with typical California beach looks, beautiful hazel eyes and perfect teeth when he smiled. But, like Pablo had thought before, something had been wrong with him. He had looked labored.

Lebuff had introduced the guest. "Pablo, this is James Haberman. He's an American."

Pablo had shaken the man's hand, which seemed to lack strength. "Hello," was his reply in perfect English. Lebuff looked as if he had a secret, with a ridiculous, hidden grin on his face, so Pablo naturally asked, "What's up?"

"James here was your chess opponent the other day. His screen name is 'Dr. Sparks.'"

Pablo's face had immediately changed to the same internal grin that Lebuff had.

"Apparently you beat him and he came here to admonish you," Lebuff had continued, "not only for your cheating, but to let me know that the character of one of my students is less than honorable. How do you think that makes me feel?"

"I see," Pablo had said.

James spoke up, "I know this seems like a triviality Pablo, I mean, what's the harm in running a program and having some fun, right? Well, that's what I came to tell you Son, that 'it is' a big problem, because when you do something like that, you not only affect others, you are selling yourself short." James looked at the boy in earnest, "You can become that computer if you try. Before that loss, I hadn't lost a game of chess since I was ten. So you understand now why I'm here. I want you to see that a person can do it. You don't need to cheat."

Pablo and Lebuff had to play poker here, otherwise this guy was going to think they were mocking him, as he was very impassioned and that would have been a huge insult.

"Well, Sir, I can see you feel very strongly about this, and I want to apologize for upsetting you so. I will get rid of the program, and I'm very sorry to have ruined your streak. Do you think we can play one game before you leave? Just to start me on the right path, so I can see how far I have to go to be great like you?"

James smiled from ear to ear, "You bet, Son, we sure can do that." He then rubbed Pablo's head in a way that was seemingly a sign of affection in the U.S.

* * *

Matt engulfed his head in his hands trying to wrap his mind around this unbelievable situation.

"So that's it? This whole thing is about retrieving someone's property out of a safe?"

"Yes," Vera answered, "in the simplest explanation, yes. That's exactly what this is about. Of course the sensitive nature of the information is what everyone is so concerned about. They think Al Qaeda or the Chinese are behind this. Those implications are scary for your country, I must admit, but this is not that. This is a private party retrieving private property that was not being returned, so don't think that this is some plot to bring the U.S. down, because that is simply not true."

Matt thought about that. "And, of course, your plan to step on that plane and disappear went out the window the minute you plunged your knife into Dr. Cooper?"

"Yes."

If what she was saying was true, then Matt realized he had just hit the "opposite lottery." In this lottery, he didn't win anything, and in fact, he got the opposite of winning; he lost everything. He had always been convinced he was slightly cursed with bad luck, but this astronomical happenstance was proof positive.

"So what Agency did those two guys work for?"

"I don't know," Vera said. "It could have been DHS or CIA or just two cops. I have no idea, because they didn't identify themselves when they grabbed me."

Matt understood now why the authorities thought he was suspicious in this, and it wasn't looking good for him. He looked like Harvey Dent of *Batman*—Two-Face.

Improbably, he really was caught up in a legitimate conspiracy, and that reality was hitting him hard now. Inexplicably, he really did have a new boss right now, even if he had never met him. Not only that, if he cooperated with these people, then a totally new life path was going to open up, and it is one that he never could have seen coming in a million years: that of a criminal.

Seriously, if someone sat me down yesterday and asked me to come up with a situation that described my worst nightmare, I would have never been so cruel to myself as to think this up. Not only am I now a criminal, I'm a traitor to boot! No man, this is all too much! He doubted this could really be happening, but the inability to make sudden decisions or grasp new realities was never among his shortcomings.

"Okay," Matt said, "I'll help you get out of the country, and I'll have to trust you to keep your word, because it doesn't look like you or I have any other choice."

Matt sat back and stared out the window from the back seat, where he remained in the shadows, since the authorities were looking for two people. His head had been spinning; both from the information he had just received and from the drug he had been forced to inhale, but it was done spinning now. What these people couldn't have known about him was that his intuitive instincts were as good as anyone's on the planet.

Although he had flunked out of the Sheriff's Academy, Matt's ability to create a coherent action plan in the midst of chaos matched the abilities of any trained agent in his position. In the threat assessment department, he was top-notch. His current assessment was not good for himself. His assessment for himself was that he was not going home. He had no illusions that these people would not hesitate to kill him the second he was in their grasp. So his final determination was that he would become an agent for his country by self-induction.

To do that, he would have to convince this girl somehow that he should not be killed, because if his plan went anywhere near right, he would probably only get one chance for martyrdom. He now doubted her statement of, "They have us ensnared." Although he didn't understand Spanish, he did understand inflection, and the kind she was using on the phone was not the inflection of someone who was subjugated. She was one of them, not ensnared at all. That meant she wasn't perfect either, because letting that information slip was a mistake.

He reflected on the things he had learned from the work of the Masters, from Tolstoy, Dumas, and of course, Sun Tzu. Matt thought of the most apt lessons. A few of the most prominent came to mind. *"To know your enemy, you must become your enemy." "Pretend inferiority and encourage his arrogance." "All warfare is based on deception."*

These people, his abductors, thought they had a Lee Harvey Oswald here, but what they were going to have was a mad saboteur, if Matt could just get the opportunity. In his movie mind, Bruce Willis' character John McClane from *Die Hard* popped in. He would strike back for his country because she was lying about more than just her status with these people.

When he pressed her about this not being used against the U.S., her denial was emphatic. Whoever had trained her had forgotten to eliminate emphatic denial as a critical part of her training as emphatic denial was a sure sign of deception. So was the fact that she looked slightly to the right when she lied. *Yes, this girl was definitely trained by someone smart, but she was no spook. So what the hell is she in all this? Well, one thing is for sure, I've enlisted myself into the employ of my government, and in the fashion of fanatics all over the world, I am going to show these assholes how much damage one man, who is willing to sacrifice himself, can do — if I get the chance.*

* * *

James had known that there were over thirteen hundred named chess openings, and he had never seen this kid's moves before. His play had been very unorthodox, as had he. It had gotten James thinking that he was more like the ugly duckling than the sheep. James could imagine the swan eventually arising, but for the time being, this Pablo Manuel was still a transitional teenager. Tall, thin, and wiry, he had soft features on his face. His nose, lips, and ears were all in proportion to his head, and no feature was out of place, but James could tell he was one of those people who did not look anything like they would as an adult.

James watched as hands that were as soft as a nun's made the next move. As Pablo had been moving, James had focused on his eyes. Now there it was, the kid's exceptional attribute, his eyes. *Oh man, the eyes on this kid were something else. The way they darted, the way they computed. They might be plain old brown, but there was nothing else ordinary about this kid's eyes. The way he looked through you when he spoke and the way he started his chess game were quite unbelievable.*

James had thought he would have some fun and use the "King's Indian Defense," but he had quickly found out that that was a mistake, and that if he weren't careful, the game could have been headed toward stalemate. *What the hell? There is no way this kid played that first game himself? Or was there?*

* * *

Beck came in sans his sport coat, dress shirt, and tie. He wore just a t-shirt and dress pants—pants with numerous wet spots still from the spot cleaning. "Well?" he growled.

Sarah Berkman was a techno geek for the Farm. The Agency had tried to use her for fieldwork, but she had not been able to handle the stress. In fieldwork one must be a good actor, and unfortunately for her, she wasn't. Her biggest weakness was that she was unable to conceal her emotions in a way that field agents must do. At 5'7" and 175 pounds, she was perfect for the field. She had that soccer mom look; a look that would have led very few even a chance to guessing her true identity.

Field failures aside, she was such an asset that the Agency quickly found a niche for her. Her work in the field of lie detection and investigation was becoming legendary, and she was Ken Beck's ace in the hole on many fronts.

"She's not hiding anything Ken. Sorry. From everything I can see, she's just as stunned as everyone else, and I doubt she knows anything consciously. Her husband seems to have led a successful double life, and now she's been thrown into this out of the blue. Sorry, but that's my initial assessment."

Beck sat down and looked at the monitor of the woman crying into her pillow and said, "Great, now what?"

Ken Beck put his head in his hands and started to think. *Okay, we know they went over the San Mateo Bridge, because the cameras caught them, but why?*

Then he had an idea. It just popped into his head. *Why didn't he think of it before?* He was going to follow this on his own. Rogers was an okay guy, but Beck had worked his way up through the ranks. He was an actual field agent, not some appointed figurehead. He called Sarah over.

"I've got an idea." Sarah knew this man, and when he said he had an idea, if someone knew what was good for them, they placed all bets on him. If not, then they'd better hope he never found out that bet wasn't placed.

Sarah somehow inherently knew this about Ken from the day she had met him as a Field Agent. She inherently knew to always have his back, and she was right, but it came with a personal price, one that was known only to her. Aside from that, every single person who had ever burned this guy had had their careers sent to the Dark Ages. Somehow the Old Man loved Ken from the get-go, and his career had been on the fast track ever since.

Sarah also knew something else, that the CIA doctrine sometimes called for sadistic, unbelievable behavior in the name of God and Country, and Ken Beck loved to live in that world. Actually, she feared that he loved it a little too much, and often wondered about his boundaries. But if she were to choose someone to go after these people, it would be

Ken Beck all the way. She listened to his instructions, took notes, and got into gear making it happen.

Within minutes, he was driving to Sacramento with a team of six people in three cars to follow his hunch. Beck always drove himself, except on official visits. Ken was in the lead car going over the very bridge that Matt Hurst's Mustang had just hours before. It was a slim chance, he thought, but it was better than sitting around and getting barfed on.

* * *

James had sat back and stared at the board. He had lost, not stalemated. He'd had to check the kid several times when they were playing, just to make sure he hadn't been wearing a wire. He hadn't. James had thought he detected a smarmy grin on both of them earlier, and now he understood why. He had been staring at the next World Champion! James said, "Nice game, but I really can't believe it."

"Why?" said Pablo. "Because I'm nothing but a kid in your eyes?"

"No," James said, "Because I'm one of the best players in the world, even if you've never heard of me before. One of my colleagues is a Grandmaster, and he cannot get past stalemate with me."

Lebuff interrupted with, "Are you trying to tell us you're a Grandmaster?"

"Yes," was James's reply, "that and a lot more..."

* * *

As the car descended into the Tahoe Basin, Matt was trying not to be awed. He wasn't in the mood for being awed, but damn it, when he saw that view, it just took his breath away. The moon was going to be full, and it was already showing in the distant sky. Lake Tahoe really was one of the wonders of the world, and the descent down Highway 50 offered the best view of the entire basin one could get without climbing up a mountain.

He really loved nature, and it occurred to him that this might be the last time he made this drive. Jan loved Tahoe. She loved it so much in fact, that they got married here. It took about forty days for her to figure out she was pregnant, but once she did, Matt had to give his roommate and high school friend a thirty-day notice to move from their shared apartment. If he wanted to see sunlight again, Jan instructed him that they'd better be wearing wedding bands when they broke this news to her dad. *Man was she ever right—he would have killed me on the spot. Will I ever see Jan again?* Suddenly it hit him what she must be going through.

* * *

Field Agent Pete Brody was calling Beck as he drove over the San Mateo Bridge heading east.

"What have you got, Pete?" Ken asked.

"Homeland went through the house with a fine tooth, nothing concrete. No foreign link, but I called with other news, our kind of news." Pete was one of Beck's underlings, and he was a very smart boy. "We might have a better situation than you think, Assistant Director, but we need to get Callahan in here right away."

"Okay Pete, I'll get that done, and then I want a detailed report. But succinctly, why do you think we need that from Ray?"

"Unless I'm wrong, Chief, I know a patriot when I see one, and this guy's no goof either—not some security guard, low mentality type. No, Assistant Director. He looks like he's self-taught in a lot of things, could be he was studying our tactics because he was aiming to join some agency in the future. I can't put my finger on it, but Ray will.

"It can easily look like this guy is home-sprung and is going to wreak some serious mayhem out there, and that's the way the Homeland guys are spinning it, but I don't think so. Part of my team is going through his former bedroom at his parent's house, and this guy is Johnny All-American. There is not a single anti-American indicator in his entire past. In fact, he is very social and well connected within his community.

"That hardly fits the profile we had established from past cases. My assessment is that our bad guys randomly grabbed this Hurst guy. By sheer happenstance, they grabbed the wrong guy, and at the very least, a guy you wouldn't want against you if you let your guard down. I just need Ray Callahan to confirm, Chief, and then I will file my report."

"You'll wait until we can file that report together, Pete," Ken replied. "First of all, we have to be very careful going against the grain here. Second, this is not going to be a by-the-numbers case, I can just feel it, so I need you outside the box. Do you understand?"

Pete Brody knew Ken Beck as well as anyone on the planet, and that familiarity was limited to knowing his title, his ability, and the fact when he told you this was off the record, you already forgot the conversation.

They hung up. With a quick call, Ken Beck had Ray Callahan en route within minutes. They had already had him out to assess both scenes at Conceptual—fortuitously, he had been on the West Coast training personnel, as had Sarah. This was a lucky break, as they were both usually in D.C. As soon as this case broke, Ken had him poring over Nancy Chavez's profile immediately. Unfortunately, the data on Hurst wasn't so readily available because he was in the private sector.

Ken drifted into reminiscing about his progression in the CIA, starting with Ray Callahan. Ray Callahan was a Farm legend. If one wanted to be in the CIA, and actually made it to Camp Peary for training, then that person would have to get by Ray Callahan at some point. Ken Beck was no exception.

Ray Callahan had never liked him. Ken knew this because the Old Man had told him so, just so that he never trusted Ray too much. Ray had thought he was brilliant, but had also viewed him as a person with a hidden agenda. Ray had always felt that a potentially psychotic personality lurked inside Ken Beck, and he was not shy to report it to Bob Thompson.

That had been his big mistake. It had been innocent enough. They had been going over test scores, and Beck's consistently high scores had drawn notice. Instead of commenting on the positive, Ray had let the boss know that this one cadet was possibly a sociopath, that in his humble opinion, this individual wanted power so badly that he might be willing to do anything to get it.

Ray could have not known that the traits he was describing were exactly what his boss was looking for. Super motivated, super ruthless, and never nice about anything—the antithesis of Bob. Regardless of Ken's ability, or Bob's commitment to cover his chosen man, Ray had tried to pull Beck's rug out more than once, especially after the Iraq fiasco, but the Old Man had always saved him.

For all his grandstanding with the whole "legendary calmness in the storm" thing, Bob Thompson loved that his Assistant Director was just the opposite. He had purposely fast-tracked Ken's career, believing that his balance would discourage complacency.

Beck's lucky break had been that Bob Thompson was very worried about the greatest potential shortcoming in his management style, which was that he could miss the time to be stalwart. Thompson knew that with Ken Beck, the moment wouldn't be missed.

So, the Old Man had overridden Ray time after time, and Ken had gotten results, time after time. Regardless, Ray Callahan was the only person who had dared go against him, because he was the only person more untouchable than Ken was in the eyes of the Old Man. So often it had been a Mexican standoff, but most of the time, he had gotten what he wanted.

Yet Ray was a man whom everyone tapped into if they wanted to succeed, and that was the thorn that Ken Beck got to stick into Ray Callahan, time and time again. He included Ray on his hardest cases, and almost always went with Ray's analysis, since it was usually spot on. So in essence, Ray Callahan helped the man he hated get promoted. It was quite the catch-22.

The rumor mill had Callahan secretly running the show for years, and if Pete Brody was right, then Ken had finally caught a break, a break that they would keep to themselves at CIA. Ray was not authorized to share information with other agencies, which meant that they could share Pete's assessment with Ray and all he could do was help. It was a very trying situation for Ray Callahan, and a very soothing one for Ken Beck. Anytime he could cause another human being suffering or angst, then that was a good day for him indeed.

Ken also knew that a prior interagency situation had caused Ray to have no inclination to help DHS, so that shouldn't be a problem anyway. He had learned more than once not to go against a DHS assessment unless he was ready have every corner of his body checked with a dental pick. Those boys were the government's face to the public, and they beat the drums according to their own needs, but rarely ever in actual pursuit of the truth. That was Ken's job, and a lot of other people behind the scenes just like him. He allowed himself a little smile. *Maybe one break will lead to others—luck happens that way.*

* * *

On the descent into the Tahoe Basin, one view was lost only to gain another. The place was so beautiful with lush rolling hills, covered with pines everywhere, and little roadside businesses selling Alpaca rugs and woodcarvings. They passed a wonderful looking golf course, which Matt knew mostly from memory from passing it all these years—although he could care less, since he hated golf.

This part of South Lake Tahoe was less chaotic than the Nevada side, where all the casinos were located and ninety-five percent of the tourist population resided. Highway 50 was littered with little cottages, chalets, and motor inns that were overflow for skiing season and summer peaks, but were sparsely populated in the off season. Since this was May, the summer rush was not yet on.

It was getting dark when they pulled into the Pine Chalet. Vera parked the car and told Matt to wait. She went in just like she had done several weeks ago. She was glad to see the white-haired Abigail still working the counter.

Abigail and her late husband Chuck had run this place for the last forty years, and she hadn't been quite ready to give up the ship after his passing.

Vera had come up to check the plane and reconnoiter, which was how she had found Abigail. Nowadays, Abigail couldn't see so well due to cataracts, so customers often helped her with the paperwork. Vera thanked her, and as she was heading out old Abigail said, "Terrible what happened today, isn't it?"

Vera turned and said sincerely that it was "a most horrible act, and I surely hope whoever did it is brought to justice." That seemed to please Abigail, so she turned and lumbered back to her chair, which was two feet in front of the blaring TV. When they got to the room, Vera told him to shower and wash his hair while she went out for some things. After getting his clothing and shoe sizes she left, but not before noting he wore a size 13 shoe. *Good looking and probably well endowed too, not bad . . .*

Matt was stunned. *She left?* He couldn't believe she left? He could just walk away, make a 911 call and play it from that point. Then *he* would have the deal to make. He knew that was important. He also knew how things worked, and they would have to believe him. The evidence would dictate it.

Then he turned on the TV, and his mind changed as quickly as this whole thing had started, not five hours before. Homeland Security had gone through his house, and although they refused to confirm anything on the TV news, all of a sudden it seemed they were labeling him as a Timothy McVeigh wannabe—like he was some kind of maniacal individual, who was extremely dangerous and should not be approached under any circumstances. In a thought of dark humor, Matt thought that he should be afraid of himself after watching the news because they had him cast as such as badass.

Of course, his mind immediately flashed to Jan playfully comment-ing about his man cave. "You better hope nobody sees all this stuff, or they'll think you're a nut," she had once said.

The news was circling again back to the start, where they were profil-ing him as a domestic terrorist, who was now armed and extremely dan-gerous. They were warning the public not to have any contact with the two of them, and to immediately call in sightings. *This can't get any worse.*

He looked at the phone, but didn't pick it up. He hadn't forgotten about his captors, or the fact that they knew who he was and had already made a veiled threat against Jan, a threat he was sure they would carry out if he picked up that phone. *Damn it!*

Thinking of any way out, he believed he picked up on something earlier. He was no intern when it came to women. He'd had steady girl-friends since the ninth grade, and he knew a look when he saw one. She liked him somehow. If he was going to stay, he needed to use her little tell to his advantage, but he had to make it look spontaneous, as she was way too smart to try to fool. As he imagined her flowing hair he thought, *not that it would be hard.* He was going to have to create a moment, some-thing he could get in her head with, but what?

*   *   *

Anyone who saw him now would think he was asleep sitting up. Pablo was always conscious of the outside world during his frequent visits to the past. Although his own form of transcendental meditation made him seem out of touch with his environment, he was not.

On the day James had lost to Pablo at chess, he had revealed a past that was difficult to fathom. This American was the heart of America's military ingenuity and military defenses. James was truly a living leg-end, and he knew where all the bones were buried.

Pablo remembered that he and Lebuff had sat stunned. What this man had just told them seemed impossible. Yet there he was, speaking of things that only someone who did them could actually know about. A quick Google search had confirmed his identity. He even had his own Wikipedia page.

This man was what Lebuff had known Pablo would grow up to be, and the two of them were there, together by fate, in the same place at the same time. Not for long though, as James had also told them of the pancreatic cancer, and the news he had received just yesterday of it spreading. Apparently, no one knew this information except the three of them and James's doctor, and it was sworn that it would stay that way. They had both promised that they had never seen nor heard of James Haberman.

Pablo had asked, "What are you going to do?"

"Well," Haberman had replied, "I was going to go back and deal with good-byes, then finish a project for a friend, kind of an important one."

"Was?"

"Yes, was, as I was doing it as an auto-response, because that is who I am. I'm the guy they can count on until the end. That's what I was programmed to do—you know, do your patriotic duty and go to the grave waving the flag. It appears life has just thrown me a curve ball though, and I'm going to go with it. So with your teacher's blessing, I would like to work with you, one on one. And let's see what you got, kid."

Lebuff hadn't been able to say, "Yes" fast enough. Then he had added, "What a tragic and wonderful opportunity. Life never ceases to amaze me." He had said this quite unexpectedly, and then run over and hugged them both for a long time.

* * *

Vera pulled out of the parking spot and drove toward town. But a block down she quickly turned left into a nearly vacant hotel parking lot and backed into a spot under a pine tree. After retrieving the rifle case from the trunk, she partially rolled down the back window and assembled her rifle in record time from the back seat. Within seconds, Vera had the door to their room under scope. Being careful to avoid detection and keeping the door covered, she used a series of quick glances to ensure she was clear. It was deserted except for the cars passing by on Highway 50, which was also nearly deserted.

She waited twenty minutes, but no cops, and he didn't try to leave. That was a good thing because it meant he was on board, which also meant that she didn't have to kill him and clean up the fallout from that move. She was also relieved for another two reasons: first, she might still need him to get out of here; and second, *well, that was something else.* That "something else" had been bothering her for the past hour, *and of all the inappropriate times for it to pop up?*

* * *

Ken looked at his caller ID and observed Sarah was calling him. *I wonder what she has,* thought Ken. "Beck here."

"Okay," Sarah replied, "based on the info you gave me, I checked the two hundred sightings over the past hour, and narrowed it to the Sacramento area as you instructed. Of those, I found one in Stockton from a doctor who was driving home. He said a black Mustang cut him off very aggressively, and then when it got caught at a red light, he pulled up to tell the driver off. The doctor says it was a guy, with a really hot chick in the back seat. He also says, it was *our* hot chick."

"Did he remember the intersection?"

"Yes, it was them for sure, as we have the camera footage from the traffic light."

"Stockton, huh? Okay Sarah, let's find these guys. Let me know what else you come up with. This kills my idea, but at least I'm physically in the neighborhood to get on this."

SIX

Simpatico

Still sitting in his trance in his corner office, Pablo's reflections of the past continued. Those three months with James had been unlike anything he had ever experienced. For the first time in his life he hadn't needed to explain his references, he was able to toggle back and forth between languages, and he was completely understood.

James had been amazing, and he had seemed stronger lately. Perhaps having taken on a pupil (or more like a dependent) had been healing him somehow? Pablo had read of such miracles. James had opened doors that would have taken years of teachers and schools to open, and he had done it in days, sometimes hours, not weeks or years.

Back then, Pablo had been sure he knew what heaven felt like as his mind had spent every day absorbed in the amazing world that James provided. Every night, as Pablo had lain in bed, sleep had come in fits, as his head spun in a million directions trying to process all that James had taught him in that day's lessons.

A bird brought Pablo out of his deep thoughts, momentarily. It was doing a very acrobatic, very graceful dive for a fish in the Guaya River. Pablo smiled at the thought of how many of his technological advancements had come from watching natural acts such as this bird.

He fell back into thought, and immediately went back to the day when he had found out about his family's murder.

Earlier that same day, something else significant happened, as Carmen Ardourel had asked him to the dance that coming Friday. He had thought she had always seemed happy when she was around him, now he knew why. Pablo just wished he had known then, that for the last time in his life, at age sixteen, he was going to fall asleep to a world of peace, innocence, and wonderment of things to come, and wake up to another reality altogether. *And I never even got to kiss the girl.*

He had learned a great deal the night his life changed forever, both about human behavior and about James Haberman. He had later found out that James had written a letter to Sandy Burroughs that night.

He let his mind roam to James, and to his thoughts that night as James told him what was going through his mind at that time, during one of their many long talks. It had been essential that James understood Pablo's need for all information, and thankfully, James had. So he had meticulously recreated happenings to satiate Pablo's need.

Pablo had known that James sometimes missed Bill Westinghouse, and his old job. James had loved the challenges and the pride he felt for bettering his country. Leaving had been hard. In the first place, it had been a challenge that took years of planning. At Conceptual, the employees' financials had been watched very closely, and it hadn't been easy funneling a hundred million dollars into Zurich. Of course that had been working on Plan Number One, the "get-more-money-than-anyone-needs" plan.

Plan Number Two had been his breakdown story to cover his needed sabbatical. He had needed time to become someone else, and to make that person rich. That had been before his yearly physical turned up some problems with his white blood cell count, and it was a good thing he had used his own doctor for that test. His original plan had been to be back in place before they got too desperate and started hunting hard for him. He had figured Bill could hold them off for at least a year. He might have stayed and tried to fight the cancer in the U.S., if stem cell treatments had been available.

After James had left them no choice by being gone so long, they brought in Cooper to complete his project. James thought it had been very possible that Cooper could do it based on the data the team already had knowledge of, which of course, was everything but his crucial battery discovery.

This had been one of the worst hardships for him, because in his entire lifetime, James Haberman had never started a project and then failed to finish it. There had been no reason to feel guilty—he had given his all for the U.S. But he had felt guilty nonetheless. His mind had molded civically, and that had been all he had ever known.

His former team had the concept, and Cooper had had a competent enough mind to make it happen, so James had never really understood one hundred percent why he had always felt so guilty. Perhaps, it had something to do with his patriotism, and perhaps it had something to do with him always having to be the best.

James had conceded that he initially had plans to introduce Pablo to his American friends once he was done training him. His plan had been to send Pablo to Westinghouse, with Burroughs in tow to explain it all. Then he would have been a hero—a posthumous hero, but a hero nonetheless. The U.S. would have benefited enormously if his successor had worked for them.

Pablo had known of the accolades James had been using when referencing him, and he had known that James felt shame because he had been constantly fighting the urge to compete rather than teach. Deep down James had confessed that he had known the competition would be one-sided. He had often said of Pablo, "Once this kid absorbs all there is, he will be at a level that mankind could only look up to and genuflect." Pablo had known that James had never felt that way about anyone in his entire life.

As a hobby, James had built an empire by setting up a puppet company in the Bahamas and then investing in the stock market. Being on the inside of all the major military breakthroughs and contract dealings, he had amassed a hundred million in two years. He had also been one of the pioneering minds behind the Internet. He had been there in the beginning, as the boys at the CIA recruited him and secretly placed him in DARPA unbeknownst to Westinghouse.

The CIA had him set up some back doors to certain entities that they deemed "problematic" if they were ever to fall into enemy hands. For every backdoor James created for them, he created one for himself too. No one had been at his level at the time, so who was going to catch him? Of course no one would have ever uncovered this information, since it was only he and Bob Thompson who had known exactly what he was doing for the Agency. No one else had known, otherwise they would have both been in jail.

Only, what Bob hadn't known was that James was rogue, and it hadn't stopped once the desired institutions were obtained for the CIA, as that had not been the way James Haberman was wired. He had been wired to never stop until the game was over. So James hadn't stopped until he had them all! He had even had NORAD and the Energy Grid System for the U.S. Nothing had been out of his reach, not even the CIA.

So when James Haberman had proclaimed, "The kid's a prodigy," he hadn't meant he would someday win a Nobel Prize or some piddly shit like that. What James had meant was that one day Pablo would cure cancer, or complete the EMP Project and make ICBM's a thing of the past, or invent time travel, something HUGE!

James's letter to Sandy Burroughs had been very specific on how the lad was to be taken care of, and how he and his family would never want for anything, ever again. Unfortunately, it was a letter James would never send, because at 2:14 in the morning, just as he was finishing that letter, his phone had rung and scared the bloody hell out of him.

It had scared him not only because of the hour, but because not many people had had his number. It couldn't have been good news—no good news came at two in the morning. He recognized the area code as local. *Ah, probably a wrong number.* He had answered, "Yes?"

During one of their many long talks about things past, James had told Pablo numerous times how that call started, and it was certainly apt how Jeremy had begun.

"It's Jeremy. You might want to sit down."

Already feeling weak, James did what he was told by Jeremy. He sat.

"Is it the boy?" he had asked before Lebuff could speak.

"James, I don't know how to say this, or what to make of it, but we just received word that Pablo's entire family has been wiped out by a band of what appear to be mercenaries. They spared no one."

Stunned silence had followed. Finally, James asked Jeremy, "Why?"

"We don't know. The only way we found out was because we donated old books and supplies to Pablo's former school. His old principal called and told us the news."

James's head had started working and he had thought of something he had learned once upon a time. *If you want the truth, follow the money.*

"Jeremy, I never asked you this before, but how does an impoverished boy from Ecuador afford to go to school here? Scholarship?"

Truthfully, Lebuff hadn't known. The teachers hadn't really cared.

Sure, they had been able to deduce who was from money and who wasn't, and Jeremy had recalled that Pablo was somewhere in the middle, but that had been all he remembered.

"I don't know, James."

"Well, you need to find out and give me a name—quickly! I have some work to do right now, but I'll be waiting for you to get back to me." James's voice held urgency.

"I don't like the tone of your voice, James. Do you know something I don't?"

"No, but who's to say whoever did this doesn't want to finish the entire job? Find me that name, Jeremy!"

* * *

When Pablo got like this, he could sit for hours and contemplate on his past, running away with his thoughts. It was especially easy when he came here and saw the very river his uncle had died on. Of course, his thoughts naturally drifted to his *tio* and his last day on the planet, a day Pablo had researched at length.

He could see Julio laughing and having a great conversation with his father, who had just gotten news about how well their Pablito was doing in France. He had bellowed to Julio on the other end.

"He's doing the same thing there as he did here, he's rewriting the books. I heard they just gave him an award for Drama. He's apparently quite the actor, too."

Julio had chuckled heartily, "We sent him there to rule the world and he got a drama award!" They had both laughed a good long one while picturing their Pablito doing the play in tights. Julio had yawned and said, "Okay, my brother, it's time for me to go, please tell the family that I said 'hi.'"

Julio had pocketed his phone, feeling really good at the moment. He had poured himself a double shot of rum and squeezed out a lime in his mouth for the after-wash. He had gulped it, and as he pulled it away, expelled an audible "ah" of pleasure. At the last second he had observed the Ninja in the reflection of the small mirror off to his left. *Well, it sure looked like a Ninja,* was the last thought he had ever had, his reactions were stupefied by alcohol.

Before he had been able to turn and verify his initial assessment, the specially sharpened garrote wire had been around his neck. In one deft move, within one second, the attacker had tightened the wire and had jammed his knee in Julio's back. The next second, his decapitated head had shattered the glass table into a million pieces. His attacker had stood over the body, the stump still spurting blood at an alarming rate, and said, "That's for Fernando, Puto."

Octavio had then bent down and picked his victim's phone out of his pocket. "Now let's see who you were talking to on the phone."

* * *

Vera came in as Matt was drying off. She could tell he worked out regularly. He was a big guy, not fat, but certainly not thin. He almost had a six-pack and little body hair, but she could tell he was working on it though. His brown hair a tufted mess, and damn, did that boy have big feet! She internally blushed.

"Hi."

"Hey," was his reply, his eyes glued on the television set.

Matt watched her remove some purchased items from her bag and said to her, "They're heating things up. So what's the rest of the plan you wanted to tell me? Because the way it looks, they've clamped down on every major way there is to get out of here."

Vera replied, "Major routes, yes, Matt, but not every way. I have a plane here."

"You fly?"

"No," she answered.

Matt tried not to be condescending, but it was hard. "I'm confused. You have a plane and you can't fly it?"

"That's correct. The government was scrutinizing potential pilots to the point where they were basically being vetted by Homeland Security, and I didn't want that scrutiny on my alias' identity. So I bought the plane, and I was planning to buy a house here. Then the cover story of why I needed the pilot's license would have worked for my covert identity."

Matt thought, *wouldn't the purchase of the plane draw scrutiny?* Her next sentence covered his thought though.

"The plane was purchased by a blind, a fake company set up for me. It's what the storage sheds are under, as well as the car we're driving."

"Okay, so we have a plane we can't fly, and everyone in the world is looking for us. What part of this is your plan?"

She opened up her shopping bags and pulled out hair color for men. It was a very light brown.

"This will be a start."

* * *

Ken Beck exited Highway 99 via Highway 4 and got off on California Street in Stockton. From there it was a short two blocks to the intersection of Weber and California, ground zero. He gathered the team.

"Okay, we know they were here, but we don't know why. My guess is that they were either here to switch cars, hit a safe house, or both. Unit One is to do a sweep of a mile radius, starting here, then two miles, then three. Look for all hotels, restaurants, and businesses they could be hiding in, just in case they were running down the rabbit hole and decided to lay low."

Ken turned to Unit Two. "Okay, you guys do the same perimeter, but look for the car or any signs of a safe house. Look for activity in back yards, garages, et cetera. I will look for auto and storage units in the vicinity. We have three more teams coming to help. And remember, stay off the radios, just group text for now. We want this on the down-low. The Agency has to have first crack at this. Make it happen, people."

He added before they left, "Sarah is continuing to chase leads in Sacramento, just in case we're barking up the wrong tree here. Remember, we're systematic for a reason. Just keep flipping the stones and something good will come from it. Now go out and find them."

* * *

Vera was drying Matt's hair and watching the TV. *Man, had they ever kicked over the hornet's nest.* The net was clamping down for sure. She handed him a sectional aeronautical map, San Francisco legend.

"What's this?"

"It's an aeronautical map. It shows things like Military Operating Zones and the classes of Airspace Operation."

"I'm listening," Matt said.

"Well, according to this, if we stay below seven hundred feet, we're below radar, and if we stay on the course I have penned on the map, we'll dodge all the MOA's all the way to the Mexican border. We have a pick-up south of the border, if we can make it."

"Wow, that's a thin plan. Are we supposed to just pull a pilot out of our ass?"

Apparently she didn't like sarcasm because she "accidentally" pulled his hair while combing it and it freaking hurt. Then she started combing again a little nicer as she continued. "I was thinking we could find a sight-seeing group and kidnap the pilot."

"That would be too high-profile," Matt said. "It would draw too much attention."

"Okay, what do you suggest?"

Matt offered, "How about an instructor from the pilot school I saw advertised on a sign at the airport when we drove by it."

Vera hadn't thought of that or seen the sign when she checked this place out the previous month. That didn't sit well with her. Apparently, she didn't have her mind completely open. "Not bad," she conceded, "we could even pay him some crazy amount for three hours or something. Then we could have a nice head start before anyone notices that we're gone. All we have to do is lay low here until tomorrow and see what we can find out." She inwardly admitted that it was a great idea. Vera was beginning to realize that Matt wasn't just another pretty face, which brought her back to the other thing, the troubling thing.

He looked in the mirror. She had changed his appearance so drastically that he hardly recognized himself, especially his hairstyle, which was now parted on the side. She found some designer shops, and he was now a very sharply dressed metrosexual male who looked ready for the casino. She completed Matt's ensemble with some wire-framed glasses, a black shirt that was certainly in the several hundred-dollar range, and some very comfortable slacks. To top it off, she had gotten him some good leather shoes with nice thick rubber soles.

"Very nice," he told her as he inspected himself in the mirror. She was making some trimming adjustments on his bangs. Their faces were very close, and some light touching was taking place as she jockeyed for a better position. She actually straddled him at one point, which electrified his body, giving him goosebumps.

She got hair in his eyes, and he clenched them in reaction. She instinctively blew it out, and then it happened. They had one of those awkward moments where their eyes locked for an inordinate amount of time, and without warning, they were embracing.

He had tried to make the timing right, and by her reaction it worked, as it wasn't just a casual embrace. There was a lot of passion coming from her. Her touch was amazing.

They mated like two frenzied animals, and didn't stop to make love for most of it. But, at some point, they stared into each other's eyes and had another awkward moment while having sex. This time it turned on him, as he gave into her passion and they actually made love for a long, long time.

* * *

Ken Beck saw it on his Google Maps. It was a twenty-four hour storage unit not two miles from his location. That would be the first tree he barked up.When he got there, the hair on the back of his neck stood up. *Damn, on the first try?*

Since he'd been a rookie field agent, he'd observed that if the hair on the back of his neck stood up, it meant they were at the right spot or after the right person or whatever it was they sought. He had a sixth sense about things that had served him well.

Ken parked and went in. Jorge Villalobos was the manager in charge when Beck identified himself. Jorge was not an easy customer though. He had never seen a CIA badge before, and quite frankly, he didn't believe it was real, especially since Beck was wearing a t-shirt.

Jorge became a believer when Ken texted Unit Two to come to the address. He needed Agent Blake's help convincing Mr. Villalobos that they were legitimate before Jorge foolishly called the local police department and tipped Rogers that he was onto a good lead. After two minutes of speaking with the 6'6", 260-pound Agent Blake, Villalobos was in more of a mood to talk.

The gate logs showed six entrances between three and six o'clock, and Ken addressed his newly cooperative friend.

"Let's see the video, Jorge." At 16:45, a black Mustang appeared and a handsome man punched the code and was let in. Beck gaped in disbelief at his luck. *Son of a bitch, there she was in the back seat!* "Jorge, what unit does this person have?"

"Unit 25, it's in the very back."

They stayed on the recording, and now they also knew what car the wanted fugitives had switched into as well. She was the one to switch the car though, and they couldn't make out a passenger as she left.

Maybe Hurst is in that shed with a bullet in his head, Ken thought. He stood and addressed Jorge. "We're going to close your facility for a few minutes, and we'll keep it low profile, no news people or anything."

They set up, and Unit One covered, as Blake moved in from Unit Two and cut the lock. He slid the bolt back, lifted the door, and slid the probe into the shed. It would detect the presence of explosives, although the word was that the stuff used at Conceptual was so sophisticated that the probe might not detect anything dangerous.

It was a go. Unit Two moved in, and Beck found Hurst's black Mustang, but no movement.

The storage unit was dark, but once they found the lights, they knew that this was a safe house. There were even clothes lockers here. These two were on the move with a new set of everything it seemed. Ken Beck had walked in and smelled the break. This place would surely yield some clues. He would get Sarah working on this right away. She would find him something, as she always did.

* * *

Pablo knew from talking to James about it many times that a seeming eternity had passed before Jeremy had called with the news of his own financial backing, even though it had actually been only a couple of hours.

"It was his uncle," Jeremy had said, clearing his throat. "All tuition is being paid for by a Julio Manuel. The transfers come out of a bank in Guayaquil, Ecuador. I suppose you think there's a connection between this uncle and what happened?"

"Not sure, Jeremy, but I would bet dollars to donuts there is."

"Dollars to donuts? You Americans are good at coming up with the weirdest expressions."

"Yeah, well, there's something else we're good at Jeremy, and that's helping friends when they need it." He had let that one sink in. "I'll call you back."

James had gone to work, and within a very short time he had been able to find a valuable piece of information. The day before, a Julio Manuel had been decapitated in his home in Guayaquil. The police had written that the murder was typical of a cartel execution, with the man garroted while his girlfriends slept. The girlfriend had been pluralized. *So at least he went out happy,* James had thought. *Until he was garroted of course, a disgusting thing to wake up to for sure.*

Immediately James made the connection. Now he knew for sure that his protégé was in real trouble. He also realized that his life was about to take a major "right turn," as he'd just become a de facto parent without warning. Suddenly, he'd had a feeling he had never known before in his entire lifetime, an awakening of parental instinct.

What had been spinning in his head had now begun churning in his stomach, and before he had known it, he had been on his feet moving for the door. Most people would have been on their feet and dealing with the immediate situation, but not James Haberman. For like Pablo, his vision in life and chess had been so far ahead of everyone else's that it couldn't even be quantified. *Suffice it to say, my plan of going home to die is not going to happen anymore,* James had mused. Then, the sobering reality had struck him. He had forgotten. *Oh yeah, I'm going to die soon.*

* * *

Matt asked first, "Where the hell did that come from?"

Vera answered with, "I don't know, I didn't plan that. Truthfully, I'm dedicated to someone, and even though I had permission to do that, I never have."

"Permission? Are you married?"

She giggled, and replied condescendingly. "No. I'm not married, but you are."

Matt answered under his breath with the intention of deception, "If you can call it that."

Vera concluded the conversation. "No more questions. It happened; now let's just try to live. You have your life and I have mine."

Matt looked at her and laid back, contemplating. *Okay, for her it was no big deal, since she didn't just betray her marriage, but I did, and it isn't exactly my modus operandi.* Back in Matt's younger days he would have one girl cross over the end of the next one, but that was when he was young, and that's what young people did. He wasn't a cheater, and he really wanted to believe that he did what he had to do. The fucked up part was that he had really enjoyed doing it, and it was already eating at his conscience.

Vera was watching the emotions dance across Matt's face. He obviously wasn't a cheater, or else he wouldn't be so wracked with guilt. She felt a little bad about it, but there it was again. The minute she thought about him with his wife, she felt jealousy? *No, it's not possible to fall in love with someone in one day—is it? I'm just confused right now by all that's been happening.* Vera decided to lighten the mood.

"If it's any consolation, we'll probably both be dead by this time tomorrow anyway."

"That's supposed to cheer me up?" Matt replied. "You're not very good at cheering people up."

Vera jumped on him. "Oh yeah? How about now?"

She put her breasts in his face while straddling him, then pulled back, and let her hair fall over him. He realized as he absorbed her essence that he was hopelessly lost in this girl. *But how can that be? I just met her.*

"Okay, now we're talking," he said with a smile.

Then her stomach grumbled loudly. "Looks like you better eat. Me, too. The last thing I had was half a pastrami, thanks to you." She looked at him puzzled. He explained, "I'll tell you later. But now let's figure out where we can eat. It's not exactly like we can go out, even in our disguises. Although I'm sure there's a drive-thru window somewhere here in Tahoe."

"No," she said. "There's a little local diner up the road, we'll be fine. Who'll be expecting the two most wanted people on the planet to be in a diner in Tahoe?"

Vera really was nonplussed. Her training told her she would be fine. Hiding in plain sight was an art. Plus, he was a light-haired fancy boy now, who was wearing glasses and driving a very expensive car with his trophy at his side. One couldn't go very far around here without seeing that combination.

They left the motel, and Vera hid the problem that was swirling around her head at the moment, a big problem for her. That tête-à-tête should have meant nothing to her. It should have just been a release from the stress, nothing more. *Then why is it bugging me?* It didn't feel casual at all, and she felt the complication manifesting as she was still imaging him inside her. She was continuing her spiral off the grid now. If she lived through the next twenty-four hours, then she really had some feelings to sort out.

Vera's former life had been so repulsive that she'd never gotten into a situation where she had "longed for the good old days." The good old days had been a horror filled nightmare that no human being should ever have to endure. Only the future was for her, because in her entire life, looking back had not been an option. The world had been a cruel and horrible place most of her life, but thanks to Pablo, she was now a force to be dealt with.

It didn't elude her that she was in a unique position, one that probably had never come up in the history of the world. One moment in time she was a whore, forced into sex with all kinds of perverted men. Now, she was going to bring mankind to its knees, not the other way around.

Now was she dealing with finding love in the midst of all this chaos? Vera couldn't believe that she allowed the word. If it were love, it would be a love that was wrought with problems and bad karma. Yet, all she could think of was that she would trade it all right now for this guy and an island, just the two of them. Maybe it was just like the Bible said. Maybe the meek really will inherit the earth. If that happens, it would definitely be because of what she and Pablo were doing here now. If they were successful, then she could make that island dream a reality. *But not if I can't get out of the fucking United States!*

* * *

Everyone handles pressure differently. Most men would be freaking out that an entire nation was looking for the woman they loved. Every agency in the American arsenal was not only looking for the woman Pablo loved, but they also sought the plans she held, plans that would change the balance of power in the world, forever. Most men would be freaking out; but not Pablo, for he had reason to believe that faith alone would see her through. That reason was that he had God on his side.

Pablo went back to remembering James and the night it had all changed for him. He knew the story well.

That fateful night, James had stood over his bed watching him sleep, knowing his life was never going to be the same. He had been twisting over how to even begin to tell someone something like that.

Pablo knew that James had played it out over and over and still hadn't been able to find the words. Lebuff had stood silent in the corner, a total loss of composure on his face. The two of them had just stood there in an indecisive mess.

Pablo had awoken, and he had seen James's silhouette illuminated off his "too bright" alarm clock. Evidently his subconscious had felt a presence in his room.

"What?" Pablo had asked, looking around. "What's going on?" He had turned his nightlight on, exposing Lebuff. Then he had looked left to James for answers.

The following moments had been some of the most difficult in all of their lives. James had known Pablo was extremely close to his family. When they had relayed the horrific news, Pablo hadn't been able to accept it. It had taken Jeremy telling him that he spoke to the principal himself to get Pablo to believe it. It had been truly horrible.

Then had come the time to tell him of his uncle's fate. James had given him the news as he read it from the police blotter. As he had read, he had seen the boy's analytical mind turn on.

James had respected his intelligence by saving his theory for another time, while Pablo had tried to accept the unacceptable. James had only been able to watch helplessly as Pablo tried to fathom a reality that was usually reserved for sensationalized media footage shown on television news—the kind of reports that showed some destroyed man telling the story of how his entire family had been in a building that some U.S. rocket had errantly blown up. But this had been no news clip, it had been Pablo's life, and he was being asked to handle something that no one should ever be asked to handle.

This had been a reality never meant to occur anywhere, and in a moment of feelings that came out of nowhere, James had begun to sob uncontrollably as well. He had hugged the boy and given the same gut-wrenching moan that had just happened the other way, not ten minutes before. James had sobbed as the revelation came to him. *How many scenes in the world have played out just like this, to people just like this boy at my hands? How much misery have I caused, just like this, in the name of the good old U.S.A.?*

James had known it must have been a lot, but he had just kept going, every new offer taken, every new contract fulfilled. He had known things, things that he shouldn't have ever allowed himself to know. There had been clearance levels he should have turned down, once they were offered. Even Bill hadn't known about several of them—not fully, anyway.

Bill had known about the EMP net, and that's the one the CIA had wanted. It had also meant they would probably kill him without hesitation if they found him and he didn't surrender immediately. Fortunately, on that front, he'd only had a few months to live, so he wouldn't be running for much longer, one way or the other.

Pablo had stroked his hair as they hugged, and James had wailed on. The thing about being *simpatico* with someone was there was no need for explanation. Pablo had been trying to comprehend the myriad of emotions James was going through, emotions that being in the killing people business had brought on.

James had obviously been having some career regret, as the type of vile deed that had happened to Pablo's family was something he must have known a lot about. Even though no words had been spoken, Pablo had intuitively understood that this man would never build a weapon again, even if he recovered by some miracle. Fortunately for Pablo, one small grain of good had arrived at his darkest hour, in the form of the discovery that he wasn't completely alone. He had inherently known that as long as these men were alive, then he still had guardians, for these men truly loved him.

He had looked at Lebuff in the corner, as James had been struggling to compose himself, and had said, "Man, you're a train wreck in a crisis."

Jeremy Lebuff had broke down and run to them both, and the three had hugged for a long time. Pablo had finally wiped his eyes and said to Lebuff with a note of seriousness, "They will come and they will come soon, so we'd better have a plan and it'd better be good."

James had interrupted, "I have the plan, and of course it's good."

* * *

Sarah called Ken Beck on his private cell, a number very few had. "Rogers called, he's pissed, Ken. He knows you're screwing him, someone on this side leaked that we're in Stockton. He wants an update and an apology. His words, not mine, Boss."

"I could care less about Rogers. I don't work for him. Okay, Sarah, so the cat's out of the bag. That was bound to happen. It's the 'what have you got for me' that I'm most concerned with at present." Ken was hoping he was playing off his unease, but he doubted he was fooling her.

"Okay Boss, the company that holds the storage unit is called Arrow Brook Distributors. They distribute fine wines and antiques from South America and sell them all over California. So I was able to get their tax returns from last year, and they had quite a few write offs: cars, computers, office furniture and—get this—a Cessna 310."

"What did you say, Sarah?"

"A Cessna 310—quite a fast propeller plane."

"Yes it is, Sarah. A twin prop plane at that, with an air speed of two hundred miles per hour."

"What's our next step, Boss?"

"Okay," he said, "all the small-plane airports are grounded, so we have some time. Find out where that plane was purchased and let's find out who bought it. Does Arrow Brook list a CEO or CFO that we can get a hold of, by any chance?"

Sarah answered, "If this is a front company, then there won't be anybody real to contact. It will just be dead end after dead end, wasting our time the whole way. It's probably part of their plan, to get us wasting time while they progress."

"Okay, forget the executives. Focus on the purchase, look for a name. We have a few hours left before the contents of the shed will be moved to a secure location for the complete overhaul."

"Okay Boss, stay cool and call Rogers—that was not a pleasant call I took for you."

Before they hung up, Sarah reminded him, "By the way, your boy Hurst flunked out of the Sheriff's Academy two years ago."

"Why?" Ken asked.

"Seems a psychiatrist there thought that he was harboring rage issues, and they labeled him with a 'predisposition for irrational violence.' Apparently there was an incident in the locker room and he got into a fight, but didn't stop when mutual combat was over. The other Cadet suffered a fractured jaw and had a concussion."

When they hung up, Ken's neck was starting to prickle, and he was sure Sarah was going to call back in a little while with the home run. He dialed Rogers and received the warmest greeting.

"We're supposed to be on the same team, Asshole. What have you found out?"

* * *

Pablo came out of his malaise over things past and decided to look to things present. He brought up his computer, and he was quite happy at what he saw. The world was scrambling, especially the U.S. He'd already made history by single-handedly bringing their air traffic to a grinding, miserable, near-standstill. That was a win, as was the fact that their President acknowledged his threat. Security checkpoints were causing delays of almost every flight, some for hours. Not to mention their whole country was looking for Vera.

He must have really struck fear into them, because their politicians didn't do that. They lied, they skirted, and although the President was "a man of the people," they didn't go on national TV and tell the truth. That is, unless it was so bad that they knew what was about to leave the country was irreplaceable.

It was not lost on Pablo that his actions were going to stain the legacy of what appeared to be a good leader. Basically, this was an act of war, and Pablo was sure that once he was briefed, the President would realize this had happened on his watch. He was now making the grievous error of exposing himself too soon, and Pablo was sure the man realized that he was now culpable in whatever outcome resulted from Vera's break-in. That's what Pablo was seeing, and it made them look weak. So in that respect, they'd made the first blunder??

Pablo looked at the stock ticker on the European NASDAQ and smiled. He observed that the Indian technology company Tanjotti rose twenty points on the news that it would launch its new communications satellite the next year. They would be using some groundbreaking technology that would revolutionize cellular communications. Tanjotti was using the Russian for-hire private space corporation Stratosphere, to launch their satellite into orbit.

The article added that Tanjotti would be using their new state-of-the-art satellite to strengthen their existing network in South America. But there was already a rumor that they would be combining with one of the big U.S. based companies to help broaden their existing range. Once that move was made, there would be a mutually beneficial merger for the shareholders of both companies, whoever that other company might be.

Pablo smiled. He had just made a cool ten million on those twenty points, and he was the one who had leaked the merger information, which was totally untrue. He owned Tanjotti and a busload of other corporations all over the world. It was amazing what one could get some players to do just by loudly and obviously moving a simple piece on the board.

No merger was planned. He had obtained this Tanjotti Company because they happened to have cheap labor, which he could use to run a profitable acquisition. He was building the actual satellite in Brazil. Tanjotti was just going to manage the legitimate, cellular business that he was appearing to run.

In the highly volatile commodities world, pieces of information or misinformation were worth millions. Pablo smiled again. Whether Vera got out or not, that satellite was going to do a lot more than communicate. But if she did make it, the production shortcuts that her cache would allow him to create would be priceless. Regardless, his orbiting wasp was going to leave quite an impression on anything it came into proximity to, with or without all the enhancements that the safe's contents would surely help enable.

Pablo had been trying to shelve the reality that Vera might not ever come back from America. He really didn't want the only family he had going and living away for two years in a foreign land, but it was the only way to get to the safe. God, how he loved her, but as she knew, it's wasn't the romantic love that she desired. She didn't understand yet that true love didn't come out of feelings of indebtedness.

True love needed to come from left field, and although she swore that that was the craziest thing he'd ever said, he had tried to convince her not to close her heart to the possibility that she could have "our love" and the spontaneous romantic love that everyone deserved as well. Pablo would always love Vera no matter what, but she really didn't know what love was, even though she thought she did.

He fondly remembered her concern.

"Even if this madness you speak of were true, what about you Pablito?" she had asked. "Where is your happiness?"

"On the love front my dear," he had replied. "God will point us to where we shall be, that's why I believe in another love for you, because my destiny is not to be 'The Lover.' My destiny is to be 'The Judgment.'"

Pablo's parents hadn't thought he had known that the last card the old woman had turned over at the carnival that fateful day was "Judgment." Judgment was a very interesting card. It focused on closing old doors and opening new ones. It talked about resurrecting old ghosts and letting them go. For him to do that, he was going to need some closure.

According to the story he had overheard his parents recant, after seeing his parents, the old Adivina had immediately closed for the day, and the next morning she was gone, even though the carnival was in town for two more days. "Judgment." It was coming for more than one unsuspecting group, whether or not Vera made it out of the U.S.

He looked in the corner contemplating his newly-purchased armament when his phone rang. It was Felipe, his Field General.

* * *

Sarah sounded elated, "I got it Ken! The Cessna, it was delivered to Tahoe, and it's registered and housed at the municipal airport up there."

Ken knew that he should immediately call this in, and that they should converge on Tahoe with all available personnel, scorching the earth looking for them. But he also knew, and believed in the mantra, "No guts, no glory."

"Sarah, hear me. I'm not asking you to torch your career here, as you've been more than loyal, so I understand if you feel the need to turn on this. I'll call bygones now, but I'm going after them and I want until tomorrow at 07:00."

Silence followed. "Why?" she finally asked.

"Because this is the one, Sarah. This is my ticket to 'the seat.' This is the defining moment for me, as I will be completely untouchable and you know it. The why's and the how's won't mean anything if we have the proof of the pudding. Come on, Sarah; don't tell me you don't know that too. Remember Alabama? This is a country of results. Plus, worst-case scenario, they get out and you have some F-15s scramble. Then it's all over. They're trapped and you know it. Now let me go in and take those two out before they know they've been made and do something like go backwoods on us, or split up."

"What about Pete Brody's assessment?"

"Hurst could be a good guy. If he is, Sarah, then he better hope he's good at conveying things quickly."

She thought about it. "How are you going to make it to Tahoe expeditiously from Stockton without raising every eyebrow there is?" she asked.

Ken chuckled. "That's right, Sarah, you've never driven with me when I'm motivated, have you? Trust me, I'll be there in less than two hours, and they're at least five hours from pulling out here. No one will know I'm gone because I'm in mobile office mode, and it's not unusual for me to be in my car at a scene for two hours or more. They'll just think I'm busy. Plus they're in gathering mode. The time for this move is right now."

"Alright—go, Ken. But God help us both if you're wrong on this."

The line went dead. Sarah thought to herself that she could always work for her sister in Atlanta. She owned a dry cleaning chain. *The only thing I hate more than the smell of dry cleaning solutions is humidity.* Sarah already had one foot out the door on Beck's whole crazy scheme, but she would be abandoning a career path that she had stuck to fastidiously.

Not only that, she had seen what happens to people who've enraged Mr. Beck. Thinking that thought reminded her that the interrogation barf scene had been recorded. She'd watched it a dozen times. It was so funny. Sarah was sure Jan Hurst would turn up dead somewhere in the near future. "Choked on her own vomit," the report would read.

Some would claim that Sarah rode Ken Beck's coattails to the top, but Sarah knew the truth that they were the dynamic duo. It wasn't so much that she rode Ken's coattails, it was more like she was the running back following the blocker. Only in this league, the blocker was the star. Even though there were things about him that gave her the creeps, so far, he hadn't let her down on the career path. No, she would roll the dice and wait out 07:00. *But damn, it was going to be a long night.*

* * *

Starving, Matt and Vera entered the diner talking about gambling in a rehearsed nonchalance. They acted as if they barely noticed the waitress while ordering coffee and perusing the menus. The TV was running at an average volume at the far end of the counter, so they couldn't hear it clearly from their booth.

The three people at the counter and their waitress were currently huddled around it watching a live broadcast from DHS, which looked to be about Matt. The waitress broke off when she glanced at them watching her, and she was back in a hurry with the coffee. She apologized for the wait, explaining that she just felt the news was "all so riveting."

Then Matt did something that immediately threw her off from suspecting them of anything. It was a move that took away the tension Vera was feeling inside. Afterward, she realized that it was quite an ingenious thing Matt had done. He had simply told the middle-aged, white waitress with the weathered face and the worn-out shoes, "It was probably them Towel Heads or those damn Chinese." Just like that, he was in with her.

She went off on some tirade about foreigners and took their order. Then she mentioned what a nice couple they were before disappearing into the kitchen.

Matt whispered to Vera in a knowing tone, "One thing you can always count on in this country, you can always find a racist when you need one."

He continued to impress her more every second. As she was looking over at the three guys sitting at the counter, she suddenly got an extremely focused look on her face. One of them was wearing an Aviator's jacket, with small wings on it, and then she noticed the pilot's hat on the counter. He was a white guy about thirty, with dark hair and average looks, build, and stature. He was "everyman": not too short, not too tall, not fat, but not skinny. Matt and Vera suddenly became very interested in his newest conversation with his counter mates.

"So, how long you grounded, Doug?" asked the fat guy on the left, who looked like a truck driver.

Doug replied, "Until the FAA says we can fly. Apparently, the big boys have the infrastructure to catch someone if they tried to get through, but we don't. Probably better off, from what I hear, be anywhere but an airport right now, especially a commercial one."

"What about your cargo?" the guy on the right asked him.

"Well, this trip I only dropped off. I was heading back to Oakland empty when this shit happened."

"Well, it could be worse," said the old man with the Walter Cronkite looks on the right. "You're in Tahoe, after all. Go throw a few dice."

Doug responded with, "Nice try, Harry. I have to be ready to go at a moment's notice. This is killing me, I had a hot date tonight."

The waitress brought their food, and Matt wolfed down his sandwich in record time. All the while they were eavesdropping on the "good-old-boy" conversation going on across the diner.

Vera had heard enough. She took a note pad out of her pocket book, wrote her plan out, and showed Matt.

Matt looked at her as if to say, "Are you sure?"

She gave him an "are you kidding me, doubting my abilities" look. He immediately capitulated.

Pablo had taught her that the simplest thing, like not having something to write on at all times, could be the difference between life and death. *Does he always have to be right? And if he is, what does that say about the hazel eyes staring back at me right now from across the table.* Matt rose, gave her a kiss on the cheek, and left. The waitress came over and said, "Where did your man get off to?"

Vera replied, "Oh, he's not my man, silly. That was my brother. Didn't you see the resemblance?"

Nadine (that's what her name tag said) uttered, "You know, now that you mention it, I surely do."

Vera knew she already had the pilot. She had noticed him eavesdropping on their conversation, and using her peripheral vision she could tell he was hooked. She got up. *Time for a trip to the bathroom.*

Douglas Sharp couldn't believe his luck or his eyes. First of all, this incredible blonde in this beautiful pants suit comes in. Her outfit had an amazing V cut in front, and it sent his mind reeling. Doug was quickly forlorn though, as she had a companion that could only be described as a "Nancy Boy" in tow.

Between trying to catch the news, and trying to casually look at her every chance he got, this was becoming a game of sorts. The game was, "Don't get caught starring at someone you can't take your eyes off of."

There were just some women that had it. They had the ability to just command attention and get any guy they wanted. She was one of them. He was a 28-year-old horn-dog who was looking to sow any and all the wild oats he could before he settled in for the death sentence of marriage. That's why he had become a pilot in the first place, so he could fuck his way across the world.

He didn't give a rat's ass about love for the air and all that crap. It was just a flying bus to him. Sure, at first, it was all exciting and such, but now a year later, it had become monotonous. He wanted to do his time here at a regional carrier like Ameraflight, then get on with the big boys and hopefully get over to the Orient, where he would be sure to get laid more often than not.

His luck had just gotten better as the dandy she was with got up, pecked her on the cheek and left. Shortly thereafter, Doug had overheard her talking with the waitress, revealing that the "half-a-fag" with her was her brother. *What a break. Damn, was she hot!*

She had got up and gone to the bathroom. As she had passed, Doug had fallen in love with every inch of her. *Oh man, what is that fragrance she's wearing?*

Matt had a few minutes to pack and tail her back to the airport. She had no gun, but she had her knife. This was all becoming too real, too soon. He packed their bag in a deft two minutes because they didn't really have much to carry, but he did note the destroyed bed and his mind drifted for a second. He decided that he would take the time to see what the heck she was carrying; but her stuff was gone. He had seen her satchel go in the backpack earlier, but now it was gone. This stupid backpack had more pockets than he had ever seen, and he was not in a mindset where he would find it anyway, so he abandoned the search. *So she trusts me, but only to a point.*

He looked at the phone. It was now or never. He needed to either pick-up that phone and take his chances that he wouldn't end up exactly like Lee Harvey Oswald, or do this with her, all the way. Then he took a moment to think about what going all he way might entail, including him against a law enforcement officer at some point.

He spoke out loud to himself. "So what will it be, Matt?" His internal voice answered, *I'm sure I will be killed before I ever get my day in court. I feel I'm somebody's patsy. Someone is looking to blame this whole thing on me in the end, there's no other way to explain why my shoplift recording of her did not exonerate me. That means the only way to exact revenge and justice is to follow the girl and see where this goes.*

The conversation with himself over, he placed the shoulder holster on and checked to see that the Beretta was in fact loaded at the chamber. It was. He sure hoped they had Federal ammo in it, as he'd jammed one of these with inferior ammo once. His weapons mentor had taught him about Federal ammo: it never failed.

As he was pulling the door shut, he had an idea, one that might get the results he desired. He took a page off the top of the provided hotel notepad and wrote, "An Intelligence Service is the ideal place for a conspiracy."

Maybe someone would get its true meaning, and if somehow she came back here and saw it, he could explain to her that it was a taunt. Matt knew that someone there, some profiler, would get his intentions, or he at least hoped that person would understand that he had the opportunity to escape. He could have righted things for himself, but he was sacrificing himself for God and Country.

He couldn't simply knock her out and turn her in. He couldn't even try to take some of the things she was smuggling and leave them behind now, as he had hoped for. Matt realized he was probably throwing away his life in vain, but he was doing it anyway, because he was sure that whatever items she had stolen were definitely going to be used to bring down the U.S. Plus he hadn't forgotten the threat to his wife and unborn child. *I have no choice.* Matt closed the door and crossed his fingers.

* * *

The sun was setting into the afternoon, and it was almost time to leave. Pablo had signed all the necessary documents, his task as owner fulfilled. The helicopter pilot had called and told him he would return from refueling in an hour. So Pablo sat back and stared out the window some more.

Pablo clearly remembered how he had sat in shock that night as they had drove. The plan had been to run to James's chateau in Switzerland.

James hadn't tried to communicate as they drove, sensing that it was not the time for words. Pablo remembered that James had initially driven ten hours from his chateau on Lake Geneva to find him after the chess game. Since then, to avoid looking suspicious, he had been living out of several different hotels and finally a flat.

James had ended up living away from his home for three months while he was tutoring. But he had told Pablo that home or not, they had been three of the greatest months of his life.

It had been a long drive back, and Pablo had known that James was truly concerned about Lebuff doing his job when the time came. Pablo had pushed up against James's car door to the point that James was hoping it held. James had said he was simultaneously wondering who their enemy was and worrying about the door.

Was it someone as powerful and far-reaching as the Colombian Cartels? Or maybe some local players, who just exacted revenge on those they could reach?

Well, Jeremy Lebuff would be the canary in the coalmine. If they came searching for him at the school, then that would be the answer: it was no regional player.

Either way, Pablo had known that after spending one day back at James's computer lab, they would have all the answers they needed.

Pablo remembered James telling him that for all intents and purposes, he felt like he was a real father that day. He had a boy to protect from some very bad people, and he was not going to let him down. He had told Pablo that the files and subfiles started opening in his head; that it was just like a chess game to him.

James had needed to put it all in perspective, to assign all this madness a plan—unorganized madness was not acceptable. From that moment on, James had vowed that they would be so far ahead of everyone in their pursuit, they would be forever untouchable.

The situation had been just like his cancer: it was happening and there wasn't shit he could do about it except go along for the ride. *Until it's over of course, there was always that.*

If he wouldn't be going back to face the music, then Plan B had been to disappear—hard, burrowing in deep. The plan for that had lain just hours ahead at the chateau. James hadn't planned on the two of them looking over their shoulders forever. He'd certainly had no intention of letting those terrorists get away with killing Pablo's family and making them live in fear.

Pablo used to make James tell the story of the car ride over and over again. He had been desperate to know what was in James's head during that time. James had seemed to understand, always making sure he conveyed all his thoughts and emotions.

The main thing James had felt at the time was that he couldn't comprehend or put into words what a horror the massacre was. It had been quite literally an indescribable thing. James had frequently wondered what one man could have done to bring down that kind of wrath.

Pablo knew James's mind also drifted to his own problems. He hadn't liked leaving friends hanging out to dry. Bill Westinghouse had been as close to a friend as one could have in that environment. To call the competition cutthroat would have been like calling Wall Street a play yard.

During the drive, James had thought of several ways he could help Bill, which in turn would be helping the very people who had been profiting from the death that he had contrived. It was on that momentous drive that James Haberman had had the life-changing epiphany that it all had to stop. He had decided that Bill Westinghouse would have to be sacrificed—even though James thought he was a decent enough warmonger, as far as warmongers go.

Decisions had been made once they reached the chateau. They had been hard decisions. One of them had been that James would need to call Sandy Burroughs and have him fly in the next day. Then James had changed his mind and had Burroughs fly out that night, as the next day was going to be a very busy day, and they would need all the time they could get.

On that ride, for the first time in his life, Pablo's mind had not been grasping the whole board. He had remembered almost coercing James to repeat the car story numerous times, to make sure he got the most information possible. Every time, Pablo had gotten a flake of information that didn't make it out the time before. He had done this to James until he was sure he had completely reconstructed that drive.

He realized now, sitting there in his glass office, that in the annals of history, their car ride from the ferry building to the Hedge would become more than a footnote. It had set things into play that would change the world forever.

He sure wished James were there. But it was probably better that he wasn't, because this was not going to go well for his country, regardless of the outcome. A small tear ran down his face as he looked down on the river and hung his head.

James had also made another decision on that drive. He had decided to turn the tables on the aggressors. He had intended to find out exactly who Pablo's enemies were and start to make life hard on them. James had been the one that motivated Pablo to find out all the things he could about Octavio Mendoza, the man who had been directly responsible for ensuring that the murders of his family were carried out. As a matter of fact, as he had found out in his constant search of the facts, at the same time they had been taking their car ride, another conversation had been going on in Peru.

* * *

The Lieutenant in charge of the group in Peru had come forward. He had been an ugly man and Octavio had hated the sight of him. *Not that I'm good looking or anything, but at least my wife can keep her eyes open while we make love. Oh, and the smell…*

"It is done, Commandant," the man had croaked out.

"Did we get them all?" Octavio had inquired.

"Yes," the Lieutenant had answered, "everyone present in the house was dispatched."

"Thank you, Eduardo. Your services are duly noted, Comrade. Was there suffering?"

"No. Just like you ordered, they all died at once—instantly."

"Very well, then."

The leader of the death squad had left, and the person he had really wanted to talk with had been standing there alone. Marco Rivera had been an IT genius. Without him, they would be light years from where they were now as a group.

The fact that he had been Octavio's son-in-law had meant he had always known where he could find him, too, and that had been a plus. His daughter, Luisa, had been as fiery as she was beautiful, and she had never allowed Marco to go anywhere alone.

Marco had said, "There's a bank account. That Indian used his real name too, just like on the lease."

"How much is in the account?"

"That's the weird part. There's only $200,000 U.S., and it appears there have only been two sources of direction for the funds. One has been to pay tuition to a school in France, and the other has been cash advances to our boy here locally, in Guayaquil. Octavio, it looks like there is one more Manuel out there. Someone has got to take a trip to France."

Octavio had sat silently for many seconds. Marco had learned to never interrupt him while he was in deep thought, so he had waited. Marco had drifted off to the scene of what had happened to the hombre who had given them Julio Manuel's name.

He had probably thought that Octavio would spare him, maybe even give him a job. Of course that belief had changed when his sadistic father-in-law had sliced the man's IV bag open and poured bleach in it. They had him restrained to the fullest, and the violent convulsions that tested those restraints and the blood-curdling scream that ensued were things that Marco would never forget. Marco would also never forget that the man who had remorselessly poured the bleach into that hombre's IV bag was no one's friend, not even *la familia*.

Octavio had finally spoken. "You are right, my Son. Someone does have to take a trip to France; it's you and I. Better pack your bags and tell your lovely wife to be waiting for you to get back, like a good wife should."

Marco had nodded acceptance and left. He hadn't liked it, because it was an unknown, and unknowns could be very dangerous. For all they had known, this could have been a trap, or it could have been as simple as this kid had no clue and "boom," they were done with the Manuel family. Knowing his luck though, he had known better. He had thought to pack a big bag.

"Oh yeah," Octavio had said before he had left, "There's one piece of good news in this. Tell our crews to scour every last inch of the grounds. I guarantee that this *payaso* has that money buried on the property. Tell them to be smart, that money is there, and if I have to come there to find it, someone is going to pay!"

Marco had left thinking two things. *One, how the hell did he deduce that the money is there based on their last conversation? And two, my wife is going to be pissed, and there's always trouble when she's pissed....*

* * *

When Vera came out of the bathroom, the Aviator's eyes were stuck on her like eye magnets. He did have a nice smile, and she gave him above average marks on the nice smile. She also noticed that the big one and the old one were at the far end of the counter now and the seats adjacent to the pilot were open.

As she was heading to her table, he said, "Hello." Then he said, "Mind if I join you?"

She turned around coyly and shot back, "That's awfully forward of you, don't you think?"

"Well, I noticed you weren't wearing a wedding ring, and I couldn't help hearing that that was your brother there, not a husband or boyfriend."

"You mean you couldn't help hearing because you were listening?"

"Okay, guilty as charged, but can you blame me? I mean look at yourself. You're like Kryptonite, lady, at least to me."

She softened. "Okay, Doug, let's sit down."

He looked confused. She swaggered over to him all cool-like, never breaking eye contact. She saw his Adam's apple contract involuntarily as she neared close enough to touch him, and then she pretended to dust off his nametag. There was that smile again.

The next thirty minutes was a quick synopsis of both their lives. His was first, and she barely listened. It was something about seeing the world, blah, blah, and blah. Hers was the made-up life of Michelle Fernandez, sales rep for Arrow Brook Distributors. It was the cover name she was going to escape with.

By the time she was done with her story, she had covered her life up to this point, and was telling him how silly she felt owning a plane she couldn't fly yet.

"That's a hell of a plane," he said. "You could have started with a single prop, you know, might have been wiser."

"Well," she said, "the salesman told me that this could carry more weight, since we'll have clients and all of their gear coming up, too. He told me it was a better buy."

He thought about that and replied. "He might have ripped you off."

"Why do you say that?"

"Well," he gulped, "salesmen have been known to take advantage of women from time to time, especially in fields they're not experts in." Backtracking he said, "I'm sure you did your homework. I'm sorry if I offended you."

"No offense, you were just being honest. I agree, most women are stupid when it comes to things in a man's world."

Doug let that go, since it could be a trap.

She asked, "Would you like to come see it and tell me what you think?"

He tried not to look as shocked as he really was. In reply, he said as coolly as he could manage, "I would love to come and see what it looks like." But he doubted that she got what he really meant, or she wouldn't be smiling so nicely.

They paid by leaving the money on the table. Nadine must have been in the back. The other two were glued to the TV and barely noticed them leave.

Finally, Matt thought. *Her note said ten minutes. How did she go from "you've got ten minutes, be waiting," to then taking over thirty minutes to extract herself from the diner? Typical woman-time behavior.*

But finally she and Fly Boy were on the move, and Matt was following behind at a safe distance. Two minutes up the road, they turned left into the airport, then swung onto the access road to the right. There Matt saw them get out and head for the middle row of six hangers.

He kept driving straight into the main airport complex, which consisted of a large single story building to the right, and a parking lot to the left, which was maybe a hundred yards long. It currently housed cars in about thirty of its one hundred potential parking spots.

The terminal was a long, single story building. It had a row of handicapped and short-term parking spaces right in front. The front steps had a few newspaper stands and a flagpole with a spotlight on the American flag, flapping gently in the breeze.

The place looked deserted, and it was only midnight. Matt went forward to the second lot entrance. He turned left into the parking lot and made a sharp U-turn. He nestled himself between two cars, inched out enough to have a full view of anyone coming in.

Matt realized that there were no less than ten private jets on the tarmac right in front of him, and it hit him why there were thirty cars in the lot this late. This was a commuter airport for rich people to get down to Vegas and the Bay Area, or even L.A. and vice versa. So with the "no-fly zone" imposed, these planes were stuck here, and whoever owned those cars was stuck in the Bay Area or L.A.

He looked in his rear view mirror, and saw nothing but blackness. Matt was pretty sure he was going to get scraped off the surface of the earth tonight, either by some missile shot out of an F-15 or some other form of high-tech death his own country would employ against him. *This plan is as thin as it gets.*

He was on that precipice again. He could hear it on the news, which he kept low in the background. They were updating their profile on him, and he was starting to sound more like Timothy McVeigh by the second. He got that feeling again of turning himself in and taking his chances.

No, he thought. *I am an agent of my country now, whether they can figure it out or not.* He was going to see this through, even if it meant getting scraped trying to make it happen. His wife's existence on this planet depended on it! He was at the ten-minute mark now, and it was time to move. He hoped she knew what she was doing. It all was on her now.

* * *

Ken was still seething. He couldn't believe that after everything he'd done for that bitch, Sarah had the nerve to call him and tell him to pick up Crawford in Sacramento. He hated the fact that they were so intertwined now that he couldn't afford to lose her anymore. So when she called and said she'd have to tell Rogers if he didn't pick up Crawford, Ken had to stow the level of anger that was mounting, anger that he had almost focused on her.

Her words echoed: "It is just too risky, Ken." *Damn her, it was no time to lose her nerve now.* But she had, and had chosen this "Field Reserve" as his companion. According to Sarah, "It covers our asses with a grape skin's worth of protection. By yourself, Ken, I think you'll lose. Either way, there's no story that will work. At least this way, it was you and your partner on a hunch."

Damn her for being right. This Crawford kid actually tried to small talk me. That won't happen twice. I guess he didn't know that I don't like people. Poor kid didn't make a sound the whole hour. Now we're here and it's time for him to listen.

* * *

Matt checked his watch. Twelve minutes left. It was almost time to make his move over to the hangers. He was reaching for the door handle, when he saw some headlights and sank back. The car slowed at the front of the terminal and made the first left into the parking lot. A few seconds later, Matt saw a small-framed man heading for the front door, looking furtively. In Matt's world, *never a good sign.*

The man stopped short of pulling at the doors, though. After listening and looking in, he left without attempting to enter, and instead headed off toward the hangers. *Damn it, who is this guy?* He slid out of the car carrying their backpack, but before he got out he switched the dome light off, trying not to become a lighthouse.

Matt went around the back of the BMW and was heading for the hangers, too. But then he saw the phone-lit silhouette of a passenger in the stranger's black Ford Expedition, which he now realized was goverment-issued.

This was a real problem. Matt needed to neutralize this person, but couldn't use his gun, or it would expose them before they could get away, not to mention notifying his partner. This was a real dilemma because the individual in the Expedition was obviously a good guy—otherwise, he wouldn't be here hunting them. Matt kept reminding himself that over the course of the past hours, he had become a bad guy now.

He looked at his watch. Nine minutes to go. He made his move to the corner of the car and realized that in ten odd minutes, they would meet regardless, so he steeled himself for that reality. This guy was going to try to kill him before he could get out any type of explanation, especially if confronted alone with the man he believed just killed two other Federal Agents.

The news had said they were Homeland Security, but how could he have known? Matt's problem, and he knew it, was that this situation had now become him acting against his country. But what they didn't understand was the threat to his family. If he didn't play this just right, these guys would kill Jan, unless he chose to believe his kidnapper was lying. *No, she wasn't lying about the threat, she was conveying.*

He adjusted himself so the driver's mirror wouldn't reveal him, when suddenly the passenger door opened and a six-foot-plus guy with striking blonde hair got out and stood looking at the hangers, like a dog looking after its Master that has gone into the bank. Then the man's phone came out again, and he went into conversation.

"Yeah, it's Crawford," he said into the phone. His voice was way deeper than Matt would have expected. "No, he's on foot, heading for one of the hangers. I'm in the parking lot waiting, where he told me to be. No, Sarah, that's not what we talked about, but he was very specific in his instruction that I am to stay here. Now, are you telling me that I'm to tell him that I need to go with him, like some kind of chaperone? The man wouldn't let me speak on the way here Sarah; he's a major reprobate. There was no way I am telling him anything. Now he said he would be back in twenty minutes, so I at least have a reason to go looking for him if it's much longer than that. Okay then, I'll get back to you when we know more, but I think it's a dead lead here. This place is deserted."

Agent Crawford hung up on his heated exchange. As he was placing his phone back into his pocket, Matt slammed the back of his skull with the butt of his Beretta. Matt had taken advantage of the phone argument to creep up on the agent. *He surely should have been trained better than that,* he thought.

Matt considered putting a sleeper hold on the man, but it was just too risky. *No, this was for keeps, and if the guy lives, then that was great, but my main concern is a dispatched enemy.* The blow was a skull-cracker. Even if he woke up, the agent was not going to be any good for fighting.

Matt forced himself to use lethal force—anything less could lead to his death. It was the reason cops didn't shoot to wound. He'd made it that far in the Academy.

A quick search of the man revealed no weapon, and no cuffs. *What kind of cop has no cuffs?* He quickly opened the vehicle's door, and the interior light revealed a Heckler and Kotch 9mm, with a silencer attached laying on the seat! *Heckler and Kotch silenced? Really?!* Now he was certain that the guy going after Vera was in the CIA. No government agency carries silenced weapons, other than the very group he had just joined as a patriot.

Suddenly he was on that fence again. This could be a good time to flip, he began to think; but then he looked down at the crumpled agent. Matt knew that by nabbing her, they would get nothing. She was just a puppet, but she was one of them, that much he knew. He was the only one that might have a chance to see who's running this operation. *Right before they kill me,* he mused. He looked at his watch. *Six minutes to go, damn.*

He grabbed the fallen agent's gun off the seat and headed for the hangers, holstering his own non-silenced weapon. Matt checked the chamber, verified that it was loaded, and removed the safety. *Someone was planning on killing us, it seems.* Matt always yelled at the characters in movies he would watch, about things like checking the chamber and safety. Now, he was in the movie. He needed to keep that in mind, because this was not the movies and he wasn't going to live if he made a single mistake tonight. He stopped short and went back to the SUV. He wrote a quick note from the notebook on the dash and left it on the seat.

* * *

They walked and laughed. Vera had him so in love with her within the space of an hour that this man would marry her tonight, and would spend the rest of his life worshiping her. *God, men are so weak.* He was prattling on about something or other, but she couldn't focus. Apparently he liked Japan, but somewhere like Singapore would be more affordable. She couldn't believe how boring he was, but his life was just about to get a whole lot more exciting. If he lived, he'd probably have more pussy than he'd know what to do with. A good story like this could get a guy laid for years—Vera was quite sure of that.

They got to the hanger. There, she punched in the seven-digit key code. The door popped open, and they were inside. Doug didn't notice that the hanger door didn't shut right, and was left slightly ajar.

The plane was as promised, a brand spanking new Cessna 310. She hadn't gotten ripped off. Well, actually, Doug wouldn't really know. He had just been bullshitting her earlier. When she had asked Doug to see the plane, all he could think about was extending time with her in any way he could. He had opened the passenger doors, looked into the spacious aircraft and said, "She still has that new car smell."

When he had turned around, she had closed the gap and was right on top of him.

Doug had started for a second at the overture, and then he had her in his embrace. *This can't be happening. I never get this lucky. Oh my God, she's such a good kisser!*

After five minutes of heavy petting, she broke off and asked about the plane again. So he tried to amaze her with what he knew about flying in general. She told him that she wanted to take guests to Ensenada, and asked if he would fly them.

Doug was giving the answer, when out of nowhere a smaller man in dress pants and a t-shirt appeared and said, "She's not going to Mexico.

Doug immediately snapped, "Who the fuck are you?" and took a fighting stance. The answer was the delivery of several, well-timed, lethal moves. The little man moved quickly, and every move he did made an impact noise. After what must have been seven unanswered blows, the last move probably ending their chances with this pilot, bouncing his head off the concrete floor of the hanger with a sickening sound. The final blow had struck the back of the pilot's neck in a chopping rabbit-punch type of move, and he had been seemingly unconscious as he hit the ground, doing nothing to protect his face from the impending impact with the hanger floor.

It was over before it started. Vera tried to run. He grabbed her hair, only ending up with her wig in his hand. She then made a shimmy move to get by him, but he was able to shove her off balance as she tried. Her body slammed into the doorframe, and she fell straight to the ground. He was then on her like a wrestler.

Although Vera was a deadly fighting machine, she was no match for Ken Beck. She quickly found out what every other person who ever tangled with him discovered. Ken Beck possessed incredible strength for a man of his stature. She fought with all her might, but the more she fought, the more he seemed to like it. As a matter of fact, she could now feel exactly how much he was "liking it."

He used his chin to wedge in her collarbone, and then he whispered, "You're going to tell me everything, Bitch." Then he smelled her hair, and his eyes went wild. He said to her, "What's that smell?" She tried with all her might to get out of that hold, but he restrained her and smelled her again. Every time he did, he grew more and more sexually charged. He finally whispered in her ear, "You're going to talk AND MORE."

She replied through gritted teeth, as he was pressing her jaw with his forearm, "No, I'm not!" That's when he pinned her arm under her back, and she felt his hand unzip her pants suit. She had chosen the kind with the zipper that goes through the crotch and she thought, *NO WAY!* Vera started to fight in a way that even surprised her. First she bit the forearm pressed against her face, and when Beck recoiled from that, she was able to free her right hand. She scratched his face with the desperation of survival, going for the eyes.

The savagery of the next two blows immediately incapacitated her. The first blow surely broke her nose. The second struck her temple with a purpose.

When she came to, he was in her! She fought pointlessly, with very little strength, well beyond stunned. She was definitely being raped! *Who was this guy? What kind of Law Enforcement Officer would do this?*

He kept on smelling her hair during the assault, and she realized that Pablo's pheromones were having an adverse effect on this man. Somehow her essence had sent him over the edge.

Then something really bad happened inside her head. All her past experiences came rushing back, thoughts that were supposed to have been erased. All the rapes, all the customers who paid to "get it rough," all the times she was passed around like less than human.

Pablo had enabled her to forget her past, and had helped her to realize that she had purpose. He had programmed her to forget about the horrors, and to look toward the future. He had even hypnotized her, making the past disappear. But now it all came flooding back, and she didn't want to live any more with these thoughts!

The whole time this savage man was engrossed in this act, he continued to interrogate her. He kept slapping her, and telling her it would stop if she told him whom she was working for. She couldn't even look at him, let alone listen, even though he was demanding it. Finally she looked at him as he threatened to punch her in the face again if she didn't look at him.

She could tell he was going to climax, and she couldn't bear to look into his smug, psychotic face, with those lifeless, fucking blue eyes. She closed her eyes again, waiting for the punch, or for him to finish a rape that was just another of the long swath of insults cast on her since she was a child. She felt his body stiffen in that familiar way that initiates climax, and then his full weight was on her. *Gross!*

But something else was wrong, and she realized her face was wet and warm. She opened her eyes and a corpse was on top of her. Part of his head was gone. She screamed insanely, throwing him off and kicking him away in an adrenaline-fueled move that actually sent the man's body skidding a little before it hit the wheel of the plane. Vera looked across the room and couldn't believe what she saw before blackness overcame her.

SEVEN

Blindside

His hands were doing it again, and Matt hated it. Every time he arrested someone, his adrenaline shot up, and his hands would shake. Once he had busted a seventy-year old woman stealing a scarf, and his hands were shaking during the arrest, most notably during the writing of the incident report. Funny as it was, he knew that if he was going to really be a cop one day, then he might have to take a hard shot. If his hands were shaking, then he wasn't going to be able to hit the target—or worse, he'd hit something else.

It was right about that time that he had met Russell Peltz. Peltz was a hard-looking man, a man who had written the book on old school. Russell had taught firearms at the local Community College, but he was no college teacher. He was a Sergeant for the Sunnyvale Police Department. He was also the SWAT team leader, and he just flat-out loved guns. So much, in fact, that he had sacrificed most of his hearing with bad decisions he had made in his youth. Peltz was pepper-haired and sixtyish, and kept his hair cut tight at all times. Matt believed Peltz could have taken anyone in the room out to the woodshed for a good beating and never broken a sweat.

The fact that Peltz had been sixty and still a Sergeant was all one had to know about his people skills. But if one loved and respected firearms, and wasn't annoying or a criminal, then Russell Peltz could be one's

125

best friend. Matt remembered looking through the class schedule, and when he saw firearms listed he had thought, *Wow, that's a funny class for school.*

Then he had noticed the prerequisite of an active twelve units of Administration of Justice to take the class. Matt had met the requirement, so he had taken the course.

The first day, Peltz had started by saying, "You've all had your backgrounds thoroughly checked to be in this class. Now I'm hoping a lot of you are fairly inexperienced, so everything you know or thought you knew about guns, is going right out the window with little resistance. I will reshape you. If you happen to be an expert already, and you came here to show off, then leave now. I have no time for novelty acts, and this class is for people who want to learn.

"If you came here to safely learn everything that I know about firearms, and you promise to listen to instructions at all times, then I'm your man. Consequently, I have no leniency toward mistakes on the firing line, as there is no margin for error. I have one main rule: never bring ammo into or load a weapon in this class or outside of the firing range. Does everyone understand this?"

Everyone responded, "Yes." The class had been a mixture of all races and sexes, including the obligatory fat, lonely, talkative guy, who had ended up working for the ATF of all things.

Peltz had continued, "The weapon in front of you is a Smith and Wesson thirty-eight caliber revolver, and I have placed it there after confirming that it is unloaded. The first rule you've probably learned that we will break is, you will pick up those guns, check them to ensure they are unloaded"—he had taken a sidebar to show how to do that properly—"and aim them at me."

"You will then practice dry firing at me. In this room, there are no bullets allowed—ever. If you're caught with even a single bullet, you will be expelled! Am I understood?"

The class had responded in unison, "Yes."

Peltz had then instructed them, "Okay, so let's pick them up and work on breathing."

That had immediately perked Matt up, and he had become a Peltz sponge for the next six months. By the time he had finished that class, he had not only known how to control his breathing, but what part of the breath to take the shot in (which was actually between breaths). He had also known how fast the bullet was going to go, what its impact would be, and what he should expect the follow through to be. Russell Peltz had been his inspiration for mastering weapons, and Matt had become the best shot he knew as a result.

He had also learned that there was nothing he could do about the shakes. They were going to happen as soon as the adrenaline flowed high. There was a lot one could do to minimize the effects on one's shooting, though, and Matt had learned all the known techniques.

He approached the hanger with two minutes left, and he was breathing heavily. It took twenty seconds to get his breathing under control before he could stealthily enter the door.

Matt immediately heard a mixture of sounds that were very confusing. Once he focused, he realized it was an interrogation. Entering the hanger, there was a small partition wall that prevented him from observing the entire hangar bay.

Rounding the entry wall, he saw the very disturbing sight: their pilot lay unconscious and the squirrel man from the front of the airport on top of Vera, horrifically raping her as he interrogated her!

So much for being on the fence, this piece of shit thinks he's in Vietnam fifty years ago! The world doesn't operate like this anymore. The CIA doesn't have the impunity to operate like this on American soil, Patriot Act or not. No, this was a rogue agent acting on his own accord, and this was not, and could not be sanctioned.

Hard decision-making had never been one of Matt's shortcomings, so he knelt, set his breath, and squeezed the shot off as the bastard was raising his head in what looked to be climax. Matt wasn't used to the powerful gun, and the shakes were bad, so the shot hit the rouge agent off to the right, and made the impact look like the Kennedy headshot. The shot caused a nasty brain spray that splattered the inside of the plane's door, which had been left open.

What also reminded Matt of the Kennedy scene was how quickly Vera shed herself of the corpse. The whole thing had a dejá vu feel about it as it played out in slow motion. He opened the electronic roll-up door and found that outside the hanger was well-lit by the full moon. Matt fought having to throw up the contents of his stomach for a good thirty seconds straight.

It wasn't that the man's exploding head grossed him out enough to lose it mentally. It was more like his nerves were on such high-alert mode. He felt like a quarterback before the big game. He turned back on the grisly scene to see Vera in a semi-conscious state and the pilot waking up.

The pilot looked up at Matt and muttered, "What the hell is going on?"

Matt wiped the saliva of his mouth with the sleeve of his shirt and pointed the gun at him as he re-entered the hangar bay. "You're flying us out of here."

The moonlight through the window illuminated the pilot's face, and Matt could see the cobwebs clearing in the man's head. "The fuck I am," was his response.

Matt's shot hit five inches from the pilot's hand. With the shakes gone, Matt's accuracy returned, combined with anger at the audacity of the pilot's statement. The cement exploded everywhere. Luckily, none of it hit the pilot in the eye. Matt wondered, *what the hell is this thing loaded with?* He re-pointed the gun at the pilot, who was rubbing his hand. "Apparently you thought that was a question. Now I reiterate, you're flying us out of here, or I will kill you right now. Do you understand?"

"Yes," Doug retorted, unsteadily putting his hands up and shielding his face. "Please stop pointing that gun at me."

"What's your name?"

"Doug."

"Okay, Doug. According to her"—he pointed toward Vera—"she called and had that plane fueled yesterday, even though she couldn't fly it. I need you to go make sure that happened. I also need you to forget the dead guy that knocked you out and carry her into the plane."

Doug froze. He looked like a man who just had an epiphany. "It's you two! You're the two from the news, I just know it!"

Matt saw him backing up. He closed the gap and raised the gun, letting Doug in on a little secret. "Your life, like ours, has become a series of events that has led to this moment. Every decision you make from this point on is going to take you on an immediate path of continued life or instant death. There is no negotiating with me, and there is no going back.

"You either do exactly as I say, or your life on this planet is over immediately, are we clear now? You need to shake off the pain, clear the cobwebs, and get working for me right now, not one hesitation. Make up your mind now, because if you live, it will only be because you've decided to let it all hang out and get us to our destination.

"I swear to you if you listen to us, we will spare you, and then we will secretly find you, and make you never want for money again. This isn't a country thing so don't listen to that shit on the news, this is a 'corporations' thing. Apparently they're stealing each other's secrets, and then stealing them back, nothing more. So Doug, now is the time, are you in my command?"

Doug nodded. His first order was to get in and check the fuel. Matt changed his mind and said he would take care of her.

Matt came up to Vera, her face caked with all sorts of horror, her pants suit revealing another. *That crazy son of a bitch, what was he doing?* She wasn't unconscious he could see, as she was pulling her eyes closed harder at times.

"Fuel's good," was Doug's response.

"Okay, help me get her in."

"I can't do it," was his response. But it wasn't disobedience, it was terror. Matt was able to scoop her up and get her in, but not before letting Doug know that his next refusal would be his last.

His newest dilemma began as he was lifting her. As he got her up, it revealed that she was lying on her small satchel. He told Doug to buckle himself in while he moved her. He had no time to wipe her face, or cover her exposed crotch. They were in survival mode, which meant seat belt only for now.

Matt quickly dragged the scumbag out of the way, his head leaving a snail-trail of nasty, his pants still down in shame. *I'm sure they're going to get the message in this one. If they don't, they're blind and screw them. Don't employ scum and you won't have to clean them up.* He retrieved the purse and had a strong urge to look inside to see what this was all about, but this was hardly the time.

Although this wasn't the time, this was also the perfect time. It just depended on what his government would do if he turned himself in. That was the big unknown. Only he knew that he was a self-inducted soldier at war with an enemy of his country. So if he carried this through, he might have a chance to get in on the inside, if he was right about her being part of their core group. And there he was, a big old tomcat that had gotten chased up a fence by a dog. Now he was walking down the middle of the fence in another tomcat's territory, not sure which side to jump to, and very uncertain of what lay ahead.

No matter how many times he considered the various scenarios in his mind, the one thing that still trumped all was the threat to his family. Before he left this world, someone was going to pay for that. Yet the best way to hurt them would be to help them, and she was his key to his survival.

This happening to her was the best thing that could have happened to strengthen his odds. Yet he was oddly torn as a patriot on one side and a lover on the other. He resisted the urge to leave one thing behind as a clue, figuring that she must have done inventory already, and that would be an inconsistency if something were found missing that she had already reported having.

Matt, the tomcat, made it to the next figurative yard. *Guess I'm going to find out what's ahead rather than jump off the fence.* As Matt turned back toward the plane, he spotted the fallen CIA agent with the ruined head and had not one ounce of remorse for whoever that asshole was.

He put the purse in the backpack, telling Doug to get out and help push the plane out of the hanger. Then he had a very serious thought. It was like he had been telling himself on the way to the hanger earlier, *if I make one mistake, I'm not going to live to see tomorrow.* He instructed Doug with an air of knowledge meant to demonstrate that he wasn't asking about something he knew nothing about, although he really was. What he knew of transponders was only what he'd seen in the movies.

"You need to disable the plane's transponder."

Doug had the look of a man who had just had his big plan ruined, and his face did not hide it well. "Okay," was all he could muster.

They pushed the plane out onto the roadway between the hangers, a hundred yards from the runway, and of course Matt had never been in a prop plane before. *Tonight was just full of firsts.*

Doug entered the plane first and buckled in. Matt followed suit after securing both the hanger and plane door, being careful not to look at the bone-flecked flesh adhering to the door's interior.

Doug asked with an air of haughtiness, "Do you have a flight plan?" Matt searched her backpack. Soon he found the pocket with the map and handed it over to Doug. Doug studied it and his response was a muttered word, "Suicide."

Matt looked at him hard and said, "Sounds better than murdered."

* * *

Pablo was trying to have faith. Faith was what had gotten him here. To waiver in his absolute belief of her escape would be a betrayal of his conviction. He steadied himself, assuring himself that she would make it out. Having no family left, his trips to the past inside his head were vital to him, because they were the only place he could visit his family, remembering all their words in an effort to stay balanced. Of all the times past he recreated in his head, the only memory Pablo had trouble recreating was the day immediately following the death of his family.

He didn't remember arriving at the chateau or how he got into bed. That always ate at him with a nagging feeling of lack of control. He just felt grateful that James had understood him and filled in his gaps with such detail, recreating and recounting, redundantly, so that Pablo could have peace. James had known that there could be no peace in his mind until the last piece of every puzzle he encountered was placed.

That next day, Sandy and James had settled down in the alcove off the kitchen. It had offered the most amazing views of Lake Geneva, truly one of the most beautiful places on earth.

"Nice view," Sandy had said, and James had drifted off for a second.

James had remembered the first time he had seen the chateau. He had been so full of promise about his first remission, and he had thought the house would be a good thing to look forward to when he got better. Of course, because of his treatments, he had to be closer to Zurich much of the time, but he had gone there whenever possible.

He had first been drawn to Yvoire for its medieval appeal. Oh sure, he had scented out and avoided the tourist part of it, but this place had been truly ancient, and he had just loved the feel of it. He had paid cash, the transfer done with a wave of his hand. In this neck of the woods, the fact he didn't haggle hadn't even been noticed by his very happy realtor.

"Are you sure, James?" Sandy has asked. "All of it? That's a god-awful amount of money to leave to a kid. He's not even of age yet."

"Sandy, you know as well as I do that Zurich doesn't operate like that," James had replied. "Plus, he'll be of age when I'm gone anyway. Look, my parents are very well off, I have no ex's, no kids. Sure I have a few charities that I like, but this kid is owed, and I have enough tabs out there that I need to pay up. So look, these are my wishes. No second-guessing me past this point. The kid gets it all!"

"Okay, James. I'm glad you flew me here and I got to hear it from you with such passion, because a hundred and ten million is an awful lot of money."

Pablo had been in James's computer room, and it had been impressive. It'd had all the bells and whistles of a good-sized agency. Evidently James had been running this massive system through a proxy server, then another and yet another. It had been untraceable, and all controlled remotely by him. It had been pure genius. James had set up a number of lofts around Europe to make it happen.

Pablo had recalled having an epiphany that day, as he had come to the realization that as long as he was with James, he no longer had a monopoly on genius.

Before ensconcing himself in the cyber world, James had given him the pass codes he needed. Then he had cut him loose. James had known him well enough to know that he had to seek answers on his own and get the real story of his own accord. Once Pablo had started, he had become an information-gathering machine, scouring the local news articles, blogs, and police documents in a way no other human could. Ultimately though, it was an e-mail he had come across that had stopped him in his tracks.

Thanks to James, Pablo had been able to look at an e-mail sent to the CIA Station Chief in Guayaquil. Apparently James had had a friend who had given him some access codes. That e-mail had sent a chill down Pablo's spine. It had been from a field agent in Quito who had said the hit on the Manuel's was ordered by the Shimmering Way Terrorist Organization in retaliation for the bloodbath in Gualaquiza.

The word had been that one of Octavio Mendoza's relatives was killed in that attack, and Luis Calderon had ordered a scorched-earth type of retaliation.

Pablo had jumped at the words he was reading. *That's my entire family the guy is nonchalantly writing about, like it's an everyday thing, just some common thing for an entire family to get wiped out.* Pablo had traced the news about the massacre in Gualaquiza, and that thread had led to a hundred more stories. Soon he'd had all the information there was to know. His uncle had stolen from a cartel. Only this cartel had been more than just a regional cartel—they had been a military organization, apparently not one to mess around with.

Julio had been involved with the people who had attacked this cartel, and somehow in the aftermath of a horrible gun battle, he must have ended up with all the drugs or money, or both.

Pablo had just sat and stared at the screen. How could his uncle have lived with himself knowing that he had created all these lies from blood money, money that Julio knew his parents never would have taken if they had known of its origins? *Regardless, what kind of people would kill everyone in my family because of the actions of one man?* These type of people had no place on earth, Pablo had decided, and he had not been afraid anymore. His mindset had shifted to vengeance.

That day in James's basement, he had been forced into many new realities. Sitting down there alone, he had come to the sad realization that whatever childhood he had had was now over. He knew James had loved him, it was obvious, but James was not his family. James, being a single man his entire life, could never have begun to understand the bonds shared in the Manuel household.

The Shimmering Way hadn't just killed his family. They had extinguished a very bright light of good that had existed in the world, the bright light that had created him. So this had not been a simple matter of revenge against bad people. Pablo had seen his plight as truly a battle of good versus evil.

A large spider came down on its web in front of the window, momentarily bringing Pablo out of his trance. Back then those *pendejos* had done everything they could to make sure he didn't live. But he did. The thought of revenge had always seemed so tiresome to him, especially seeing all the people throughout history that had fallen to its siren song.

He always thought those people were weak, ruled by such emotion as to blindly walk into their doom willingly, all in the name of "honor." He now understood it, he had to admit. Now that he knew what it was like to be last person in his bloodline, the act of revenge was a foregone conclusion. He was going to have his revenge. The rage was building inside of him, and God help those responsible.

The spider decided that its new web was going to be in front of Pablo's office window. He watched it carefully design the trap that the next unsuspecting insect would find. Its web, much like his plan, was intricately woven to perfectly catch whatever prey haphazardly came its way.

The great Bobby Fischer had won his World Chess Championship by aggressively thinking outside the box. That was the same type of ambitious attack Pablo was going to use to extract revenge for his family while immersed in enacting his intricate plan for the world.

It wasn't easy changing the way his thought process normally worked. But knowing that justice had to be served, he obtained the knowledge to help him understand how to deal with this quagmire.

To achieve his purposes, the one book that really grabbed him was *War and Peace*. There were so many words and accolades one could give the greatest book ever, but none can ever match it. Tolstoy was able to make his readers part of the families he wrote about.

One of the lessons that Pablo had been unable to shake was the lesson in honor that that book revealed. He had read the novel before the atrocity to his family. At that time, he couldn't quantify its profoundness, because he had not yet endured the type of hardship that one must endure to truly understand the need for protecting one's "Family Honor."

Pablo remembered the momentous day when he had shut off the monitor on James's computer system. He had read enough. His family had been desecrated and someone was going to have to pay. He had known then that he would do as he always did. He would align his pieces, then he would attack, and there would be a checkmate—one way or the other.

At lunch later that day, James and Sandy had made their revelation to Pablo. The boy had listened, and the tears had started to run down his face as they concluded. Sandy had reached out to the boy and put his hand on his shoulder, saying, "I know, Son. It sure is a lot to take in. You've been through so much, and becoming so rich overnight like this, it must be a big burden for you, especially at a weird time like this."

Pablo had been about to correct him when James had spoken. "He's not crying because of the money, Sandy. He's crying because I'm dying, and you just reminded him of it, one hundred million times."

James had held his arms out for the boy, and soon had had him sobbing in his clutch. Life could be so unfair, so cruel in its decisions on who gets to live and who gets to die. All three of them had cried together for a very long time. Lunch had barely been touched.

They had tied up all the loose ends, especially the part where Pablo would become the sole heir when James passed. They also had determined that no one was to be notified of his death. James had been about to become Amelia Earhart. Sandy hadn't liked that part, but James had told him he had his reasons, and that had been good enough.

Sandy had checked his bank account that morning and had discovered a transfer of five million deposited the day before. Five million! *Whoa man, is the Taxman going to love me.*

Sandy had felt the manifesting hardship of parting with them. James had been such a good man. *He is going to die soon and leave this boy behind, and also leave a lot of people wondering what ever happened to the greatest mind of all time. Well according to James, that mind is trying to pop a pimple in the mirror right now.*

James had made sure that Burroughs had understood he was to be Pablo's lifeline. He had also made Sandy vow that he would honor his memory by looking out for the kid. James had assured him that he was on board to help Pablo, no matter what. Sandy had accepted his "knighthood."

They had taken Route D'Excenevex, the short drive to the Ferry Building in Yvoire. There, Sandy had dropped off Franc LaForte and Arturo Castanada, both with dual Swiss and French citizenship. James had mastered the fake passport game long ago, and he'd had several aliases already set up. It had taken all night, but by morning, Pablo's new identity had been ready.

Pablo had left his real passport and ID in the safe at the chateau, and they had closed the door on his old life. They had shaken hands with Sandy once more before heading for Nyon on the Swiss side of the lake. They had left everything about them and their old lives behind. For James, this was the second time he had made someone disappear, and he had been getting quite good at it.

As the ferry had made its way across the lake, James had leaned on the rail and looked back across the lake, gazing at his chateau in the distance. He had felt a deep remorse. In another life, this place would have been an amazing place to live. Then he had stopped for a second and just taken in where he was, letting nature and history just wash over him. This was the same lake that inspired Hemingway after all, and he could feel it every time he allowed himself, when he wasn't so preoccupied that he forgot where he was. He had watched the boy in similar deep thought and had been left wondering. *Why does life have to be so short?*

Pablo came out of his daydream and watched the Guaya flow its nice steady march to the Pacific. It never ceased to amaze him how much water flowed by every day, not just here, but in rivers all around the world.

Pablo knew from his reconstruction of the past that just after they had gotten off that ferry ride in Switzerland, Jeremy Lebuff had been correcting papers alone in his office. Pablo switched channels in his thoughts, and pondered about Jeremy.

James had also had the presence of mind to fill him in on all the things he had known about Jeremy. James had possessed a clear picture of what had been going on back at the school, as he had a way of communicating with Jeremy that only the two of them knew of.

On one such occasion, James had recounted that Jeremy had been just about ready to head home from the school when he had felt a presence. He had looked up to find an average looking man standing there. The man had had a dark complexion and had been wearing a fedora, round glasses, and a full-length trench coat, even though it really wasn't coat weather.

"Good evening," he had said, "I hope I didn't startle you."

Jeremy had answered, "Well you did. Haven't I answered enough of your guys' questions, today? How much attention are you giving one runaway boy anyway?"

The man had hesitated and then simply stated, "I'm not from Interpol. I represent a private group trying to help the boy. We were hired by friends of his late uncle."

"Well, I'll tell you the same thing I told them. The kid was a loner. He didn't socialize much, had no real friends, and I could barely get a word out of him. That's really all I know. I have no idea of where he went or even the places he liked to hang out, and I was his favorite teacher, I'm told."

The man had handed Lebuff a number. "Would you mind calling me if you hear anything about his whereabouts?"

Lebuff had hesitated, as James had taught him to do. Then it had rolled out: "What's in it for me?"

"Of course there will be personal compensation for you, Mr. Lebuff. Just make that call."

He had been able to act relieved and portray that the man's response was what he had wanted to hear. He had assured the man that if he heard anything, he would be the first to know, even before Interpol.

The man had smiled. The business card had said his name was Enrique Dominguez, but Jeremy had doubted that was even real. The stranger had left saying, "Thank you, Mr. Lebuff."

"No, thank you, Mr. Dominguez. I will keep my eyes and ears alert."

The man had left. As Pablo and James had told Jeremy, if his act had been believable, then he wouldn't be kidnapped that night and tortured to death. Jeremy patted the pepper spray in his pants pocket. After closing the door, he had taken a moment to come out of character and have a little breakdown. He certainly hadn't been cut out for this type of shit, and thank God he didn't really know where they went. He had been quite sure if he had known, it would have shown on his forehead in neon. He had taken another moment to reflect on his friends, wondering if they were safe.

* * *

Sarah was filled with angst. She pondered in her head, over and over again, *why, Ken, why? Why does your need for advancement, and more truthfully, approval, oftentimes block your big picture ability? I guess that's why behind every great man, there is a great woman saving his ass. But not this time, this time he went too far, and at the wrong time, so now I'm going to have to go into cover-my-ass mode.*

She knew she could have a chopper up there in thirty minutes out of Sacramento. That would cause all kinds of problems and raise all kinds of issues, especially if Rogers found out that Beck was screwing him again. That would get a phone call from the White House faster than shit through a goose. No, she was going to have to take precious resources out of an active search. *Well, what choice do I have? Damn him for this!*

She dispatched Webster and Macon to get up there and make contact with Assistant Director Beck. She was more than a little nervous about this, and felt guilty as hell about having to cover her ass because she should trust her "Superman." She was always supposed to trust him to come through—Ken Beck had promised he'd never let her down.

She remembered the night six years ago when that promise had been made. They had been working on tracking down a terrorist cell together. They had been dispatched from D.C. to the area around Troy, Alabama to shake things up on a slowly-progressing case. The chatter, which had been through the roof, had died down, and the assessment had been that whatever threat had been developing had gone away, for whatever reason.

They had both walked out of that assessment meeting secretly disagreeing with the team's assessment that it was a foreign threat that had gone away. Based on their hunch, they formulated a new plan. Their investigation had ended up yielding a homegrown-terrorist sect that had been getting ready to pull off some pretty heinous things in the name of Islam.

All of it had been an attempt to get people moving against anyone of Middle Eastern descent, and these nuts had been recruiting like mad, only in a different sector of the populous. Sarah had only had to spend a week biker blogging before she had arranged a meeting for Beck. He had gone in alone, and Sarah had been his remote backup.

Prior to the meeting, he had been fully tattooed and pierced. The fake tattoos had been applied with a special Agency dye that wouldn't wear off for months. It had been Beck's idea to overkill the tattoos so that they couldn't place a brand on him. He had even done his penis.

He hadn't shaved or showered for a week, and he had stunk. He had ridden a Harley into the meeting. Even his own mother would not have recognized him.

The group had let him in based on fake prison information he gave them. Some drunken asshole had helped him out as they dragged him out of a crowd and asked, "Do you know this dude?" The guy had stared and said, "Yeah, I know him. We did time together."

That had been it. They had never pushed it past that. No one had talked about where they were from other than the city or state, so he had been cool.

For a month Beck had become one of them, but only after being vetted properly. He had always been able to pretend inhale when it came to Sherms or weed, so that had been no issue at all. Plus, his eyes had been so red from the constant smoke of one kind or another that that faking being stoned had been no problem.

But on his fourth night, after he had drunk the punch that was handed to him, the real Ken Beck had come out. He had gotten into two fights with much bigger opponents. Fortunately, he had remembered not to use martial arts, but his opponents had lost anyway. He had shagged numerous girls of all types, and after what seemed like hours of fucking and fighting, he had finally run out into the yard and started firing rounds off into the night sky. He had been buck-naked, screaming like a madman. The next morning, the group had nicknamed him "Madman." That had cost him six months of active duty after his debriefing, when it emerged that the punch had been laced with Ecstasy. It also emerged that he might have contracted an STD and was tested monthly during his hiatus.

After it had all been over, they had been back in Washington putting it all in narrative and preparing for the prosecution. One night they had finished off a long shift of paperwork in a local bar. It was there that their true bond had been established, although from Sarah's perspective, it had been partly out of fear as well. They had sat in a corner booth and had gotten pretty drunk. Soon they had really opened up about everything, including sex, lack of sex, family, friends, and work.

They had spilled all their hopes, dreams, and fears. That's when he had told her to follow him no matter what.

The words hung over her now that she was doubting his abilities. Based on his past, this should be an easy slam-dunk, and she has no reason to doubt him professionally. He should be calling any moment, and they should be moving offices soon. Sarah took a quick second to fantasize about what her new office in Langley was going to look like.

* * *

The plane rose. Matt could see the area like daylight. *What a night for a full moon.*

He looked back and saw that Vera was still unresponsive. He went through the backpack and found a myriad of items, including a medical kit and some large strips of fabric, which he could only assume were meant to tie-off a wound.

He also found a bottle of water and some ibuprofen. He took four for himself and made his pilot take four as well, knowing it wouldn't be long before his headache kicked in. He asked him, "How are you?"

Doug replied, "I'm sore. That asshole really messed me up. Who was he? Did he do to her what I think I saw?"

"Yes, he did, and that proves to you what I said. This isn't about law and order. This is about corporations doing whatever the hell they want. They're getting to be stronger than nations, Doug. That's why I'm not kidding you when I say you will be let go and compensated. These guys are businessmen, resorting to violence only when necessary." Matt could see he found comfort and logic in that.

"You said, 'these guys.' Aren't you with them?"

"Let's just say, I'm a special contractor to a lot of people, and we'll leave it at that. Now, we'll all be okay if we relax and you do your job, which is to simply fly us at treetop level seven hundred miles through at least two military zones. Do that and we're all set." Matt concluded his pronouncement by slapping Doug on the shoulder.

Doug gave him the look someone gives when they're trying to figure out if they're dealing with a dry-witted individual, or a certified nut job. Matt didn't let him off the hook.

Matt unbuckled himself and went back to her, asking Doug to keep it steady for a few minutes, if possible. *God, she was a mess.* There was brain matter all over her, and the inside door of the plane, which had been open when he took the shot. He started with her hair. He had to pick out the fleshy particles, as there was just no other way.

He got what he could see and then started to clean her face. Her eyes opened with a start when he touched her face with the cool of the wound cloths he had converted into a damp wipe. She seemed to be coming back to reality. *Thank God.* He gave her a slight touch on the cheek. There was no more reaction from her after that. She remained completely catatonic.

She had a pair of shorts and a t-shirt in the backpack, but no underwear. Matt unbuckled her and undressed her, manipulating her out of her pants suit and ripped underwear, discarding them near the smattered door. He wiggled her into her shorts and manipulated the shirt on, trying not to be so lame as to think about sex with her. Much to his chagrin, when her breasts inadvertently touched his face, he got aroused. *What is wrong with me thinking of sex at a time and circumstance such as this?*

Then he caught a faint whiff of her fragrance and realized that something about her aroma was intrinsic to his infatuation. He didn't know why, but he never wanted to be without that scent again.

The whole process took a good fifteen minutes. He could tell she was going to be of no use from this point forward.

Then he remembered his first aid training. She was in shock and needed warmth. The plane had been stocked with a first-aid kit, and fortunately there were two blankets as well. He took them both and wrapped her as best he could. Then he used the cotton swabs in the kit to clean the blood out of her swollen nose. He could tell she was not breathing well.

If it hurt he couldn't tell, since she never flinched. But when the plane bucked and the jolt almost killed her, he decided it was time to call an end to the cleanup session. He belted her back in and made his way back up to the cockpit.

Once settled in, he asked Doug, "How's it going?"

* * *

The problem with being able to recount the past in the way that Pablo did was that he sometimes fused two realities. He would come out of a fugue believing James was still alive, and then he had to deal with his death all over again. It was an unfortunate side effect of his ability to enter into deep thought.

He got up, stretched his arms and looked around his very modern office. It was time to go. He loathed this part.

He had only been to his own company twice, arriving by helicopter both times, which had built walls between him and the common folk running the place. Pablo really hated projecting such an image, but he had no desire to meet the people. Juanita was a good, loyal secretary, whom he actually let run the place as if she were the CEO. For all intents and purposes, she was.

All his companies turned a profit, and this one was no exception. He carefully chose the secretary for each company in light of what their jobs would really entail. Secretaries could run most offices of their own accord anyway. This simplified things for Pablo, since less people would be asking questions.

Today Juanita's reward for a job well done was a set of keys handed to her with an address on the tag. Pablo told her that she had a new house, and that she should go enjoy it right away. He left the stunned woman sitting at her desk. He was sure that the minute he was gone, the buzzing would start. He was also sure Juanita was going to be keeping her new address secret from curious gossipers.

After some of the warehouse guys loaded his contraption, the chopper lifted off. He watched the building and the river get smaller and smaller, and then finally fade away.

His phone rang. The display read "Felipe." He answered.

Felipe asked, "Have you heard from her, Pablo?"

"No, I haven't heard from her since the last call, but that doesn't mean she's off schedule. We need to add more resources, since she might have to go off course and use one of the alternates. Felipe, do not fail me, spare no expense, and don't forget where I told her to go first. You have your control station set up?"

"Yes, Pablo."

"Okay. If I'm not back in time to take control, you know what to do."

"Yes, Pablo. It's such bad timing that something brought you away."

"Although the timing was bad, Felipe, after setting this up for as long as I did, there was no delaying this meeting."

"I hope it was a good meeting, *Jefe*."

"Oh, it was, Felipe, it was. But now, we need her out."

He hung up the phone and looked up at his laptop. The world news was getting serious, as well it should be. The *payasos* have figured out that whatever was in the safe was as serious as it gets. Little did they know the real reason he went into the safe had nothing to do with the EMP technology and everything to do with James's back door access drive—a drive that could access every institution known to man.

In their time together, James had given him all his warfare knowledge firsthand, but he had not been able to give him the drive. The coding had been too much to try to convey while he was teaching him everything else. Time had been a barrier.

In the two years since then, he had already gotten ahead of his mentor's EMP work. He was already in the production stages of a couple of new kinds of weapons. Well, at least they were new in the way he would deploy them. No, it wasn't the EMP technology he was after.

The back-door codes were a little different. James had had insider knowledge of the Internet when it was young. He had gotten in and placed back doors before a lot of security was even invented. He had been a true "Ghost in the Machine." Pablo desired that absolute power even more than his other aspirations.

Speaking of power, sitting in the back seat of the chopper, he looked back at the power. Not too many men ever came close to wielding this kind of power. It terrified his soul to think that it must be used.

His Russian friend had thought he was insane for even inquiring about the thing, until he told him the truth about how he planned to use it. Then the impossible became possible. No matter if Vera succeeded or failed, nothing was going to stop him from finishing what he started with that "suitcase," as it was called.

He had come here to buy the suitcase, and that had been successful.

Now he hoped that by the time he made it back to the compound (he no longer called it a hacienda), he would either hear from her or find out that she failed.

He settled back and looked at the screen once more. But he wasn't into it, so he closed it and drifted back into his thoughts of things past, of him and James embarking on a new life.

They had crossed the lake with ease, taking in the scenery, but in a private, contemplative way. Immigration had been a breeze, and their car was parked in the marina parking lot. James had purchased a long-term spot there and had left a car with Swiss plates on it, just to make things easier while he was traveling back and forth to Zurich frequently.

They had both leaned on the marina rail, looking back one more time and saying goodbye to the life they had known. Every step was now going to be a whole new experience for Pablo, forcing the past out.

He'd had a flashback of his sister Jasmine, who had been the next youngest after him. One time his family had traveled to a mountain lake. He remembered their Papa had been playing with them. They had been running from the "monster," played by their Papa. He had chased them around while they screamed. *How could it be true? How could a whole family get wiped out? How could anyone be so callous as to murder my Jasmine?* The tears fell. He had known it would take months, or years even to stop crying all the time. He had also known that when the tears dried, when he got his resolve back, then the pieces would move forward and he would get some closure.

Inherently, he had known that revenge would only make him feel half-good at best. That he got to exact his God-given right for blood would only satiate his immediate needs—but what then? He would need to feel better than that.

Pablo's head had been down and he had been praying hard. For some reason it had just made him feel better. Pablo had been praying harder than he ever had in his life, pleading for God to help him.

Suddenly he had seemed to be lifted out of his body. At first he had thought he was going to pass out, he was so light headed. He had chided himself for leaning on the rail too hard and making the blood rush to his head, which was how he tried to explain it.

It was at that moment that the Divine Plan had been inserted into his head. There was no other way to describe it: there had suddenly been knowledge there that wasn't there before.

Then he had received confirmation. Just as he had been about to turn around and leave in stunned confusion, he had heard a girl's loud scream to his right, which scared the hell out of him. Then he had seen the girl by the rail of the dock, running for her life. Her father had been lumbering after her in Frankenstein-like fashion as she ran and hid behind what must have been her Mama—just like Jasmine had used to do.

Talk about a message from God! It hadn't happened like a bolt of lightning. It had been more like stepping through a really thick cloud. Once through, the energy had shot through him with the intensity of a laser. He had needed to send a statement to the world that this type of behavior would not be stood for anymore. Not just from "his" bad guys, but from all who oppressed others for money or to further themselves by stepping on *las ovejas*.

Holy shit, he had thought, *I think God is really talking through me. I get it, checkmate!* Pablo's download had been complete. He had known what he had to do. They had killed the meekest people in the world. They had murdered sheep in their sleep, and the Bible clearly said that, "The meek shall inherit the earth." *So apparently I am to represent the meek? I am supposed to be the Harbinger of Change?*

Pablo had known that it must be—otherwise God would not have cleared all that he held dear out of the way. Pablo had now been able to see clearly that God had removed all that would stand in his way, so that he could enforce the harsh responsibilities of this "Harbinger of Change." *Why else would this have happened?*

He had decided to start a memoir, and this moment would need to be recorded as "the" moment. It would reflect the exact place and time that his mission was set forth to him by God. Not in a dream, as was the usual in the Bible, but right there, in the parking lot of the Nyon Ferry building at Lake Geneva, Switzerland.

James had thought he saw him staring at a small family. He hadn't realized the boy had been in a trance-like state. He had put his hand on Pablo's shoulder and said, "We have to go, Son."

Pablo had jolted. Then he had turned and looked at James deeply and said, "It's going to be okay, Papa. I'm going to be okay. Now it's time for you." Because of their many talks, Pablo had known what James was feeling during those moments, and it had helped fill in his daydream. James had become very weak, and he had been thankful to know how perceptive Pablo was. He had also been secretly happy to have a son, but under such tragic circumstances, it had been bittersweet at best. This had been a small source of shame, he had later revealed.

As James had pulled out onto the roadway from the ferry building, Pablo had known that he was thinking about how he'd set up this type of situation a thousand times in a hundred places around the world, him and his death-dealing cohorts. He had thought to himself, *it's time to pay the piper, Jimmy.*

From that point on, James Haberman's mindset had become, *at least I'm going to my grave having done some good here to offset the horrors. The boy understands I might not have long, and that's good, because I don't. At least I picked a beautiful place to die with someone I love. A lot of people have a lot less.*

* * *

They were coming up on the first military zone, according to Vera's map. Matt looked back, and saw that Vera was still out of it. The map he had in hand now was for Northern California, but he also had a second map for the Southern part of the state, *if they made it that far.* He had also found two cell phones in the backpack, and had turned one on to see if it had any saved data, such as contacts or previous calls. It didn't. Matt didn't know what he would say even if he could use it.

Suddenly the plane hit a wind current that reminded him they were flying for their lives here, not on some commercial airline flight. He placed the phone back in the backpack, keeping his eyes on the scary, half-lit world outside.

She had three places in Mexico marked on the southern map. Earlier, with the pilot, they had noticed that she had circled a place to go just east of Mexicali. Matt wasn't sure, but he thought he had driven through there once, and he remembered the area was sparsely populated, which was good. She had mentioned that they had a pick-up there.

He so badly wanted to take time and reflect over the past twelve hours, but he fought the urge. Too much had happened, and he just felt a small wave of fatigue. *God, not now.* He needed to keep his wits about him. It was crunch time. The two-minute warning was coming up, and they were out of time-outs.

"Okay, Doug," he said, "you've seen it on TV, just like I have. If we're detected, then we're going to have an F-15 Escort faster than you can say it, just like old Payne Stewart."

Doug knew that Professional Golfer Payne Stewart's plane had gone off course due to a faulty window seal. Within minutes, two F-16's had been dispatched and had pulled up on the wayward private jet, only to see all on board dead.

Doug replied, "I see."

Matt answered, "I'm glad you see, Doug. Now let's see how low we can get this thing to go without dying."

The past hour-and-a-half had been the most tedious Matt could ever remember. He couldn't stop his fear. He had no idea how Doug was handling it, but he had made it out of the Sierra's on guts and will alone, at two hundred miles per hour. Matt thought to himself, *this guy is not rolling over, he wants to live!*

* * *

Sarah's cell phone rang, and she got a call that she never thought she would get. She was Teflon after all, and the "career ender calls" were for guys at Beck's level, not hers. *Well, that's all changed now, hasn't it?*

The team she had sent to Tahoe had just found her rookie, Agent Crawford, crumpled on the ground next to Beck's SUV, his head crushed in, barely alive. Beck was missing.

She hung up, disconnecting her call from the agent in Tahoe, numb. Out of survival instinct she then dialed Roger's cell phone number. Her only chance at possibly staying out of jail was to come clean one hundred percent, right now.

The phone rang on the other end, and she wished this would all just go away.

"Kirk Rogers here."

Rogers listened and computed while he heard her out. *This is not good. First of all, Beck was done, his career completely over in a wisp. What was that fool thinking? Didn't he realize the resources we could have put on that area? Of course he did, that's why that cowboy is done! At least Sarah did the right thing and told me now, before she told the Old Man. Once she did that, Beck's true treachery might have never been revealed. Apparently Sarah couldn't have that on her conscience.*

DHS Assistant Director Kirk Rogers sincerely thanked Sarah before he hung up. He knew she had just upended her career to do the right thing, and he let her know that there was a place in their Bureau for a person such as her.

With those words coming from a man as knowledgeable and experienced as Rogers, Sarah didn't even have to read between the lines to know she had just been informed that her career with the CIA was probably over. After they hung up, Sarah thought about that revelation. *Well, I'm fairly well off being single. I've been spending wisely and investing wisely. I could retire now, if I got a part-time job.* She thought about her last move and decided that it had pretty much sealed her fate. Her upward climb was over, along with Beck's career. She picked up the phone and called Bob Thompson.

Bob Thompson was very reserved under pressure. At 68 years old, he had learned some tact and dignity, giving him a composure that sometimes bordered on arrogance. Others would never see him lose it. Even during 9/11 he had been rock solid. His reputation for maintaining his calm had started much earlier. Once upon a time, he had been a Field Agent during the Cold War, and later the Station Chief in Moscow. He had been around the block and back, and he had known the enemy. Or, at least he had thought he did, before 9/11 happened and the Department of Homeland Security (DHS) had been born.

Since then, his job had never been more important. Yet at the same time, DHS had clouded the waters. The two agencies had missions that covered some of the same ground. This required interagency cooperation to avoid crossing each other's jurisdictions and impeding each other. Predictably, they often competed against each other, and frequently held back information from each other until it was convenient to release it. However, Bob knew the situation Sarah was explaining was completely different, involving much more than some over-competitive agents trying to be first to close the case.

Bob looked out over the room he was in. There were more than twenty dedicated agents, doing whatever they could to bring this to an end. But the question that wouldn't go away was whether any one of them would resort to such madness as Beck had perpetrated in order to obtain resolution on a case. Bob knew the answer was no, and that Ken Beck had officially jumped off the deep end. Regardless of the outcome, Beck was going to be relieved of duty immediately.

After mentioning that she had informed Rogers first, Sarah patiently waited through the ensuing silence.

Bob thought long and hard before he responded to her. "It was good that you informed Rogers first," he began, "that way they can't claim conspiracy. But by doing that, you risked your own neck for sure." He let that sink in. "Brilliant and daring, seeing that you didn't know how I would react."

She felt slightly relieved, but she was not off the hook. He said to her in a conciliatory tone, "I know Ken. He's my monster, Sarah, and I'll have to deal with his fallout. You were just another in a long line of people he used to get to the top. I allowed it because he always got the job done, but this time he went too far. There are too many people watching. So the Agency owes you. But our day is hardly done here. So let's get back to work and find Ken Beck and our bad guys, so we can bring this thing to a close."

Right then his other line buzzed. "Mr. Director, it's Webster in Tahoe."

"Put him through, Carol. Stay on speaker, Sarah. Hello, Webster, what do you have?"

"We found Beck, Mr. Director. He's dead. He was in a hanger with half his head blown off. That's not all; we think they're airborne."

"How long airborne?"

"About one and a half hours, Mr. Director. There's no control tower, and the only pilot inside was sleeping when he heard a plane take off about an hour and a half ago. He had no idea of which direction it was headed. There's something else—two things really. First, we found another note. Second, Assistant Director Beck was found literally with his pants down, underwear too. We're having a team do a complete work-up, including a rape kit. We don't know what happened to him."

Before they hung up, Bob Thompson asked Webster what the note said.

"It said, 'At least we're getting the kind of experience we need for the next war.'"

They hung up, and Bob said, "Sarah?"

"Yeah?" was her weak response.

"Don't let those words affect you. We have no idea what all of this means, so please hold judgment about Ken until we know the facts. I'm so sorry you have to work through this. I'm sure you would like to have time to sort out your feelings, but right now, more than ever, I need you to do your job better than you've ever done it before. I need you to figure out where they're heading and get us out of this. If there's anyone I know who can do it, it's you."

Damn, she thought, *was he really that cool?* Someone would think he had just ordered dinner at a quiet restaurant or was giving his niece a pep talk for the SATs. Well, he wouldn't be so cool if he knew why that news had left her thunderstruck. He probably thought that it was about the loss of Ken Beck, but he couldn't have guessed in a million years that the real reason was the use of the word "rape" associated with that man.

They hung up, and Bob hit the comm button for Carol.

"Get me Stan LaRue right away, Carol."

"Yes, Mr. Director," was her snap response. Carol knew her boss, and she knew when he wanted to see a high level of get-to-it-ness. Even though he was cool as a cucumber, that didn't mean he wanted everyone else to act that way.

* * *

The city was long gone, and the world above and below was dark. Rain had come, and Pablo's trip back home to Ibarra was well under way, but now the mood was slightly more ominous due to Mother Nature. Every now and then, some trace of light would shine out of the clouds that tried to keep it back, and he realized that he was much like that sun ray. In a dark world, they were both trying their hardest to bring some light.

He listened to the blades slicing through the rain. The helicopter remained strong, and the blades did not sound labored. The wind was not heavy, so they kept a nice steady pace. The monotonous sound of the blades soon had him daydreaming again.

Soon his mind drifted back to him and James in the backcountry of Switzerland. The drive to the Hedge had been long, and it had been the perfect time for heartfelt conversation. There had been much to plan as they rolled over the Swiss countryside, taking in the lush greenery and what seemed to be the right mixture of farms, vineyards and people. One certainly didn't feel overcrowded there.

He had looked at James and hadn't liked what he saw. The past twenty-four hours had taken a toll on his friend.

Halfway through the trip, it had become evident that James needed a nap. It had seemed like no big deal that he was going to have to drive for the first time. Pablo remembered thinking, *I'm the greatest mind of all time; I can drive the car.*

James had looked with suspicion upon his request to drive the rest of the way, and had asked, "You know how to drive?"

Pablo had looked at him as if to say, "Hello!"

James had capitulated without a fight. He hadn't even seemed to notice the rough starts and stops, as the greatest mind in the world learned how to operate a car on his own. It hadn't been pretty, but several hours later, they had pulled into the Green Hedge. The GPS had announced that they were at their destination.

The Green Hedge had been a Bed and Breakfast located in Gebenstorf, a beautiful town in the middle of an agricultural area. It had sat at the confluence of the Ruess and Limmat Rivers, right where they flowed into the Aare. The Inn itself had not been too many yards from the Limmat.

James had slept the whole second leg of the trip and had awoken abruptly when the car stopped. "We made it alive?"

Pablo had mustered a condescending look in response. It was obvious James hadn't believed the "I can drive" speech, but he had been too frail at the time to protest. And they had made it alive, after all.

"So how did you find this place?" Pablo had asked.

"I needed a place to stay during treatments," James had answered. "Don't forget, there are people who want me too, so I had to keep a low profile. This place is about as low-profile as one can get."

"Can we trust it still?"

"The owners are friends. The first time I stayed here I played the dumb American, so they spoke French liberally around me, thinking I couldn't understand. Consequently, I found out some really personal things about them."

"Like?"

"Like they were in serious financial trouble, and their daughter had come close to having sex with a former occupant. With the tourism industry being so down, they were worried about losing the place."

"They were?"

"Yeah, it's a couple and their teenage daughter—Eva and Yon Heldergarten, daughter is Eva, too. I guess he really loves his wife—and he should, too, she's a beautiful, blonde-haired woman. They're real salt of the earth people, Son. They don't even own a TV or subscribe to the paper. If you stay here and want news, then you have to go to the nearest store a few miles away, or have a cellular option. They love it that way.

"So, after a couple of weeks here, I let them in on the secret. They were very embarrassed at first, but truthfully, I had never actually said I didn't speak French—they just assumed it because all I attempted was English. So one morning I said *merci beaucoup* when handed my coffee.

"Frau Heldergarten jokingly asked, *'Parlez-vous français?'* My reply was in fluent French, and she almost fainted. Fortunately, they liked me, and had only kind things to say about me, so we didn't have too awkward of a moment."

"So now you've become their friend, huh?"

"Let's just say that they'll never worry about money again and they're free to live life to the fullest. They also know the truth about me, to some degree. They know I'm dying—I was very weak from my treatments. It's hard to mask sickness, and I'm not a good liar. They also know they're not allowed to acknowledge they ever met me, for their own good, and if somehow that ever happens, their story is they thought I only spoke English. We're safe.

"I'll have them open the garage, then I'll park the car if you don't mind." James had then done that annoying head-rubbing thing—which Pablo was actually becoming fond of—before heading for the Hedge, as he affectionately called the Heldergarten's Inn.

* * *

The President looked across the collected minds of his military advisors. "Do we have anything yet?"

"No, Mr. President. We're still trying to figure out which way they went, and if they're even still airborne. We're currently checking with all the small airports in the Sierras, but the assumption is that they are still airborne."

Lawrence looked at the man speaking. It was Steve Hatten, Head Chief of the Air Force, who continued, "We've scrambled recons from Nellis Air Force Base, both east and southwest. We also have the northern top covered by Beale Air Force Base, the middle covered by the National Guard out of Fresno, and Charley is scouring the area around Stumps with his Air Corps. Past him to the south, Mark has El Centro and San Diego running constant sorties."

United States Army General Mitch Osborne, who was Chairman of the Joint Chiefs and the guy that was usually quiet, spoke up early on this one. Normally, General Hatten and Rear Admiral Anders had him aimed in a certain direction prior to going in, with the three forming a like-minded alliance. But apparently that was not the case today. There was too much riding on things, and the spotlights were out looking for scapegoats.

General Hatten watched Mitch, and he knew this was a time of great trepidation for him. He spied the empty chair on his left, a chair that had used to seat his ally, Vice Chairman Richard Reis, until a fatal heart attack two months ago. The chair had not yet been refilled. Since Reis' heart attack, Mitch had become more aloof and withdrawn. This unchoreographed outburst was just more evidence of his mental instability and of their crumbling alliance.

Osborne spoke to the President. "It's a needle in a haystack. We have re-configured one of our Army Satellites to do a fly-over on a high-probability area down south, but we're really just grasping."

Steve Hatten chimed back in, "We figured their maximum airspeed at 200 miles per hour, which puts them approximately 300 miles out. My people are telling me that they doubt the path is down south—too many military zones, and too much populace. They feel we should be focused on the Canadian border. We believe that we should be able to pick them up soon as they lose the cover of the mountains, which should be any minute now."

Lawrence looked at his Air Force Chief and asked, "What was the name of that millionaire who crashed in the Sierras some time ago? He was a big contributor of my opponent's campaign."

"You mean Steve Fosset?"

"Yeah, that's the guy. How long did it take to find him again?"

"Over a year, Mr. President, I believe," Hatten croaked out, shrinking as he sensed a tone of impending reprimand.

"Over a year and a half, Steve, that's right." Caulfield's voice was rising. "It was over a year and half that half the Free World was looking for him in that same area. So the next time you want to tell me what you anticipate 'might happen,' I will have you removed from this room. Am I understood?"

Before Hatten could get the reply out, the President's voice brought the room to a halt.

"Gentlemen, let's get this straight right now, seeing this is the first time we're in the war room together, formally. Now, other than Mitch here, who happens to know me from college, none of you know what kind of man I really am. So let's get all the congeniality and Southern hospitality you have me typecast as, and throw them right out the window! I'm the Commander-in-Chief, and I do my homework. So understand this now: I give no breaks from this point forward for any failures to inform me of facts. The same goes for insufficient facts. I'm making decisions that hundreds of millions of people depend on. Bring me information I can act on, or hold your tongue."

Hatten did just that, as did Osborne, as did the rest, and they went on about their business. The President thought, *General Hatten's ego is bruised, but he'll get over it. It was a slip of the tongue for sure, just thinking out loud probably, but I set the tone exactly the way Kim wanted me to.* President Caulfield had just been waiting for one of them to slip up so that he could take the opportunity to assert himself in a room full of lifetime warriors who didn't much believe in him.

He had heard the grumblings and read the pundits questioning his military ability. Their favorite charge was, "He's never even served." But this charge failed to take into account the President's advisor Kim Sullivan, who was more than just his Chief of Staff, but was also the smartest person he'd ever known.

Caulfield's friends at TJAC had been tracking her since high school. At thirty-five, she was the youngest Chief of Staff in U.S. history. She was also a person who could answer any question on any topic and give a reply that was not only informed, but laced with helpful insight. He had been very reluctant when they presented her, first because he had been thinking, *okay, here comes the hook. I knew this was too good to be true.*

The night they had recruited him in his office on the Hill, the smarmy man behind the knowing smile in his office had been Chase Viana. Viana was CEO of the Teledine Corporation in his day job, and Chairman of the Board to the TJAC Corporation in his spare time.

TJAC didn't exist in the sense of being a corporation that manufactured something or paid taxes. There was no public face to their enterprise. As a matter of fact, only eleven people even knew what the acronym meant, or that the company existed at all.

Chase, as most billionaires, had enjoyed the good life that successful capitalism afforded. It was there in his perfect bubble that he had gotten an honest look at just how corrupt the top really was. It bothered him.

It had started consuming all his thoughts. He had decided to clean his own house. It had been a painful experience, one that had cost him things he thought were honest partnerships, and in some cases, friendships.

In one case, one of his subsidiaries being run by a "trusted friend" had turned out to be a Ponzi scheme. That had cost his shareholders $500 million to set straight, and his former friend had hung himself in jail. It had taken over five years to clean house completely. But clean house Chase had.

Like most conglomerates, they had absorbed untold businesses along the way to get to their current size, and many had never been vetted properly. They couldn't have been, because they had all been acquired too quickly, mostly because they owned some piece of proprietary equipment or software that was needed. Their growth had happened too expeditiously for there to be any real regulatory controls. Chase knew if it had happened to him, then it must have been happening elsewhere.

Thus, his house cleaning had not been enough to satiate his need for good. Chase had known that there was so much more out there that could be done. But what the hell could he really do about the big overall picture? Chase Viana was not a comic book crime fighter, for Christ's sake, he was a businessman.

Somehow, when one is right and good, word got around. True to that, another kindred spirit had come out of the woodwork at intermission during a performance of *Phantom*.

Jason Evans had been a CEO from Virginia. His defense firm had made circuit boards for an assortment of military devices. His company, ICB, had been ranked thirtieth on Forbes list of the top 100 companies in the U.S.

Chase had seen Jason at functions, and they had tipped nods from time to time. He was very surprised to have Jason Evans approach him and introduce himself without his wife, who coincidentally, was talking to Chase's wife. The two had hit it off instantly after Evans' opening line, "Word is you cleaned your house up pretty good."

After some witty banter and discovering what mutual relationships they shared, they had set up a lunch date. After that they had met every month. TJAC had been born ten months later, in the garden at Chase's Estate, over Arnold Palmers and BLT's.

Caulfield knew the story now like he'd heard it a million times, and it felt like it was close to that. Back then he'd had no inside knowledge about Kim. All he had known was that they were asking him to do something they had promised not to do.

He remembered it had been Evans who had gotten him into a meeting and said, "Look, if you don't like her, then say 'no.' No one is telling you what to do. All we're asking is that you interview her fairly, not taking into consideration her gender, age, or past experience. Actually, her past experience has been handled very carefully, molded if you will, to serve a man such as you. But that aside, just be unbiased."

He had agreed, and the rest had been history. She was amazing, not too attractive, and not too homely. Kim knew how to dress to look more mature, especially by pulling her hair back in a bun, which perfectly complimented her round face and gave her a no-nonsense appearance. Complimenting this quality, she never lost eye contact in a conversation with someone, and as a result, she was an expert lie detector.

Her answers were so automatic and good that Lawrence had to make up a couple of impossible scenarios, just to watch her trip up, just to make sure he was seeing what he was seeing and hearing what he was hearing. Her abilities seemed impossible.

His thoughts snapped back to the war room. *These militaristic pinheads have no clue just how much I've learned about them. Not only about their tactics, but also about how each one of them thinks, acts, eats, and shits. Kim insisted that I review each one like a fighter reviews the films before a big fight.*

Now those months of late nights were paying off—the nights where Lawrence had had to pore over all their bios when all he wanted to do was sleep. Like all things that took time to accomplish, there would be a time when it paid off, and that time was now.

That was how he knew to try to push Hatten's buttons first if he could. Hatten was the "ringleader," as Kim had put it. She had instilled in him the belief that, "They all have weaknesses, and you need to know how to exploit them when the time comes." She was his Angelo Dundee. Hopefully he had some Mohammad Ali in him. *How could someone so young be so smart about everything? Thank God, she's on my side.* Lawrence slid out of his tangent thoughts, and stepped back into the game a little stronger.

* * *

Pablo was jarred back to the present by a pick up in the wind, caused by the changing landscape below. The chopper lurched as the pilot turned and aimed them toward their destination. They were minutes from Ibarra now. Soon he would be home, and hopefully in time to be of service to her. His heart was elevating, and he couldn't contain it. He was failing to control his escalating anxiety, and the lack of control bothered him, so he purposely went back to his daydream, to avoid the coming reality.

The chopper calmed back down, and Pablo drifted back to the past. He remembered he could immediately see the plusses of "Life behind the Hedge," as James had so eloquently put it. The food was good, the company was needed, and the daughter was really good-looking.

Because of his mourning soul, it was hard not to think about her without guilt. Yet it was impossible not to. When she walked by after breakfast was cleared, Pablo tracked her every movement with lust. Her straight blonde hair falling midway down her back was hypnotizing. She was a slightly plump girl, with big boobs. Maybe plump was the wrong word—thick was more like it—as he stared at her ass, too. Suddenly he was racked with overwhelming guilt, and he put his face into his hands.

James had leaned over and said, "Easy boy, you can't help living. Pablo, look at me." Pablo had remembered looking at the floor. "You will never be able to erase tragedy. It will loom, but you can also never stop living, or what is life for? Don't you see? I could have done so much good with my mind, but instead I was suckered in by some rich boy, with some of daddy's money to throw around. I got caught up in all the flag waving and big contracts. Hell, even after I made my fortune, I stayed. I could have traveled the earth dropping goodwill and cash on all I crossed, but I chose not to truly live. I chose to continue to try to get more, always more. So no matter the task you have, or the tragedies you endure, if you truly want to live, be your own man and never feel guilty for wanting to enjoy every second of your life. If I would have done that, I wouldn't feel like I do now."

"Do you believe in God?"

"Why do you ask? Because I'm dying and you want to know if I'm going to go from atheist to Bible clutcher in my waning moments?" James spat his words out with a little too much drama, he realized after they had already left his mouth.

Pablo had smiled. "Been holding that in a while, huh?"

James had rubbed his head in that annoying American way Pablo both hated and loved.

"Okay, Kid. Seriously, there's a good argument for both sides of that issue, but I have to lean toward the science, although a few things still sit in the back of my mind."

"Like?"

"Like, if you could go to the end of the known universe, what would the end be? And what would be on the other side? You know, things science can't come close to answering. What's this about anyway?"

Before Pablo had been able to answer, Eva had walked back into the alcove, and the conversation had changed directions to her, and where she was heading for school in the fall.

James had observed that the boy never took his eyes off of her. *So maybe there's a chance he will have a family after all.*

* * *

Their path took Matt and Vera's plane over Bishop and down into Death Valley. Once in the valley the plane was able to stay low, thanks to a friendly moon. Matt looked back at Vera, and she still had the thousand-yard-stare.

"What next?" he asked Doug.

Doug replied, "When we come out of here, we'll be smack-dab in the middle of several military bases. You do realize that once they figure out we're below radar, they'll start flying sorties all over."

Matt thought about that and said, "We're still a needle in a haystack because no one knows which direction we left in." He thought he detected a glimmer of something in Doug, and it looked like hope. It was time for Doug to have a refresher course in Threats 101.

"Doug, if we get an escort, I'm not going to be turning myself in, so be prepared if that happens. Seriously, if I see an escort, it's time to get your affairs with the Big Guy in order. I'm just saying."

Doug was floored. It was like this guy could read his mind. *Was this guy for real? He talks like Al Qaeda, but he's a white guy. Damn my neck hurts, what a night! Who could have ever seen this one coming? Actually, I should have seen this one coming because no chick that hot has ever talked to me. That should have been clue Number One.*

Doug wondered how many times in history a man had been led to his untimely death at the hands of a woman with ulterior motives? Well, he was now one of the countless fools, and he hated himself for still being able to feel her against him. The few minutes he had gotten to be with her were the most amazing time he'd ever had with a woman, and they hadn't even made it. Then "Psycho Boy" had showed up. *Who the hell was he?*

Doug remembered that as he had been coming to, he had heard the man yelling, "Look at me!" He had heard slapping and whimpering, and then finally a pop, like a champagne cork. It was that pop that opened his eyes.

He looked at Matt and analyzed him. *This guy killed that guy, sure as shit.* That both pleased and terrified Doug, because he knew that he was not in a bluff type of situation with this guy.

On the other hand, he couldn't think of a better person to have been killed than that asshole, whoever he had been. Maybe this guy was right, if the attacker had been a cop, then he would have identified himself, and he wouldn't have hurt him or the girl.

This was all adding up to be something right out of a novel.

He had too much left to do to give his life away so that some trade secrets didn't get stolen or re-stolen, depending on whose version of the story you believed. *Hell, I've never even had two chicks at the same time yet, and that's definitely on my bucket list.* Doug realized that it had to be as this Matt Hurst said. He needed to make up his mind right now if he wanted to live or die, because if he wanted to live, it would be because he was going to have to leave it all hanging out.

He thought hard about that, and the last sentence where this guy had made it clear that there would be no surrender. *Maybe drifting above seven hundred feet and getting spotted wasn't the best idea after all.*

Doug was no dummy, and he knew that his ass wouldn't mean shit to the government, or whoever it was that wanted these two. He also knew that the lines between the private sector and the government, were merging at an alarming rate. He reflected on that whole Blackwater deal, as well as every politician in Washington who was on the payroll of some special interest group. For sure, if he wanted to live, then he would have to fight for it and trust that this guy wasn't full of shit.

He banked the plane down as they cleared the mountains and headed across the open desert at near full throttle.

* * *

The Bahnhofstrasse is one of the premier places to shop in the entire world, hosting all the usual high-end retailers: Armani, Tommy Hilfiger, Rolex, and a prestigious list of others. It also hosts the famous Swiss banks that drug smugglers love so much. Because of this, James had not been able to just walk up and deposit a big bag of cash, as had been possible at one time.

The Swiss banks had adopted a policy to "know your customer." This is why James had had to become a master forger, way before he ever became sick. He had needed a different identification to start his Wall Street endeavor, so he had gone with the nationality that he wanted to put his money into, Swiss. He had been able to create a whole new identity. Then he had gotten a job in Zurich as an Information Technology Manager for an exporter.

He had carefully sought a job where he was able to work off-site. Then he had bought property. He had finally been able to deposit more than $250,000 without scrutiny. It had been shortly after that when he had started feeling ill and had gone to his doctor.

James had known that there were only two ways to get money into a Zurich bank, and if he hadn't done it this way, he would have had to pay an exorbitant broker fee, which wouldn't have done for one of the smartest men in the world. Later, all those moves had looked like Divine Intervention.

They had pulled up at UBS Bank. Pablo had never seen anything like it. The building looked Gothic, with three ornate head sculptures flanked by serpents climbing what appeared to be poles, standing as sentinels over the entrance. He had known that serpents usually meant medicine in Greek mythology, but he hadn't been sure what it meant in a bank. The inside had been very stuffy, with the feel and look of a museum, not a bank.

The woman at the giant desk in the front could not have been more bemused by them, or their request to see their host. To the right of her desk had been the normal banking counters, and to the left had been a beautifully decorated waiting room that even had an Espresso Machine. That was where Pablo and James had waited.

They hadn't waited long, though, before a towering blond man in a very nicely tailored suit had appeared. After exchanging initial congenialities, he had led them off. Pablo had noticed that the man's feet must have been at least a size 18.

The man's name had been Adolph Ludgow, and he had been James's personal banker at UBS. James had known him for the past year-and-a-half and hadn't known a single thing about the man other than that he was a Senior Bank Officer. As a matter of fact, that's what James had loved most about this man, his absolute lack of curiosity. Adolph had already been prepped about the nature of the visit, and had already been given the preliminary information the day before.

The visit had lasted less than an hour, culminating with Pablo receiving unlimited access to the account. It had been finalized with Pablo receiving his account access number and his fingerprints being digitally recorded. Technology had advanced a little further since James had last visited, requiring both of them to give a retinal scan before they left. Apparently, this had been reserved for very large accounts such as theirs.

In less than an hour, Pablo Jairo Manuel had joined a very elite group of people in the world that had more money than they could spend in a lifetime. The valet had pulled the car up, and James had tipped him as they had gotten into the car and left. As James had pulled into traffic, Pablo had looked back at the entrance of the bank toward the ornate statues again.

He had wondered what the significance of having them there was, and had told himself to obtain that knowledge later. Pablo had been getting to the point that he believed he knew everything, and it really bothered him to have something staring at him that he had no file for.

Just like that, they had pulled away, and it had been done.

James had asked, "Are you hungry?" Pablo had been.

After lunch, they had gone shopping and opened a regular bank account for Pablo's new alias, Arturo Castanada, at Habib Bank. They had created it complete with Pablo's first ATM card (even if his real name hadn't been on it). The initial deposit had been $100,000.

On the ride back to the Hedge, they had both been quiet again, which seemed to have been happening more often. Pablo had noticed that James barely touched his lunch. Everywhere they had gone, if there was a place to sit, James would take advantage of it.

Even though Pablo had known so much, he had found out on a simple outing that he knew so little, too. Yes, it was true that Jeremy had taught him a lot of social graces in two years, but he had been a long way from polished. He had been a quick learner, though, he had thought, allowing himself a small grin.

He had looked at his reflection in the mirror on the visor of the passenger seat, pretending to get out a bothersome eyelash. The reflection looking back at him had been a scared man/boy, a man/boy who would soon be on his own, barring a miracle. Pablo had looked deeper into the mirror and began to have that sensation again. The fear and anxiety had been gone. Soon he had been standing alone at the top of the world, looking down, unafraid. He had begun having a real vision again.

He had felt that sensation of walking through a thick cloud, and suddenly he had been on the other side. He had been on some ethereal plane, and now he had been walking through a thickly wooded area. The path had been well worn, and every now and then, snakes had darted across the trail. More and more of them had darted as he had made his way toward what appeared to be a clearing. Each and every time one had crossed his path, he'd had a feeling of foreboding.

He had entered the clearing, and there had been his family having an outing inside a white gazebo. All of them had been there. He had tried to communicate, but he had not been in their realm. His mama and papa had been sitting in the gazebo drinking tea, and the kids had been eating cake. They had been talking about something funny, laughing periodically.

Pablo had been so transfixed that he had never seen Jasmine sneak up and stand next to him, but when he had gone to take a step he had almost toppled over her. After righting himself, he had noticed that she could see him. Before he had been able to talk to her, she had said one sentence, and then he had been released from the vision.

His conscious-self had popped back into the car with James. He had been in shock at the reality of what had just happened. He had been about to tell James when the gravity of what she said had hit him with full force: "He chose you." Three words were all she had said, but it was three words that shook Pablo to the core of his religious beliefs.

In that fugue, he had also gotten an unshakable confirmation that he was going to be used as the messenger and executioner of God's Will, that he was now the voice and hammer of the Meek.

The power that existed on earth that had upset Jesus the most was money. Like everyone else, Pablo had known the story of Him turning over the tables at the Temple, and of the Rich Man who had gone away sad when Jesus had told him to sell his possessions and give the money to the poor if he wanted to be perfect.

These were stories that Pablo had heard over and over, but now he had been able to feel that these were not wives' tales after all, but real stories. This hadn't been some hunch, either. It had been something in his gut that had been telling him this had not been like any other kind of intuition he'd ever felt. It had felt more like a direct message from God, in the form of a fugue-like state where time had no meaning.

He had felt what seemed like an hour pass, but in reality, it had been mere minutes when he had come back. He'd had no sensation, other than a feeling of low voltage that coursed through his body, voltage that kept him aware he was in a dreamlike state. A living being was not supposed to be in that realm, and the voltage, he had inferred, had meant that he was the one out of place there.

His family members had been where they were supposed to be, while he had been out of place. That was when he had realized that Julio was not there. What significance that held, he hadn't been sure. There had been no doubt that in the end, once back on this side, he'd had information that had not been there before the fugue. The best explanation he had been able to come up with was that God gave him a download, and one that was a doozy.

The vision seemed to have communicated some pretty definite things he was supposed to accomplish, yet with little clue as to how to accomplish them. Pablo had held the knowledge in his head as if he'd learned it in school, only he hadn't. He'd had a pretty good idea of where the knowledge came from, and although it had been mystifying, Pablo had been left with no doubt that the information had been inspired.

He had been given the direction that he was to stand high on a mountain and look down on the world. He was to see all that was unfolding from as high of a vantage point as he could get to, so that there was a separation between him and the earth. In his non-fugue state, he had already thought of a way he could get even higher than a mountain, at least with his eyes. He was to stand as the Judge, which really made a lot of sense.

But then something inside the fugue happened that hadn't made sense at all. A hand had slipped into his, and he had been able to clearly see her face. She had been lovely, and they had looked down together. *I'm not to do this alone? How can I do the job if I'm tethered by love? Isn't that why my family was taken?*

Pablo had been about to make some hard choices, which would cause some to vilify him as the world's next megalomaniac. So how could he be tied to someone else? He was about to devastate the elite, making him a champion to the other ninety-five percent of the earth's population.

Feeling the lightheadedness of the fugue fade, Pablo had looked out the window as they were passing the perfect little farm. The whole family had happened to be out. Their pre-teen kids had been washing a dog that looked more like a horse than a dog. They had been laughing, and the boy had just hosed the girl unexpectedly. The girl had been protesting and attempting to retaliate by throwing a wet cloth, but it had missed badly to the left, which had earned her another spraying.

The parents had been loading the contents of their harvest out of a pull-cart and into their truck. Pablo had been able to see writing on the panel of the truck door advertising that the truck was powered by natural gas. These people had been ahead of the game. Sooner rather than later, this would be the norm for mankind, not the exception.

Pablo had realized that all man really needed was to return to a simple existence. All this technology and money were just ideas that were bad, and no one had stopped them. Money was a way for evil people to gain power over other people—good people never sought to lord over anyone. Pablo had known this because he had never sought to lord over anyone. His plan, once initiated, would take on a life of its own, and no one could stop it once the ball was rolling. *Truthfully, no one could've stopped me before, and that was before God's Will was being played out through my hands.*

He had looked at James and said, "We need to talk."

* * *

Bob Thompson spoke across the desk to Steve Hatten. They were in a room set aside for telecommunications, and it awarded them some needed privacy away from the war room.

"We've focused on the Great Basin up to Oregon and Colorado with our Recon 2 Satellite. We won't have pass over on Number 1 and the southern area for thirty minutes. We've decided on the area around Baker. Our analysts say that the sparsely populated desert is a probable route."

Steve Hatten had had his wings singed today more times than he could count, and he was in the mood to give some back, so it was without pleasantness that he addressed Bob. His slightly reddish hair was a match for his face. In fact, it was his tell. General Hatten's face flushed as soon as he became passionate about an issue, and it usually stayed that way from that point on.

"Well, Bob, that's fine and dandy, but what if they hopped over to Bishop or Mammoth? They both have small airports. If that's the case, Bob, then they could be on their way to Oregon in a minivan, or having a fire in their cabin not a half hour from there. What shouldn't have happened was them getting airborne, that was a very bad thing."

Bob knew that wouldn't take long. *Beck's treachery has disgraced the Agency.*

"Listen Steve, I'm sorry the Chief got on you, but you're an old hat, you don't need to be told what that was about. Now let's not start pointing fingers. Every agency, or branch is subject to personnel malfunctions and nothing can be done about it. People fail. It's an imperfect world, Steve, and you know it. Now if we put our minds together, we can catch these scumbags, and this can be in the rearview mirror, soon to be replaced by the next crisis. I have a feeling they're trying to get out of the pool rather than hunker down. We just have to figure out where."

* * *

Doug had flown over the mountains what felt like a million times over the past year. He had flown all over the state, but on Ameraflight trade routes, and with flight plans. He had always wanted to free fly like that, just like a bush pilot. He had to admit, he felt very alive for a guy who was as close to dying as he was.

"So, Matt, what do we do when we get to the circle on that map? Do you know where the airfield is? Do you know who's going to meet us?"

Matt looked confused. Then he realized that Doug knew his name even though he had never told it to him. Doug caught the look and asked, "What?"

Matt admitted to Doug that he was momentarily thrown off when he used his first name, because he knew he had never provided it. Then he remembered the TV in the diner.

"Well, at least I know you're a sharp one," Doug replied, laughing at him. "You're currently the most wanted man in American history! The President asked the people to turn the country into an episode of *America's Most Wanted* to look for you. Everyone is going to know your name. Your working for 'many people' days might be over, unless you have a good plastic surgeon."

Matt thought about that. "Hmm, I guess there might even be a movie in the works for this one. I hope someone cool plays me."

Doug thought about that too and added, "Yeah, I wouldn't mind Christian Slater to play my part. He's always so cool."

They allowed a brief bonding moment, but before it could go further, the phone in Vera's backpack began to ring. Apparently, he had not turned it off when he had replaced it, and now it was ringing from a blocked number.

Matt answered unsteadily, "Hello?"

"*¿Dónde está Vera?*"

"Um, do you speak English?"

"*No hablo English. ¿Dónde está Vera?*"

Matt turned to Doug. "Do you know any Spanish?"

"No," Doug replied.

He looked back at Vera. There was no way she would be able to talk, but he tried. He unbuckled and went back.

"Vera, hey, can you talk to these guys?" He held up the phone. "Vera?"

Nothing. He quickly abandoned her and went back to his seat, saying one word into the receiver, "Bategues. We go to Bategues." Matt used a fake Spanish accent that came out whenever he was trying to speak Spanglish to a person that didn't speak English very well. *Like that's going to help. It's about as useful as talking louder.*

As soon as he was done, he opened the phone, took out the battery, and broke the phone with his bare hands.

"Why did you do that?" Doug asked.

"She did it earlier," Matt replied. "I don't know if it worked or not, but at least there's a chance now they know we're coming."

Matt thought about that for a second and decided that he would turn the other phone on, since they hadn't used it yet.

* * *

James had looked more than quizzical. "You want me to seriously believe this? You're not playing some elaborate hoax to bring some kind of 'God Experience' to my life?"

One look from the boy and he had known it was no joke, but this had been too much. James had needed time to absorb this information. He had broken off to think in his room.

Divine Intervention? Will of God? James, of all the people in the world, had understood the full scope of what could be if this child were to become hell-bent on something like revenge. But this had been different, and Pablo's belief in the reality of his vision had been unwavering.

James had been doing a lot of thinking about God lately, like most dying people. People wanted to believe so badly that the lights just didn't go out, or as Stephen Hawking put it, that the computer didn't just power down one last time. Now this boy was claiming that he was a Biblical character, that he was the Harbinger of Change, appointed by the Hand of God! The kid had been through so much, and it would have been so easy to write this off as some fantasy, or some kind of coping mechanism. Except that this kid had not been an average teenager.

As a matter of fact, he had been like no teenager that had ever walked the earth. James had felt that Pablo was so far ahead of where he was at the same age, that it was like comparing a five-year-old against an adult.

James had pondered the boy's exact recount of the visions, or fugues, or whatever they were. The visions had been very detailed, and the plan that had been put forth into Pablo's head had been very specific. *A plan Pablo will need my help with to pull off the right way. Lord above, though, what would really happen to the world if that really transpired?* James had fallen asleep after that, thinking to himself, *God, what would really happen if that transpired?*

As it turned out, he had found out that night in his sleep. Like in the Bible, it came in the form of a dream. Waking up from that dream, the next morning James had become the Agent for the "Harbinger of Change."

A shocked and bewildered Pablo had sat at the breakfast alcove and asked, "What the hell, James? It wasn't like I was asking you to borrow the car here. I'm asking you to help change the world, and that change will be especially hard on the U.S., a very spoiled place, and a place where your parents still live. Now I have to ask you, what gives? Why would you just cave in on this without trying to talk me out of it? We're the two greatest minds in the world, how can you just accept this so easily? I expected to win this argument over a period of time, not just have you agree carte blanche. This is too easy, and it reeks of you placating me for some reason. So please tell me now what that reason is."

He had looked at the boy, who definitely had his hackles up. He had imparted as much empathy as he could in a glance of sincerity. He had simply said, "You're not the only one with dreams, boy, both aspirationally and literally."

Pablo had gotten it. James had had his own epiphany, and had come on board! And then it had clicked, all of it, James included. It had been God's set-up for him from the start. All of it had been destined to be from the time he was born—as long as James was being sincere, that was.

He had pondered the reality that his master was really his servant. Right then Eva had dropped a wonderful plate of eggs, potatoes, and sausage in front of him, which of course tore his mind out of thought. She had also given him his first smile in a while, as she showed a little cleavage when she bent down. He was a teenage boy after all, and that better have caught his attention, or they'd have to check him for a pulse.

She had walked out of the breakfast alcove, and he had looked at James one more time and resumed, "So, I tell you a fantastic tale of God and purpose the day you give me access to a hundred and ten million dollars. You not only didn't go to the bank first thing this morning and undo what you did, but now you're trying to tell me you're on board with a cryptic sentence and a pat on the back? Why must you be so mired in subterfuge? I told you my biggest secret, one that could make me look crazy, and you won't tell me yours?!"

"Okay, Son, calm down, and I'll tell you. I had a dream, too. Actually, my last thought before I fell asleep last night was, what would the world you described be like? The answer that was placed in this dream surprised me, because I thought for sure it would have brought chaos."

"Placed?"

"Yes Son, placed. You know, I was raised Catholic, so my understanding and take on religion is skewed, but I know a vision when I see and feel one. I'd never had a dream like this before. I went back in time and saw the scenes of my childhood playing out in an accelerated mode. I always saw so much good trying to happen, coupled with so much frustration from those who could never achieve it."

James had adjusted in his chair and taken a big mouthful of potatoes. Pablo patiently waited during the pause.

James had continued, "There was always some disgruntled human under the guise of being close to God, who would stop all growth and all good. They were people who were angry, frustrated, and blocking any positive that might arise, always perverting even the most innocent of human behaviors into sin. My fifth grade teacher, Sister Connors, was the most-bitter person that ever misused the Bible."

This time it was eggs and ham that caused the pause, followed by a bite of bread and a drink of coffee.

"Sister Conners was responsible for more inferiority complexes in the boys than a high-school cheerleader with a put-down mouth. She just had this way of getting in your head, and soon you believed the things she was saying about you were going to come to fruition. So, Son, I tell you this because it's the reason I turned away from the Church, turned away from religion. So for me, James Haberman, to sit here and pontificate the merits of anything to do with God, is in and of itself a miracle. There was a time, I was maybe eight or nine, when they hadn't stolen my faith yet, and I remember feeling untouchable.

"With someone as powerful as God on my side, I was truly invincible. As I grew, I saw the poverty and injustice everywhere, and not only in my country, but throughout the world. My parents watched the five o'clock news every day of my life and were totally oblivious that they were terrifying their child with war, death, and crime on a daily basis. Being as astute as I was, I started to comprehend at a very early age. When my classmates didn't know what the Vietnam War was, I did.

"Those experiences alone killed any thought I had that God was real. All the other myths of my childhood were lies, so why not God too? Forced into Catholic School, I felt like an observer who was not emotionally attached to the scene in any way whatsoever, and, through the years, I had seen enough abuse of God that I determined it was just a way to exercise power over people, and nothing more."

Pablo had looked earnestly at his mentor and said, "James, that's how I feel about money right now."

He had looked back at the boy—such an innocent face, and such an innocent boy. "Son, I was serious when I said I believe in something extraterrestrial was at work here in my dream. Maybe we come from an alien race spreading their seed on inhabitable planets, or maybe there is an overseer of us all. Whatever you want to call God, Pablo, I do believe that the God particle will never be found."

James had stopped talking and had stared out the window at the little section he could see of the Limmat, breaking the eye contact they had been sharing. A tear had run down his cheek. "I spent a lot of time angry at the Church, Pablo, and angry at God. I didn't want my place in heaven. I didn't believe I deserved it. You know what I've done in my adult life. I'm not so sure that there's a place for the 'perfector of death' in heaven."

"Listen, Son," he said, looking back into Pablo's eyes again, "I swear this, on the very same God we speak of, that I never built any weapon with the intent of hurting an innocent person. I only built things to defend my country, and to make money, of course. As smart as I was, I tried to be naïve to the fact that there were people that would use some things I made for evil. I say, 'tried,' because I knew the truth, deep down. I knew we did things in the name of freedom that would not be sanctioned by God. Until last night, I thought that I lost my place in any of the places you would find God; that my business of death condemned me to the place Sister Connors always said I would end up."

"James, what happened last night?"

"I can't quantify what happened the way you can, because I don't believe in your God, Pablo. All I can tell you is that whatever Supreme Being is controlling this world, that Being wants me to help you."

* * *

Pablo had known from James that at the same time they were having that conversation, Jeremy had seen the tails and had known he was being followed. This time a hurried lane change from behind had caught his eye. Three left turns had confirmed it. He had been sure they had been bugging him too. These guys obviously had far reaching resources. They had seemed sure the boy had been about to reach out to one of his teachers.

Jeremy had been thankful that James and Pablo had been smart enough to know all this in advance. It had saved his life, he was sure of it. He had known that his friends would never be safe, though, because these guys would never stop. It had been a month now, and the school had been abuzz with many rumors, but he had known better than to partake in them.

Jeremy had contemplated leaking the story to AP or Reuters and letting the chips fall where they may, but then he had thought better of it. *Who knows how many lives that would cost?* He had decided he would just have to endure the countless intrusions and harassments until they stopped.

Jeremy had seen the tail pull in behind him and park as soon as he did. His fear had been that they would find some thread that linked him to this whole mess, and then the guys tailing him would be doing a lot more than that. He had nervously looked in his side mirror down the street to make sure nobody was advancing on him.

His hands had been shaking as he had pulled the car keys out of the ignition and he dropped them on the floorboard. As he was bending down to pick them up he had assured himself, *I'm sure the bad guys are just doing their homework and checking out all the school's personnel, where they live, who their relatives are, and who could be hiding the boy.*

Thankfully he hadn't qualified for threats against his family, since he had been alone since his parents passed. They had both died in old age—they had been in their late forties when he had been born, and had been gone by the time he was 28. No, they hadn't got a chance of getting to him that way, and he was thankful for that. These were not nice people. He had just hoped they would never be able to get to his friends.

* * *

Pablo had also known from his research into everything that at the same time Jeremy was being followed, the leaders of his oppressors had been planning his demise.

"Well?" Luis said.

"He eludes us," Octavio replied.

"How?" Luis asked. "He's just a boy, alone."

"Well Luis, he's here because he's special. We found out that his old school principal called here when he got word of the family. When informed, the boy just ran. No one has seen him since."

"He'll come back Octavio. He'll come back to the place he feels safe, just wait him out."

Luis chided his number one killer. "The money was never found on the compound. For once, my friend, you were wrong. But your *yerno* just found another account. Thank God you have him in the family."

"He's a good boy, my angry daughter is very lucky. Is all the money there, Luis?"

"We're not sure, as the bank is in Zurich. We will have to call in favors, but you know we will have it soon enough. So while we're working on it, take a couple of days off. Leave your wonderful son-in-law to watch for the kid, and go get a feel for this place. The bank is called the Habib Bank. We have some friends in Zurich, so it shouldn't be long. I had another thought, my friend. What if the boy has access to his uncle's account?"

"Okay Luis, I will get back to you. I'll scope things out, take a day or two to clear my head, and if you need me to, I can make your withdrawal."

"Good, Octavio. Go out and have a meal. I hear the restaurants are some of the finest in the world."

"Don't worry, Luis. I'll get him. You know I will. I always get my man."

Luis had retorted, "In this case it's only a boy, my friend—only half a job."

They had shared a laugh, but they had both known that every day the boy lived, the example and fear they had tried to instill in the locals was being mocked. Word had traveled back to Ecuador that the boy lived, and they had heard rumors that the people were forming an underground prayer movement. That had to be avoided at all costs. Octavio had known that something like that could cause the sheep to think that they had options, and that resistance could garner them a victory.

No, they had been facing more than half a job, and both of them had known it. This had been the type of shit that causes planes to fall out of the sky—one minute the plane was cruising along, the next a small bolt had worked free, causing a short that caused a failure of another component, and before you knew it, the plane was down. *This thinking is crazy. Why do I have such a bad feeling about this?*

"Okay, Luis," Octavio concluded. "I'll be in touch. I get it. We have to get him."

* * *

Ibarra was below, and it would be scant minutes until Pablo Manuel found out if he was going to become the single most powerful person to ever live or not. Actually, he could be powerful even without Vera, but not as overwhelmingly so as if she would be able to get him his "needed things." Not a bad accomplishment for someone in his twenties, especially considering that no one knew Pablo's name. A lot of people were in for some surprises in the not too distant future.

Pablo was now at the part of the game where he only needed one more move in his favor, and the game would be over. He could see it so clearly, just like he could see and hear the past verbatim, as if it were yesterday.

As he watched Ibarra go by, his immediate future lay ahead in the dark, and his thoughts fell back to James and the past. Pablo remembered asking, "So what did you see of my world?"

James had pondered the best way to get this out. "Well, when I was in college, they forced us to take philosophy, and the professors were all hippies who were into the concept of Utopia. I thought it was the biggest load of crap I'd ever heard in my life. Utopia indeed! We also had the Socialists and Communists, and I couldn't help but notice that there were no capitalist philosophers. My take was that these guys were all losers, people who wanted to be poor so they could act sanctimonious and ponder this world without greed or money. They were trying to live the song 'Imagine,' and I was surely not going to fall into that quagmire of anti-patriotic, anti-capitalist jargon, designed to confuse the developing mind. I was going to get my money."

Pablo had looked confused. "I don't understand where you're going with all this?"

"Patience, Son," James had explained, "I was getting to it. Well, last night, I actually saw this Utopia that the hippie philosophers all mused could exist. It was most bizarre. People still went to work, just like they do now. If you needed something you didn't pay, you just went and got it. Greed, envy, and crime disappeared. Pretty soon people were working hard just for each other, and a true revolution of thought evolved. It was so appealing that I wanted to stay, but I was pulled out. It was like I was only going to get a small glimpse of paradise before it was taken away. It was evident that if I wanted any more, then I have to help make it happen. I was allowed to oversee, and I felt the pride of being the enabler."

"How?" Pablo asked, riveted.

"By helping you, of course. Son, you've been chosen by the Cosmos to change the world."

EIGHT

Stampede

Doug saw the big challenge right away when he mapped his course. He wasn't a very gifted athlete, which was why he had first gravitated toward mechanics and then towards becoming a pilot. It was a way to get the same kind of clout with women as an athlete, but without all the arthritis later.

One of the few physical things he excelled at, though, was rock climbing. His high school friends had gone on a camping trip to Yucca Valley once, and had dragged him along. They had ended up in a place called Hidden Valley, and Doug had been hooked from that day forward.

It had been mile after mile of rock formations of every kind, for every kind of climber. There were the simple boulder areas, and then there were the serious rope climb spots. Doug had done both. Joshua Tree National Monument was the "Wonderland of Rocks" and he had lost himself there.

There had been something about the myriad of rock formations that let his imagination roll. His mind had just run away as he had gotten lost in all the formations. They had gone back twice every winter (the rocks were too hot in the summer) until he was in his mid-twenties.

One day he had been free climbing a rock called Black Sabbath, and as he was moving across an exposed ledge, an incident had happened

173

that had brought him to his current thought in the first place. His arms and legs had been splayed, each seeking its own hand or foot hold on a ledge only ten inches wide. He'd still had another fifty feet to saddle when suddenly a shadow had appeared on the rock.

It had been startling, but he had been stable with good handholds, so he had been in no immediate danger of falling to his certain death. But then the fighter jet had screamed by at a really low altitude followed by the wash. Good hold or not, the wash of a low-flying jet when he was on a rock with no ropes, perched on a ten inch ledge, had tightened his sphincter.

The jet had come from the Twentynine Palms Marine base, which was dead in the center of their path right now, Doug knew with certainty. As they traversed the desert east of there, he just hoped and prayed that one of those very same low-flying jets wasn't around.

Once they cleared Death Valley, the landscape became the same, mile after mile of rolling hills of white. Their plane stayed low, and they were perfectly camouflaged from the one thing that their enemies were hoping for: a shot from the spy satellite searching for them, or a blip from the AWACS.

They made their way over the vast Mojave National Preserve within an hour, and they were now parallel to the Twentynine Palms Marine base, so far without incident.

Unbeknownst to them, their timing was just right to avoid a recon plane as they dipped into a valley maybe five miles long. Doug was doing what he thought right to stay alive, becoming a bush pilot in his mind. So many nights this would have ended in tragedy, with their plane flying right into the side of a mountain, but not tonight. Doug thought, *These two certainly have good luck, and that's always a plus.*

Doug was starting to get weary, and his eyes were fatigued. He looked at his watch: three o'clock in the morning. They would still barely have the cover of dark when they landed. He knew once they cleared this stretch, it was another hour over the same type of terrain they had just come out of over the Mojave, only a lot hillier with less desert and more mountains.

Doug asked, "Did she happen to bring a coke or some other form of caffeine?"

It took Matt three minutes, but he produced a small bottle of an energy boost drink. Matt said admiringly, "She actually had three of them stored." He was more impressed by the minute with this girl.

They both eagerly drank it. Matt stowed the empty containers back in the backpack.

Doug asked, "What do you think is wrong with her?"

"I'm no doctor," Matt answered, "but she's obviously in shock. I didn't see any vaginal bleeding or anything unusual when I dressed her, so I don't think she has a medical issue."

Doug thought about that before he spoke. "We were making out before we were attacked, pretty hot and heavy. I take it that was part of the ruse?"

"I'm afraid so, Doug." Matt could see that he was hurt by that. "Well Doug, based on your theory, you have nothing to feel bad about. Apparently the attraction must have been mutual, otherwise she would have suffered physical injury during her rape."

Neither spoke again for the next hour after that horrid revelation. By then they had cleared the Marine base, and they had a straight shot to the border.

Doug looked over at him and announced, "It's go time." Then they elevated to adjust for the upcoming mountain.

* * *

The mood was not good in the war room. All efforts had failed. Satellites had failed, recon had failed, AWACS had failed, and even good old ground spotting had failed.

President Caulfield addressed the room: "Gentlemen, we need to consider at this point that the plane was a ruse, a way to make us chase our tails while the bad guys got out the back door. At this point, I'd say we've obliged them pretty well. But they're not out the back door yet!" exclaimed the President. "I believe I should declare martial law in the Northwest immediately! It will at least slow down their ability to move about freely."

Before the first mumbles began, he pre-empted his critics with a strong follow up. "And I don't want to hear one person in this room even mumble 'unprecedented' or any other hyperboles, because according to Bob Thompson over there, what they stole is 'unprecedented,' and I'm not going down in history as the guy who didn't recognize the time to act.

"Now, John Q. Public will do better than you think, that's not what I'm worried about. I'm worried about the inner cities, so we need to have a show of force to prevent rioting. There's always going to be some who take advantage, no matter the situation. So have all active and available regular Army back up the Reserves immediately. I want this moving now! Let's not make this easy. I will go on and address the nation. I'm sure Kim's already having the speech written."

Bob Thompson, who was talking into his Bluetooth, raised his hand. "Mr. President, I have Sarah Berkman on the line. We're putting her through on the comm. Go ahead, Sarah."

"I got them, Bob. They're headed out toward the Mexican border in their prop plane, to a place called Bategues."

Steve Hatten shot in sharply, "How do you know this? That pathway was heavily scrutinized."

"We deciphered a cell phone transmission. Let me play it for you."

The Generals and their Chief listened to the conversation between Matt and Felipe, but they were not completely swayed.

"That could have been anything," said five-star Army General William "Duke" Early.

"Well," said Sarah, "we matched the English voice to recordings we had of Hurst, and it's a 100 percent match!"

"Jesus Christ," muttered Rear Admiral Mark Anders, as he picked up his phone. He dialed a number and said, "Get me the Base Commander for El Centro on the line right away!"

* * *

Pablo had known that every army has generals, every powerful team has leaders, and everyone who has ever tried to take over the world has had devotees. True followers were hard to come by. People always had to have motives to drive them, or they become uncaring.

When he had originally found Vera, Pablo had had an inkling that her captors would be of more use to him alive than dead. Something had told him to follow his instincts on this.

He had seen something in the face of one of her tattooed handlers that had intrigued him. The man had been short, only 5'4" at the most. He had obviously been on a mission to make sure that every single inch of his body was covered in tattoos. He had been bald except for a ponytail that ran mid-back with periodic knots. He had worn a headscarf. His head had also been tattooed. He had worn no expression as he had sat and smoked his hand-held cigarette.

Pablo had been drawn to him, and then it had hit him why. This guy knew death. It was something Pablo was going to have to face very soon as well. He hadn't known death, other than the tragedy that had befallen him. But he was going to have to kill some people himself soon. Even though these people didn't deserve to live, he would still need the nerve to kill someone.

Sure, he had already bought a protection force that could do it for him; but just today, they made a mistake and lost him, at least for a while. He had purposely gotten into the wrong limo to test their ability to find him if things went wrong. He had vowed he would never be a victim again, so he sometimes tested his well-paid army. He had seen their vehicles setting up around him. It had looked like they were good for the task once again, albeit late.

Regardless, they'd lost him for two minutes, and a lot could happen in two minutes. He'd had different drills for them, and this was their kidnap drill. He'd had to call their performance a miserable failure at that point. Two minutes was an eternity.

He had already given his errant driver $100 to be quiet and sit still. His focus had gone back to the tattooed man.

He had reminded himself that his mission from God was to be done mostly on instinct. There had been information on what he was to become, but no specific path set in the fugue on how to get there. Some things had just felt wrong, and other things had just felt very right. That's how he was going to play it.

Thinking many moves ahead, he had seen what he needed in this tattooed man. He had only come to Rio to set up yet another blind, yet another company that was part of a web of worldwide acquisitions that would serve his end purpose.

The limo driver's mistaken interpretation of his directions ended up bringing him to Vera at the Favela da Grota. She had been lined up outside a bar talking to four other girls, and the moment he saw her, he had known that God was at work again. Yet she had been a captive, a slave to some obviously vicious people—people who lived for one reason only, to perpetrate hatred toward all of humanity; people who turned to deadly violence when even slightly provoked. *How can I talk reason to a group that only understands violence?*

It turned out that Felipe Benitez had been the leader of the Anthill Gang, and Pablo had had an idea. Rather than make a phone call to have Felipe killed and simply take her, he had decided to try another approach. He had needed zealots, not mercenaries. Mercenaries were only useful to a point, because they had no loyalty. What he had needed done would require more than what money could buy.

He had gotten out of the limo and approached the tattooed man, his team on high alert. After recovering from the initial shock of being approached by such a soft and out-of-place individual as Pablo, Felipe had given him five minutes.

In that three hundred second span, what Felipe had heard was so unheard of and so impossible, that he had just agreed in a state of shock. He had agreed that the man would return tomorrow and take their little gold mine away.

As Felipe had watched the man calmly walk out, his second-in-command had asked, "What just happened, Felipe?"

Felipe had replied, "That soft-looking man who just left said he will go and kill all of the Reds by morning, if I give Vera to him."

"What, how?"

"He asked me about our worst enemy, people we wished were gone from the face of the earth. So I told him about those assholes. He says there will be plenty to replace her, because the new girls' captors will be dead by morning."

João had not replied. He had been a man of few words, and almost nothing in this world had been capable of shocking him. He and Felipe had been on the streets together almost their whole lives, killing, stealing, and taking.

"Why?" João had finally said.

Felipe had replied, "He said that after tonight, we work for him, and we will never be second again."

"Why didn't you kill that fucker right there, Felipe? Don't you see he's trying to take us over!"

"No, João, that's where you're wrong," Felipe had answered. "He already took us over, we just don't know it yet. Didn't you see his eyes? They had no fear and he never raised his voice or his heart rate, he just spoke of what was to be. He said after the Reds are gone, we won't have long before our 'great mission' starts. He said tell the girl nothing and enjoy the next few months, for no one will dare rival us for the Reds' territory, not after tonight."

João had looked at him very confused. "What great mission?"

The phone rang, pulling Pablo out of his daydream and back into the present. "Felipe, speak to me."

"We don't know what happened. She didn't call at the appointed time, so we called the numbers. Phone Three answered, it was a *gringo*, *'no habla español'*"

"No one was there with you who spoke English?"

"No, Enrique is at Site One."

"So did you get anything?"

"Oh yes, Boss. Sorry, we did, he said 'Bategues.'"

"Where's that?"

"It's a small farm town near pick up two, right near me."

"Jesus, something has happened to her, but why is the *gringo* is still carrying it out?"

"I don't know, Boss. I thought you would have that information."

"No, I don't Felipe, but what you got was valuable. We can start now, make sure you're set up in case I'm late!"

They hung up as the helicopter landed and Pablo made his way off of the landing pad. He instructed João to have his canvas-covered contraption stored in Felipe's office, and he made his way to the "Penthouse" as he affectionately called it. It was really a war room like nothing else in the world, and it sat on top of his mountain. The whole place was dug out and reinforced as sturdily as the strongest bunker.

The only way up was an elevator that only three people had access to. The only other way out was an emergency exit that literally took one out on top of the mountain. Its only Achilles' heel was the bulletproof 20' x 20' glass wall that let Pablo see out. Eventually, he would stand there and look down on mankind.

He sat at the middle chair of the three that were positioned before the screens. The screens stretched out a full 15 feet in a semi-circle. He focused on the main screen, and entered the code to take over the drones at his disposal. The screen he was looking at was showing his video display that read *"El Centro."* He also had the ability to listen on their frequency, and he was getting the control tower at present. He called the number on the second cell phone.

Matt's hunch paid off as the phone he turned on was ringing. "Yes," he answered.

"Is she alive?" the voice asked in English.

"Yes, but hurt," Matt replied.

"Can I talk to her?"

"No, she's in shock."

"Do you know where you're at?"

"No, but the pilot might; here he is."

Doug said, "Hello." Then he got stoic and listened. He answered that he could see the lights of what must be Holtville or El Centro up to his left. He listened more intently and said "yes" about six more times and hung up.

Then he addressed Matt. "He said to destroy the phone."

Matt did as instructed. "Okay, what's the plan?"

"Well you were close in your estimation, we're just altering it a little. Plus, he told me something I'd forgotten about."

"What's that, Doug?"

"There's a naval air facility really close to here, and we're in a lot of trouble. He said if I listen, we might live."

Doug angled the plane downward, heading toward the city lights at a very low altitude.

* * *

"Tango Foxtrot, this is Gold Base, come in Tango."

"Ah, this is Tango Foxtrot, go Base."

"Tango, we have a possible locale for the Bogie. Its known heading is southbound at low altitude. Last known heading was northeast of El Centro."

"Roger, Leader. Foxtrot Tango and Alfa are coming back."

That eased Commander Spence Prior's nerves. He was scrambling his birds as fast as he could, following orders to get them all in the air looking for these two. That was what Rear Admiral Anders had ordered him to do, and the tone was urgent. He was up in the tower when the first F18-Hornet was ready for takeoff.

"Foxtrot Oscar, you are cleared for takeoff."

"Roger, Tower."

Spence watched the bird lift off, and he wondered just what it was that those two had stolen to be so hotly pursued.

The Hornet just cleared the airfield when suddenly a streak of electricity that looked like an elongated ball flashed, followed by an explosion. Something happened to the plane. Spence saw the ejector seat launch the pilot into the air, and the jet crashed with a huge boom. The surrounding population was sparse, so there were no ground deaths.

"What the hell was that?" Spence boomed. "Did you see that? Was that a Bogie?! Seriously, people, what was that?"

"There was nothing on radar, Commander. It might have been an electrical malfunction. Should we still continue scrambling?"

Spence Prior had been a pilot for thirty years and had never seen anything like that before. "No. Get me Tango and Alfa now."

Look Down/Shoot Down Radar is the most imperfect kind of radar, and Lt. Russ Halprin knew this, but was thankful every day for the guys that gave them this advantage. The fact those pukes had made it this far was a miracle, but the miracle ends now. He hit the comm to talk to his pilot.

"They're well inside range, Skip, not optimal, but close enough, and we're closing in with every second." Russ knew the radar could filter out ground clutter and focus on only moving targets—the closer the better—which was fine.

Jeff Simpson had his target. "Foxtrot Tango to Base, target acquired at 20 miles out from our location. Target is three clicks northeast of El Centro, heading south at 700 feet, I estimate they will intersect with Mexican Airspace in approximately five minutes."

"Tango, this is Base. Engage the target. We've been grounded temporarily, so use afterburners to go after them with cannons if the missile fails."

"Roger that, Base."

Without hesitation, the AIM-7 Sparrow left the rack with angry intent. With a kill rate over 90 percent, the bogie was sure to perish. Following the missile, they punched it into afterburner. This was going to come to a head quickly. The missile would find its mark in less than half a minute. If it failed, that bogie would find his six-barrel, 20-mm cannon less forgiving.

Simpson watched the missile's trail, and wondered why Base had said "if" his missile failed, as if they expected it? He also wondered, *What the hell could have grounded them in the first place?*

* * *

Matt saw a massive explosion up ahead, way over to their right, "Did you see that? What was that?!" he exclaimed. "That can't be a good sign," he added.

"It surely can't be," Doug replied.

Within two minutes, they had pulled straight across from the explosion, with El Centro coming up on the left. Doug observed, "I'm sure that's going to wake some people up."

The sky was just cracking a hint of daylight, and they could see civilization signs up ahead, when something suddenly buzzed by them, missing their plane by mere feet. They never even got a glimpse of what it was, or how big, only that it was very fast and very quiet. Matt thought it was grayish in color.

Five seconds later, the sky lit up like a giant flashbulb. Three seconds after that, there was a large explosion on the ground, parallel to them.

Doug said ominously, "Looks like they know we're here, Matt, I'm parking this fucker on the nearest street down there. We're done flying."

"You might want to hold off on that Doug," Matt replied. "It looks like we have some help."

No sooner did those words leave his mouth than two more objects zipped by them in the same exact same way. As they anxiously awaited the report the two projectiles were sure to carry, they made their way over El Centro.

* * *

"Tango Foxtrot to Base. The Sparrow failed, repeat, the Sparrow failed. Have targets in range, but it's too late to engage in U.S. airspace."

"Base to Tango Foxtrot. Engage and destroy bogie. Disregard airspace violation. *Great, now I'm declaring war on Mexico,* Spence thought. *This shit just got out of hand quickly.* He was unable to take his eyes off the radar screen.

"Roger, Base. Will engage in..."

* * *

Pablo remembered how the month with James had been spent playing chess and talking about life, love, and how things were going to be for people like the Heldergartens after the hammer came down. They had decided they would bend the rules, warn Sandy and James's parents, and make sure the Heldergartens were taken care of. They had taken long walks and gazed at the intersecting waterways, theorizing that those waterways were much like society. Pretty soon, all the waterways would be a single river. Pablo still had trouble believing that this great man, with this great mind, was really on board to go through with this.

Although Jeremy had imparted philosophy as expertly as he could, he had known that unless a teacher was on the same level or above his student, then it wouldn't quite translate. With James and Pablo, it had clicked. Life had been good for a moment. But then James's pain had started, mild at first, then becoming unbearable. The doctor in Zurich had given him an ambulatory pain management infusion pump, and he had started on morphine.

That's when the secret lessons had begun, the ones that James had saved for his last days. Pablo had sensed the urgency in his friend when the lessons had gotten tough, and they had covered things at their highest levels. These were the lessons he had needed to become the Harbinger, the ones that would lead him into what he was destined to become.

For weeks they had gone at it, with James reaching deep within himself to try to extract all his files and download them to Pablo. During this process, James had finally realized that Pablo's retention really was near 100 percent; that he was actually downloading himself into Pablo like an event people 50 years from now would know as "singularity."

Basically, singularity was the act of downloading your brain into a computer. James had taught him the theory and had predicted that one day people would be able to download their brains into a specially made computer. Pablo had remembered James saying, "But we will only be teaching the computer to do what you are doing now, son."

Pablo had known this was exactly what James needed. James had needed to feel that he'd left something behind. He had often said what an amazing opportunity the cosmos had given him by delivering Pablo. With Pablo's retention, James had realized that he was ensuring his mind would live on for as long as Pablo's did.

Pablo remembered James's notice of how his enthusiasm had spiked when they'd covered the subject of cybernetics. James had given him extra time on that topic. Pablo inwardly smiled as he reflected on how James never would have guessed how far he had come, especially how fast he'd made it to grasping the singularity concept.

As Pablo looked back, singularity had been mainly a lab concept then. It had been he and James theorizing. It had been amazing what two years had done for him with the right funds and resources.

It had been a hot day, and after theorizing, they had played a game of chess to stalemate. Shortly thereafter, it had started to cloud up. Pablo had opened the window so they could smell the ozone, knowing that James loved the smell of it prior to the rain. The clouds had burst, and then he had heard the sound of his friend activating the pain-management button on the pump. It had beeped and given an accelerated motor action.

The button had been for when the pain became intolerable. After the dose, James had lain back and listened to the rain, smiling from the relief the morphine had allowed. He had just lain there enjoying the sounds and smell of a summer rain. He had been content that the download was complete and that his protégé would ensure that his influence on the world would continue.

Pablo had sat and watched him, like he had done every night, except this night his breathing had been more labored than ever. James had seemed to be gulping for air at some points. Pablo's concern had been so tense that every muscle in his body was taut. He had sat in the loveseat in a trance and watched James breathe.

The nightlight had illuminated a bookshelf with numerous titles, and he had observed *War and Peace* sitting there. He had so loved that book, and now he could relate to the loss of family that some of the characters had to endure, especially Petya Rostov's family.

There had been another book he had taken a sudden interest in, and he had gotten up and retrieved it. It was Robert Graves' *Greek Mythology*. Pablo had remembered the Bank in Zurich. It had been months ago, but it had felt like yesterday that the two of them were there and he had thought to himself one day soon to obtain knowledge of the statues he had seen. Somehow, among all the things he had learned, he still hadn't known what those statues meant.

James had shown him so much. In their many talks, they had theorized about James's work, and in their breakdowns, Pablo had been able to enhance almost all of James's theories, much to James's amazement, seeing his redevelopment of others people's work had been *his* claim to fame. Pablo's knowledge of nuclear physics and EMP technology had reached its own plateau thanks to his mentor.

Pablo had flipped the pages and there they had been: his statues. He had read the page and learned that they represented the daughters of Asclepius, the Greek god of medicine and healing. Their names were Hygieia, the goddess of health; Meditrina, the goddess of longevity; and Panacea, the goddess of healing.

Panacea had been the one who had grabbed him. She was the one that had the magic potion to cure all. If he'd had it, he could have just given it to James and they could have walked away into the sunset.

He had set the book down. Nothing had been able to stop him from twisting up inside. Somehow the rhythm of the rain had seduced him into a fitful sleep, but it had been broken by a vicious lightning strike and a thunderclap that had woken him with a start. He had half-expected it to have waken James as well.

It was then that he had noticed the struggled breathing had stopped. He had waited anxiously, hoping that James was just more under control. But there had been no heaving of his chest at all.

Pablo had sat the entire night by his side. He had been afraid to take the next step into his life, afraid to move from the place where he sat.

The next morning Eva had come in, and it hadn't taken long for her to figure it out. She had hugged him softly and given him truthful compassion. Then he had let it all out. He had let out months of rage and anger with just plain screaming. She had waved off her parents, who had immediately gotten ahold of the pre-arranged number James had left.

Pablo had been distraught even after the undertaker had arrived and taken James away. Eva had held Pablo while he cried "Papa" over and over. It had been horrible for her to watch. It had even been physically hard on the ears at times. She had never seen someone so distraught, so inconsolable in her entire life. Eva stayed with him that day and night, never leaving his side.

* * *

Matt was trying to crane his neck to get a view of what happened, but the rear view in a Cessna was very limited. These explosions were different than the first. They were more massive and carried a shock wave that reverberated through the cabin of the plane.

"Whatever those were, they were even more wicked than the ones before," Doug said.

Matt replied, "They were different for sure. The first ones made a lightning flash, and had a small explosion."

"Well, those two went boom," Doug said. He believed the last one had been an exploding aircraft, possibly a fighter jet. Whoever was on their side was taking on the U.S. military now! Never a good idea—Doug wanted off this ride, immediately!

Doug followed the directions he had been given by the man on the phone. They crossed the border, guiding the plane by the landmarks the man had identified. Soon they saw the makeshift runway lights, even over the awakening sky in the background. A minute later they were down. *It was over!*

* * *

Spence looked at the screen and couldn't believe what he saw, although it confirmed that his hunch was right: there were enemy aircraft involved in this. There had to be for this to have happened. *Someone just declared war on the United States of America!* Worse, he feared the pilot had been cut off mid-sentence, which meant he hadn't ejected.

"Get me Rear Admiral Anders," Spence barked. Two seconds later Rear Admiral Mark Anders was on the line.

"What have you got, Commander?"

"Nothing good, Rear Admiral. They got away, into Mexican airspace."

"What?! How, Commander?"

"They attacked our airbase with some kind of EMP technology. One of our Hornets was attacked on takeoff, which grounded us. We thought fortune was on our side because we had two F-18s up already. Unfortunately, that did us little good. First, they disabled the Sparrow shot at them. Then they used an unknown technology to down both our planes. And Mark, there were no ejections—the pilots never saw it coming."

"Looks like the Ruskies are restarting the Cold War," said Anders.

"Maybe," said Spence.

Anders added, "Or maybe our smiling trade commerce buddies to the East. Whoever it is, they just grabbed the tiger's tail."

"Commander, what's our damage at the base?"

"We lost a Hornet on takeoff. The pilot got out on that one; no other damage."

"Okay, Commander, I don't need to tell you the priority on this one. Homeland Security has a facility near you; bring them in. We're waiting for all the data you can get. I saw the President already heading for an international conversation with our neighbors to the south."

"Okay, Rear Admiral. I'll get right back to you as we unfold this."

"Okay, Commander, stop wasting time on me."

* * *

"Ray, what do you have?" CIA Director Bob Thompson asked.

"I have a Freudian nightmare, Mr. Director, with some disturbing discoveries, and some interesting ones, too."

"Ray, you know me and normally, I love your long winded version of things, but we don't have the time right now. I need succinct, please."

"Sorry, Mr. Director." Ray gave the boss what he wanted, succinctly. "Okay, so Beck was not the victim of a rape, he was the perpetrator. We found scratch marks consistent with the type caused by someone defending himself or herself on his face, and he had a bite mark on his left forearm, too. So almost certainly when the DNA analysis comes back, it will be that of Nancy Chavez."

"So what does that mean, Ray? How does that fit in here?"

"We also found trace of a second person's blood, near the nose of the plane. Not enough to think there was a fatality, so more like a bloody nose. I think that our man Beck caught them off guard, knocked Hurst out, and then raped and interrogated our suspect. I think Perp Two, Hurst, woke up during the rape, and killed Beck. Then, the two flew out of there.

"You know, Mr. Director, I had this guy profiled as a possible megalomaniac years ago. Not trying to be an 'I told you so' type, but you knew he was to be watched more closely as he rose to power. You, yourself, had expressed concern that he might do anything to get to the top, and it looks like we were both right. If he did this, then he was a sociopath, much worse than even we thought."

A moment of thought passed before Ray then asked, "Mr. Director would you like to hear the good news?"

"What good news, Ray?"

"You have an agent on the inside of this case, is that good enough news for you?"

"What are you talking about, Ray?"

Ray spun the story the way he did when he was focused, like he was talking to someone in particular physically, but he was really talking to himself. "The possible downside is, seeing he's not in on this with them, he will have to survive once they all get in the same place. So you could lose that agent just as fast as you got him. His critical trial is happening right now."

"What Ray? Who? What are you talking about? And make sense this time!"

"You have an agent on the inside of this case and his name is Matt Hurst."

"I told you that I didn't have time for one of our conjecture sessions Ray. What part of that wasn't clear?"

"It's going in my official report. I believe we should put him on the payroll."

The look Bob gave Ray was like a husband might give his wife right before he called the authorities to have a forced psychiatric evaluation done on her because she had just boiled the cat for dinner.

"Listen carefully Ray, you've had a great career, but one of your men just went Norman Bates on us, and your word is not going to carry a lot of weight right now." Bob Thompson took on his fatherly expression, "Especially if you go around saying we should put the most sought after criminal in U.S. history on the payroll, then you are going to get the gun sights set on you for sure. Why do you think that anyway?"

Ray took those words in before replying, "Do you remember the story of Allen Dulles?"

"You mean Eisenhower's CIA Director? Of course I do, what has that got to do with this?"

"Those two notes Hurst left were Dulles quotes."

Bob's train of thought froze, and he began to remember his history. "Do you really think he's that smart?" he asked. "He's an untrained civilian."

"Civilian, yes; untrained, no. We know he has training in surveillance. We also found a certificate from an interrogation school that he graduated from. But more than that, it's what we found at his office, house, and in his computer that would indicate a greater awareness of things outside than that of Joe Citizen. He's a wild card, and I believe he joined our ranks as a patriot."

"Then why not just leave that note?"

"Because he wanted me to figure this out. He figured if he could lure me into solving this, then I would be his advocate. Plus, it was safer in case someone else found it, due to its ambiguity."

"Okay Ray, there's no way this kid figured out *you* exist."

"Don't be ridiculous, Bob. I meant my position. He knows it exists. So my final piece of evidence is Ron Crawford. Listen, he knows that Dulles was the perfect example of a patriot pushed into a position of looking like a traitor. Those in the know, of course, have the real story of how Dulles and his friends were intrinsic in the downfall of Nazi Germany."

"Crawford? You mean the kid whose head was smashed in by Hurst, that Ron Crawford? The one fighting for his life right now?"

"Yes Bob, and here's why he's the proof that Hurst was no hired professional. We figured Crawford stayed behind in the parking lot while Beck hunted for them. Sarah confirmed Crawford was alone on Beck's order. We found the second note on Beck's car seat, so it was surely Hurst who crushed Crawford's skull, and then ran to get her and get out. They must have been prepping the plane when Beck found them, before they could escape."

"So how does this exonerate Hurst?" the Director asked. "It actually makes him clearly an accomplice in this because it shows he acted on free will. He wasn't under any duress or forced to hit that agent."

"Great observation, Mr. Director. No he wasn't, and that's why Crawford being alive to tell the tale is my final piece of evidence!"

"How is that? Because he didn't shoot the boy, Ray? If he shot him, then the Cavalry comes a running, so he had to smash him. The fact he lived was happenstance."

"I don't buy that, because he took Crawford's HK. His silenced HK. One silenced double tap and Crawford's history. No, Mr. Director, this kid left us a trail of clues that he was sucked into this, and now he is going to finish it from his end or die trying. Maybe there's a variable we don't know about. It could be they're threatening his family—that would certainly account for Crawford being alive. That's my take on this, Mr. Director, and it's unwavering."

"I hear you, Ray. I will think about sharing this assessment, but for sure, it won't be popular. He killed two DHS agents in cold blood."

"He defended his life against unknown assailants under the color of authority. Mr. Director, my report is coming, and it won't be altered because Beck was able to hide his true nature from us—from me. I can't let this boy down. He needs us as much as we need him."

* * *

Pablo's conversation with the *gringo* replayed in his head. "She's in shock," Matt had said, reporting on Vera's condition. Pablo's head was swimming with possibilities—too many, so he drifted his thoughts back to the Hedge, and James—anything to take his mind off of this waiting.

He remembered being in the alcove eating as he looked at the laptop. How could a month have passed since James died? Eva had been hovering over him, helicopter-loving him.

He had taken her hand, saying to her in French, "It's okay, I'll be alright. I'm just going into town to take care of a couple of errands, and then I'll be right back. I'll be alright, thanks to you, my dear." He had seen her worried face. "Seriously, I'll be okay." He had pulled her down whispering in her ear, *"Je t'aime."*

She had blushed, getting goosebumps over her arms. She had quickly put more potatoes on his plate and kissed his forehead.

As Eva had walked away, she had been lost in thought. She was thinking to herself that he was such a wonderful lover, and his accent in Spanish was so romantic. She had made him use it while they made love. She just loved to daydream about the day they could be one forever. He had told her that he had a mission in life that he must accomplish, but when it was over, there might be a small chance they could be together.

It wasn't her, he had wanted her to know. It was just something that would take a couple of years to accomplish and he didn't know where he would be when it all came down. He never wanted to hurt her, or lie to her. Plus, she was young and had a life to live, who was he to hold her down? She had thought about it a whole night before she had come back to him.

"I never wanted to live life looking for what's up ahead and forgetting to live now," she had said, "but you have changed my perspective. It will be whatever it will be, but no matter what, I will wait for you."

She had waved as he had backed out, turning out onto the road. He had become a little better driver than he had been his first driving trip, but still a little worse than most drivers. Pablo had traveled over the same road as he and James had the last time they had come back from Zurich. That had been the day they had acquired the pain management pump. He would be returning the pump that day, and then was going to go get some cash from the Habib Bank.

He had been playing the Market and had already turned $100,000 into a quarter of a million. The front desk receptionist had taken the pump, giving her insincere condolences. Then he was gone—rid of the last of James's medical articles.

The bank was large and on the corner of the block. It had a huge sweeping granite staircase that led up to the entrance. There had been no parking, so he had parked around the corner as the walk was short and the day was awesome. Pablo had enjoyed the scenery all the way to the bank—for some reason, being out at this time felt like the right thing to do. All of a sudden, he had begun having premonitions that he'd never had before—like he was in the right place at the right time.

* * *

Octavio had tied his black leather shoes on snugly. They had looked to be in need of a shining. *Zurich, what the hell is really here? Why would the boy have access to the uncle's account? It was a long shot at best.* He had secured his ceramic 9mm in his waistband. The preferred Israeli weapon was designed to get through metal detectors. So far, it had, everywhere except the airports, which would have been foolish to try—as well as unnecessary, since under his alias as a jeweler, he was allowed to check it.

Octavio had decided he would go out and get some lunch so that he could at least get the layout of the place, thinking also that maybe he would find one of the European call girls he'd heard so much about. He had left the hotel room and headed for an elevator, heading to the restaurant Bärengasse, as the concierge said it was *the* place for veal. He had hoped so—he would have hated to have to kill someone over bad food advice. As he pushed "G" button, he awarded himself a small smile as the elevator door closed.

* * *

Cars pulled up from seemingly every direction, and suddenly there was a small army of heavily-armed men quickly setting up a perimeter around Matt, Doug, and Vera. The back door of a black SUV opened, and a man exited who looked out of place. He was smaller than the others, and he had tattoos all over his arms and face. He didn't look like a professional. He looked more like a hardened criminal.

The man came around and opened the door. Matt and Doug were immediately taken out at gunpoint. They were held down at the feet of their captors, gun barrels pointed at their heads. Vera was brought out and carried to the vehicle by the short man with the tattoos. As he was passing his new hostages, he muttered to his men, *"Mátenlos."*

Suddenly Vera sprang to life. Her limp, lifeless body instantly bolted cat-like toward them, throwing her arms around Matt.

"No lo mates, me salvo la vida!"

Felipe saw the situation as a no-win. He barked the order, *"Atenlo y subanlo al avión,"* and it was done. Doug was tied up and left with the plane, and Matt was taken with her.

Matt looked back at Doug very glad they spared him. After all, he had let it all hang out to get them here. Suddenly something was placed over his head, and the rest of his trip was spent disoriented and uncomfortable.

* * *

Assistant Director of Homeland Security Kirk Rogers had just gotten off the phone with Director Stan LaRue, and he was not happy with what he had just been told. He now addressed his subordinate to update him.

"Those fuckers got out."

Stunned, DHS West Coast Regional Director, Gregory Bird, was speechless.

"Worse," Rogers continued, "they attacked El Centro Naval Air Facility with EMP technology and downed three Hornets in all—one on takeoff and two in combat."

Bird spat, "Combat? They were in a Cessna!"

"I know, Regional Director. It's hard to fathom. Obviously they've had some help here. Apparently, one of them knew how to fly pretty well to get them over the Sierras at treetop."

Bird's comm line signaled. When he picked it up, the voice on the other end said, "Mr. Director, it's Henderson, I hate to bother you, but I think Assistant Director Rogers needs to take this call."

Bird was not in the mood for the unusual. "Who is it, Henderson?" he asked impatiently.

"It's a civilian and she won't speak to anyone but Assistant Director Rogers. Someone gave her his name as the person in charge."

"Why on earth would Assistant Director Rogers take that call, Henderson? Why are you on my phone now? Get rid of her, and I want you to report to me before you go home today."

Seeing that his career was already toast, Dave Henderson took the only step he could think of to save it. "Mr. Director, she says she has info on Tahoe."

After a long pause, Bird said, "Put her through."

The phone rang, and Bird put it on speakerphone. Rogers controlled the conversation.

"Hello, this is Assistant Director Rogers speaking, and whom might I be speaking with?"

Gregory heard the nasal twang of simple folk and thought, *God, if this was some kind of a turd hunt, Henderson will be in Montana by morning.*

"Hello, Sir. My name is Nadine, Nadine May, and I know one of those pilots that left Tahoe last night."

* * *

President Caulfield took in what CIA Director Bob Thompson had just said to him. "Well that's a pretty thin line, Bob," he replied.

LaRue piped in. "You mean to tell me that Ray Callahan, the Farm's very own legend, not only missed a sociopath right under his nose, but he now thinks another, much more treacherous sociopath, is on our side because of some notes he left?"

"It's more than that, Stan, and you know it," Thompson said, almost losing some emotion. "There are too many coincidences here to just disallow it."

The President spoke with certainty. "Well, when we recover the plane we'll know more. If Hurst's body's in there, then Ray might be right, but my guess is that he'll be gone. If he is gone, Bob, then that means he was part of it, and anything he left Ray was smoke and mirrors to buy time and lead us off on the wrong scent."

As Director Thompson listened, he knew that Ray Callahan would be diminished by Beck's treachery. He just hoped President Caulfield would change his mind and listen to Ray instead of the growing number of voices counter to that thought. He knew one person that would understand, and he was going straight to her the second this meeting was over.

Bob unconsciously looked over at her observation room—a room no one was supposed to know about, but they all did. *I guess I won't have to go far.* The more he thought about it, the more he believed in Ray's assessment.

Right then LaRue's assistant in California came in on the comm. The situation room was waiting for the response as Director LaRue asked, "What have you got, Kirk?"

* * *

The American President spoke with some diplomacy. "That's right, *Señor Presidente.* There's an American citizen involved in this now, too. He was kidnapped in Tahoe by the two we seek, then brought out with them. We believe he was the pilot and was coerced to fly them out. We doubt they will leave him alive, but we sure need that plane back, with or without him in it."

The man on the other end of the phone spoke to the American President with an air of indignation that only came from royalty or leaders of countries. "We're looking for the plane. When we find it, and it is determined that no Mexican laws have been broken, then the plane will be returned."

"President Delgadillo, look, I know we've had some recent trade disagreements, but it's nothing that can't be worked out. We need your total cooperation here, no holding back. I'm sure we'll work out everything we need to at our upcoming North American Summit."

Albertine Delgadillo was no fool. He knew this politician would do anything to get that plane back, and he would make sure Mexico got something good for this one.

"You have my word, Mr. President."

"Great, thank you very much. We'll talk soon."

To the untrained man, that was just a conversation. To the trained man, this was a big promise. *I believe the American legal system calls that a quid quo pro,* President Delgadillo thought, *but I just call it diplomacy at its finest.*

* * *

$50,000 U.S. had sure looked like a lot more than Pablo thought it would. It had been one thing to see all his wealth on spreadsheets and interest reports, but it was quite another to see more cash than he'd ever seen in his lifetime spread out right in front of him.

Pablo had tried to act like he'd been there before to the banker as he placed the money carefully into his specialized "cash carrying" briefcase. He had thanked the office manager, grateful this transaction was done in private. Then he had grabbed his money and left the bank quite happy.

Seeing this had been the start of his mission, he had felt the glow of God's sun on his face in a special way as he had trotted down the rounded staircase at a left angle. The man coming toward Pablo had possessed a familiar face, oddly. He had scanned his memory and identified him as one of the Shimmering Way. In fact, he had identified him as their General, Octavio Mendoza.

Octavio had been doing the same thing. He had been studying the boy's school picture for weeks, but it had just seemed too good to be true. By the time he had truly identified him they were very close. *But why does the boy seem to recognize me too?*

Pablo had seen the man reach behind into his waistband, and it had all seemed too surreal. The next thing he knew, his instincts had kicked in, and he had jump-kicked the man right back down the stairs, with dramatic effect as Octavio went end-over-end down about twenty steps.

Pablo had been running already as Octavio had hit the third step backward. By the time he had hit the ground, Pablo had already covered half the distance to the sidewalk. Two good bounds of three steps each, a dart left, and he had been running for the corner. The briefcase had made him a little slower—$50,000 was a bit heavier than he would have thought.

As he had made it within twenty feet of the end of the block, he had heard the shot. Immediately, every bird within a quarter mile had gone airborne. He had also felt the hottest sensation in his left leg, like someone had stuck a hot iron in him. It had initially caused him to stutter, and then he didn't have his stride anymore.

He had limped around the corner, making his way expeditiously to his car, maybe 100 feet away. He had touched his leg, and his hand had come back with blood on it.

Pablo had gotten into the car and shakily inserted the key into the ignition. His hands had been shaking uncontrollably as he had looked in the side mirror, expecting to see his executioner coming at a clipped pace, but no one had been there. He had started the car and was gone, his survival mode's surge of adrenaline suddenly transforming him into a better driver.

He'd had tissues in the car, and despite the fact they were not ideal, he had been able to use them to clean his wound enough after he pulled over to assess that there was no arterial damage. The shot had passed outside the bone as well, so that had been good—no need for the hospital emergency room.

He had packed the wound to put pressure on it, and had driven to the Hedge with a feeling he was not expecting: absolute rage!

He had not been afraid anymore, but he would also not go unarmed anywhere ever again! As a matter of fact, he had decided, it was time to learn how to use a gun and also hire his own security team. He was not fucking around anymore.

Pablo had taken his briefcase with him and gone into the inn. Well, it wasn't really an inn anymore—the owners had decided to live life a little as of late. They had left for a trip to Paris.

Eva had seen him pull up and had met him at the door with her usual cheerfulness. But once she had seen him limping with the bloodstain on his pants, she had gone into instant repair mode. One of her strengths had been that she was good in a crisis. More importantly, she had known enough to save the questions for later.

* * *

The kick to the chest had hurt, and somewhere during his third revolution downward, Octavio had felt the snap in his left knee. It had twisted horribly and he was certain it was ruined. His head had bounced off the concrete once he reached the bottom. He had felt blood pouring out of the cut on the back of his head. He had reached back to feel the cut, his hand coming back confirming his suspicion with crimson certainty.

The one thing he had done right was not losing grip of the gun. He had aimed from his side, which was not the best position, but he was a marksman. He had practiced from all positions, left-handed and right-handed. He'd only had a microsecond to set, and he had squeezed the shot as best he could, given his pain and disorientation. It had hit its mark, and his target had lurched when the shot connected. But he could see his shot had gone low and missed any vitals, and the boy had stumbled around the corner. Unless he had gotten lucky enough to clip an artery, the boy would live.

The shot had been loud, with no silencer, and his ears had been ringing very badly. Still hazy from the fall, he had tried to rise to his broken legs, but there had been no way to get away. His knee was completely ruined. Octavio had unloaded the Glock to set it down on the steps as he waited for the police.

He had known they would be looking for his robber pretty soon. Surely there would have been witnesses that would have seen a vehicle and other details. Octavio had known that as soon as they identified the vehicle, he would have that information as well. He hadn't been worried about the weapon, since he was simply an international jeweler, and this was a robbery attempt.

He had now learned that the kid was aware of them also. He had mused to himself, *so he is gifted and now he is going to be harder than ever to catch. Hopefully, the local authorities can be the help I need.*

* * *

The minutes of waiting were excruciating. The President of the United States was not accustomed to waiting for answers he needed. In the "get it now" world of information streams, this felt like an intentional stall on President Delgadillo's part. Such a move would be an unfortunate diplomatic oversight on the Mexican leader's part, one that would surely cost his country dearly.

The phone finally rang after fifty agonizing minutes.

The Mexican President told President Caulfield, "We have the plane, and your pilot is alive."

Stunned, Caulfield was nearly speechless. "When can we have them back?"

* * *

Jan sat and watched in disbelief. Something had happened east of San Diego. Witnesses said there was a series of explosions, one of them near the Navy Base at El Centro, and the other two east of there. According to the truck driver they interviewed, he had been putting gas in his tanker when he the heard the explosion. He had gotten his phone out and started filming. That's when he had seen the two explosions that looked like the space shuttle exploding, only twice as big. Jan somehow knew this was related to Matt, and she hoped he was still alive.

The weirdest part about this whole thing was that somehow Jan knew Matt was going to be okay. She was probably just fooling herself, but she didn't have the gut feeling she'd had earlier about getting the news her husband was dead. She truly wondered, how could this all be real? She reasoned that maybe she was having an acid flashback. There had been that time in high school.

She slipped into bed exhausted and started to doze off. Her hope was maybe when she woke up this would all end up being a bad trip, or a nightmare. *I knew I shouldn't have eaten so close to bedtime, but Ben and Jerry are both misogynist geniuses.*

* * *

Sandy had watched the TV in rapt attention. *It's the boy!* It had been two years since James passed. Two years since the warning that had been as ominous as it was absolute.

It had actually changed the way Sandy lived. The first thing he had done was sell his beloved property on Russian Hill. Although he had sold at the wrong time, property values on Russian Hill were never off too much. He had received fair market value for his home of the past thirty years.

After relocating to a house in Marin County, he had become a naturalist and taken to small organic farming. He had been retired a year now, shocking his client list and his friends. He had been a man who lived for work, forsaking even a wife to dedicate the right amount of time to his job and his clients.

One dramatic call from James had set all this in motion, and now he saw that it had started. Now as then, Sandy wasn't in a place to agree or disagree; he was simply in the middle of something larger than himself.

Although he had the same feelings that James had had about Pablo, anyone asking one to believe a story like that would take a lot of persuasive clout. James had had that clout with Sandy, but how had the boy had that much clout with James? Sandy, never a religious man, had somehow believed Pablo also, but never with the conviction that James had. It had been too incredible not to believe, knowing the intelligence of the person delivering the message, but how many people truly act when someone tells them God has a message?

James had put it the best way possible: "Sandy, you've done it all. There's nothing left for you to accomplish in the materialistic world. You have a new calling now."

"What will I do?" he had asked James.

"You will take a wife and become a small farmer, or at least that would be my serious recommendation. Sandy, let me put it to you this way: you can't afford to be on the wrong side of this."

As soon as he saw the news of the "break-in" at Conceptual Labs, he knew that listening to James had been a wise thing.

The call of a woman's voice came from outside. "Sandy, it looks like you have some tomatoes ready."

Claire was calling from the garden. They'd been married a little under a year now. She'd been his secretary for the past twenty years. Three years ago her marriage ended with the death of her husband.

Although there had been times before James's call that he'd thought about asking her out, when he had felt the same desire coming from her, he had been married to the job and had always found reasons for putting it off. But finally, one day he had showed up for work and proposed to her. Never having learned many social graces with women, he had believed cutting to the chase was the best way to handle it.

Fortunately, he had asked a woman who knew him better than a wife would have. She had told him she was sure one day something like this was going to happen, unless her other thought had been correct. They were, after all, in the gayest city in the U.S., and she had often ribbed him during the postcoital recounts of their story. He certainly wouldn't have been the first gay man to hide his homosexuality for career's sake. It was the times when he appeared to have something to say though, but couldn't find the words. That had been what had led her to believe he would one day make an awkward advance. She had been looking for it so she could help him along, but she had never expected what she got!

He smiled as he turned the TV off and headed out to see the newly ripened tomatoes. *It's all in God's hands now.*

* * *

Doug regained consciousness again. His eyes remained shut, but his mind was awake. He had slept a little on his trip back to the U.S., but it had been an uneasy sleep, and he had a headache like nothing else. This time he was in a bright room of some kind, where someone was trying to keep him awake. He heard the conversation, but he was not fully lucid yet.

"He's definitely suffered a concussion," someone was saying, "multiple contusions. There's a laceration of the scalp, probably caused by a blow from behind." Doug felt a gloved hand touching the top of his head. "He also has a nearly broken nose and two chipped teeth."

Doug was thinking, *don't forget about the ribs,* but couldn't talk.

He heard the voice continue, asking, "How many people did this to him again?"

Then someone gently took his shoulders in their hands, "Doug, wake up, it's Doctor Clark. You've suffered a concussion and we can't let you go to sleep just yet, okay?"

Lights were trying to shine in his eyes and he was hating this Dr. Clark at the moment, but Doug mustered a grudging, "Okay."

"Good. I'm going to send in some nurses to clean you up and help keep you awake."

Doug was about to doze back off immediately when two nurses came in and started to undress him, tending to his wounds. He noticed the water was cold, and it was starting to shrink his manhood. He finally muttered, "Can we warm the water up, please?"

Nurse One was just about to answer when a voice said, "It's supposed to be cold."

Disoriented, squinting, he uttered to the unseen man, "Who are you my friend, and would you mind telling me where I am?"

"I'm Ray Callahan and you're in a Homeland Security base not far from the border."

"That's good news. I feel safer already—not that I don't trust those Mexican authorities." He whispered to Nurse One, "I don't."

Doug forced himself to focus his eyes so he could see who he was talking to. He saw a short guy with glasses and short, curly black hair.

"So Ray Callahan, what's your spiel? Are you a doc?"

"In a way. I'm in a specialized field of medicine."

"I see. Well, Ray, do you have any aspirin?"

"That would not be wise to take in your condition, Doug."

"Well, Ray Callahan, you're a little late, because I already took some earlier."

"That was unwise. You're lucky that bump on your head wasn't worse or those aspirins would have killed you."

"Oh wait, it was ibuprofen, my bad. Guess I will live after all."

Ray Callahan did not look amused in the slightest. Doug got that this was an uptight time.

This Ray Callahan doesn't have much in the way of a sense of humor and right now I'm so happy to be alive that my jocularity can't be contained. Who wouldn't be after living through what I just did? Sure, I realized all along that these guys will try to call me a coward for not just letting them kill me, but they would have all done the same thing. All I have in this world is my life, and I'm not going to give it up for an unknown cause.

"Doug, we need to debrief you," Callahan said. "We know you've been through a lot and probably would like the time to recover, but time is the one thing we don't have. So I have to ask you to please suck it up, and let's get through this tonight."

Doug lifted his ass so the nurse could slide his underwear on. He didn't care what situation he was in, the feel of a woman touching him was stimulating, and Nurse Two was a solid 9, which didn't hurt.

"Well Ray Callahan of specialized medicine, we might as well do this as it looks like I'm going to be up anyway," Doug said, giving a lustful look in the direction of Nurse Two.

* * *

The President heard Bob Thompson out completely. One of his greatest strengths was that he did not interrupt people, even when they went off on tangents. He figured that to get to this level, a person had to be smart, and hopefully the speaker had a reason to stray off. He always allowed they would be back to make a point. If not, then they looked disjointed and disorganized, which was no sweat off his back.

It was a very good characteristic that he learned from his father, who'd had five kids to adjudicate over. Lawrence's father had learned the hard way, as every good father did, that he had better hear both sides of the story and not presume to know the next words out of someone's mouth. On many occasions a kid had been improperly punished in the Caulfield house until Samuel had learned the proper way to do things. Traits like that just stuck. It still took every bit of that learned skill not to cut Bob off at least three times during his diatribe.

As soon as he was finished, Lawrence announced, "Gentlemen, as far as I'm concerned, that seals it. Matt Hurst was a conspirator in this crime. He had opportunity after opportunity to get himself out of this. He had control of a gun once he disabled Agent Crawford, and we know he had control of the situation in the hanger after he killed Beck. Doug Sharp confirmed that Hurst fired a round at him—the casing and round were recovered—and we know it came from Crawford's gun. That shot was done to coerce Doug Sharp into flying that mission. And lastly, Hurst ordered him to fly on a flight plan that he pulled out of a backpack he controlled."

President Caulfield immediately put his hand up to stop Bob. He didn't care who owned the backpack, which was what Bob was trying to interject. He'd had his turn, and now the Commander-in-Chief was speaking. "From this point on, I do not want to hear any more conjecture that Matt Hurst is a good guy, or a patriot in any way!" the President declared. "He just set us back and strengthened our enemy. The dictionary says there's only one definition of treason and that is it! So Bob, you tell Callahan that he's free to file that report, and he's also free to retire right after that."

Bob stiffened before calmly responding to the maelstrom. "You can't suggest that, Mr. President, and you know it."

The level of Caulfield's voice, and the manner in which he was handling Bob, left no doubt to his detractors in the room that he and not Kim, was really in charge. With menacing eyes he told the Old Man, "The hell I can't, Bob. I'm the fucking President of the United States! I can order you to kill people, so retiring an overzealous shrink shouldn't be that hard."

The look of displeasure on the Old Man's face was evident, but only if one knew him. His poker face was legendary, and he only had one tell. His only true friend at that table saw his left eye twitch ever so slightly. Stan LaRue knew what that meant.

It meant Bob didn't agree with the assessment, and he was going to prove it wrong. Stan held his information, knowing that if he spoke now it would pile onto his friend's misery.

Bob sucked up his pride and replied, "Of course, Mr. President. I will suggest to Ray that he take a more conventional approach."

President Caulfield wasted no time. "Settled. I want this guy's whole life put under a microscope. We need to find out all the trips Hurst has taken, who he e-mails, Facebook, hell, even look for foreign correspondence via dating sites, anything that could lead us to a thread to follow. A truck driver shot a video of the two Hornets getting erased and it's gone viral now, but we have his phone and have blocked access to the sites showing it. It's not so grainy, as it was shot on a newer iPhone, but initially it's believed that the early dawn light was not enough to make out too much detail."

The President refocused the group. "People, we will play this by the numbers and we will find out who did this to us. Then we will respond in kind. I don't care who they are!"

That drew the hidden smiles of every war man at the table. *Maybe I could learn to like this President after all*, thought Steve Hatten.

"Stan, let's give Homeland a shot at Hurst's wife," the President continued, "she's got to know something, even if she doesn't know she knows. I want reports back from everyone, but none more than from the Navy Forensics Team. I want to know what hit us, then I want to know who hit us. Now let's get at it."

As the room emptied of people heading out to get things done, Stan LaRue strode by Bob Thompson and said, "We need to talk."

No sooner had Bob settled at his desk, than his visitor was with him in his office. LaRue cleared his voice before speaking, "I didn't want to say this in open court just yet."

"I appreciate that, Stan," Thompson replied, "since I can only assume you are covering my ass here or something."

"Not exactly, just muddying the waters a bit, but I knew your wise old ass would think of a why."

"Okay, let's hear it."

LaRue began, "Our team in Tahoe was doing its due diligence and found the room Hurst and Chavez occupied for a few hours. You guys were briefed on almost all of it, but there was one thing that you were not."

"What's that? And by the way, good find. How did you guys find it so quickly?"

"Well, first, we found semen trace on the sheets. We're matching it to Hurst's DNA, but it looks like they were lovers after all. We found it so quickly because one of our agents was 'almost as pretty as the lady in 104, only her hair was blonde.' Fortunately the agent who heard that compliment didn't just take it and go, especially seeing the lady behind the counter was nearly blind. The agent inquired more about the 'pretty lady,' asked to see the registry, and it went from there."

"Nice," Bob responded. However, the other information was not as nice. Those two being lovers was a really telling thing. *But what did it tell?* LaRue looked at him working it out.

"Well?" LaRue asked. "What do you think about it? Because I was leaning in with you and Ray, but if this information was available, your situation in there would have been worse."

"Agreed. How long do I have before this goes mainstream?"

"Only hours, but it's really moot at this point. Your angle has already been shelved."

"Yes, it has, Stan. And if I'm ever going to get it un-shelved, then I'm going to have to figure out yet one more problem. I really appreciate the heads-up on this. I'm not sure where it's going to lead, but I've never known Ray to be wrong about something he felt so strongly about. And you know, Stan, I hate it when they so quickly forget that Ray has paid his dues and has earned a place of respect in our community."

Stan knew the story and he agreed—that's why he was here. They shook hands. While Stan was departing, Bob thought, *LaRue will never know the kind of loyalty he just earned to watch his back—that is, as long as I'm around, which could be in jeopardy if my luck doesn't change soon.* Bob Thompson knew that Stan coming here had been unheard of, especially after the way Ken Beck did those guys at DHS. *I guess good guys are that way no matter what.*

* * *

Pablo was listening to their military chatter from multiple sources. He had hurt them. Now they were angry and they were scrambling. The Mexican authorities had put on a show of force, but to no avail, and Vera had made it out of their country quite easily. *Soon she will be here. I can finally see her.*

Until now, his internal conflict with Eva had been on the backburner, but having Vera so close to being here made him think of her, and the way he had left her two years before. It wasn't easy being a woman in his life, or hell, anyone else in his life, for that matter. People tended to not last long around him. It had taken a while for Pablo to figure out how to fill the void of his absence for Eva, and then he had realized exactly how he could do it. It had also occurred to him that his intended action could serve another purpose as well.

He had recently purchased a company in Japan that was already near beta on some very advanced robots. Pablo had taken over their engineering department after the purchase, and things had been moving along.

At first his Japanese subordinates had thought it was some kind of joke, but they had soon learned he held the keys to gates they would otherwise have been unlocking twenty years from today. His side project had cost him sleep as he brought it to fruition, but it would be well worth it.

It had not been easy building something this complicated alongside all the other things he was doing. But then it had been finished, and he had been proud of his accomplishment. *This might actually be my finest work to date*, he had thought. His special project crates would have arrived at the Hedge by now. He had known Eva was technically challenged, so he had left a set of instructions for her to follow, wording the enclosed letter to be tailored to her brand of logic and intellect. He could only hope what laid within could be a balm for her soul. He longed for her touch, but he knew it was pointless as they were still far off from a reunion.

He had drifted one last time to that day he had been shot. He remembered it had hurt like hell to get shot. Pablo had never been the kid that got hurt—that had been his brother's Ernesto's job as the daredevil of the family. Pablo remembered one year when Ernesto had gotten a Superman cape for Christmas. He had run around like he was invincible until one of the neighborhood kids had dared him to jump off the fence. So Ernesto had climbed up and jumped to fly, falling straight down and hitting his head on a rock. As soon as he had gotten up, blood had just started pouring out of his forehead. All the kids there had scattered in an instant, like in a cartoon.

Pablo had never been that kid, and when he had gotten shot, it had hurt like he had never felt before. At least he had never felt that kind of physical pain—his soul was another matter.

He remembered the last night they had been together, Eva had been asleep to his left snoring contently, her face cherubic. He had loved to watch her sleep. He had been saddened that he would have to leave her, but he had been resolved to do so. She was a sheep, and the wolves would rip her to pieces if they knew of their connection.

He would return to France and James's chateau. The only reasons they had left at all were James's treatments, the banks, and the fact that there were so many people around Yvoire all the time. James had just figured that the long-term chances of going undetected were better behind the Hedge.

Pablo had loved Eva immensely, so he was confused how God could have chosen someone else for him to do this with. He had seen the woman's face in the fugue, and it was definitely not Eva. Pablo had just connected the biblical reference, realizing that Eva sure was close to Eve. But it was not her that God had chosen for this. It was another woman who had held his hand in the fugue. Eva apparently had not been in his immediate future, so he had needed to protect her from the wolves by leaving her alone.

Pablo had remembered that physically, he had recovered quickly. Her butterfly sutures had been perfect for letting some air in the wound to help it heal. She had kept it clean constantly, saying, "A clean wound heals."

Some women say they love a man, but do little in the way to show it. Eva Heldergarten had not been one of them. She had been a hard working woman, who went that extra mile for her man, making leaving her both heart-wrenching and physically unbearable at times for Pablo. He had suddenly found himself in a huge house with no one but himself and James's unbelievable computer system. He might have sunk into depression if he hadn't had a mission to complete.

Alone with his thoughts, he had realized that dying quickly was too good for those *diablos,* so he was going to have to find a way for them to have a *muerte lenta.* Then he'd had another idea all together, one that would be more *rapido,* but still slow enough to have the prolonged suffering they deserved.

He'd heard of rumors that such a weapon had been for sale in the past. Now he'd had the money to try to buy it, or in the more difficult scenario, make one himself.

Speaking of that, it was time to make a $110 million into a hundred times that. He was going to need a lot more money to pull this off.

In the now, Pablo stood in the place where God instructed him to be. He was now looking down, and he had never felt more connected to this mission.

To his right, outside on the window frame, another spider had built a web. He could see that a hapless insect had flown into this new spider's web. It struggled helplessly as its maker descended on it, its piercing bite inflicting a deathblow. Pablo then watched the spider's legs expertly spin its helpless victim into a cocoon with startling rapidity. It quickly pulled the insect back into its lair. Pablo observed that the spider didn't even take the time to enjoy his meal before repairing its web for the next unsuspecting victim.

Pablo's mind drifted back to the day he had been shot in Zurich. For some reason it had taken him two full weeks to think it through. He reasoned now that it might have been the sex that had clouded his mind. Never before had his mind been so controlled by one thing.

A month after James died, Eva's parents had taken a trip at her urging. They had known she was coming of age, and being European they had not had an issue with the honesty and love in the situation. She had been amazing, and he had offered all the plentiful exuberance of youth.

He had gotten lost in her. Sometimes at night, when he had lain in her arms, the buzzing had stopped, and he had gone peacefully to sleep without having to connect the thousand strains of thought and tie them to the right storage files. He realized he was doing it again just thinking about her. He refocused.

Pablo's mind went back to the bank, replaying every minute detail. When he got to the stairs and replayed the scene in his head, he clearly saw the man was surprised. *He was surprised that I was there and that I recognized him. So why was he there if not to be hunting for me?*

Pablo thought it out in his special way, and within minutes he had the answer. His uncle had hidden money in the Habib Bank, and they had been tracking it down. *How improbable!* It was definitely the work of God and the Devil playing it out on Earth: one trying to advance, the other trying to stop him, and all his followers.

He remembered so clearly that he could just feel the otherworldly residue on the day, like he was supposed to have been there for a reason. Now he knew what that reason was. Pablo was absolutely certain the incident at the bank had been no happenstance. He had interpreted it as a reminder that since the beginning of time, anyone who has tried to serve the Word of God on earth has been persecuted by whatever regime held power.

The first issue he had to deal with was getting rid of the alias Arturo Castanada. That meant the money, the bank, and the name James created were all dead now. Pablo's real identity still lay in the safe in Yvoire, but from this moment on, he decided to have a web of names and blinds that would take a small army of hackers just to get through the first passcode.

Pablo would build his empire by acquiring companies that could help grow his funds, and his endeavors—companies all purchased to provide one piece of the needed puzzle. It wouldn't be a crash and burn operation. He'd make sure that he purchased wisely, growing the companies so he could fund his endeavor without budget concerns.

Pablo had watched in disbelief as another insect flew into the spider's web. His thoughts immediately jumped to his future military action, and he wondered if his enemies would also be so dumb. In his life, Pablo had now played both roles, predator and prey. He had been the insect in the web, but unlike the insects he was witnessing now, he had gotten away. *That man with the hat, Octavio Mendoza, he hunts me like that spider today, but tomorrow, I will make sure he knows what that feels like, as I build my web for him.*

Pablo came out of his daydream and was done walking through the past. Today was the day of what the future holds, so he made a vow to give the past a rest for a while and work on his future.

* * *

Bob Thompson told Stan's tale to Ray Callahan. In conclusion he asked, "So what do you think?"

"I don't think it means what you think it does, Bob," Ray replied. "I think it strengthens my case."

"Strengthens your case? I think you're taking the 'glass is half full' concept a little far here. Don't you, Ray?"

"No, not at all. Not if we're accepting that this above-average person understood our role and methods when he enlisted himself into the service of his country. Bob, Matt was drafted, but he wasn't drafted into the Army. He enlisted himself into a field where deep-cover agents are trained a very specific way, a way that absolutely immerses them into a culture, sometimes for years, with languages almost always involved. Listen, if this kid is the real deal, and we're assuming that he is, then he obviously took the opportunity to curry closeness with her to garner her trust; trust that will gain him the inside. Face it, he did very well, better than we ever could have hoped for. Crawford will live, and he killed Beck on purpose, I believe. Don't you see this?"

Ray slid a file across the desk to Bob.

After looking over the file, Bob said, "So what's this prove? He was a good community college student?"

"Look at the last class: firearms with Russell Peltz. He got an A, Bob."

"Point being, Ray?"

"Point being, Beck was so far outside the lines that the kid sent a message that we weren't getting. Beck had a dark criminal mind, and Hurst wanted us to know that. I think he believed killing him was a favor that circumstance allowed. He removed a cancer from us, at least in his mind. He could have disabled Beck easily at that range, but he didn't, because Beck's behavior disgusted him to the point of no return. I believe I know why he was released from the Sheriff's Academy now. We just need to get a hold of the cadet he got into a fight with so we can find out the truth of why they argued that day. I have a hunch, Bob, that this kid has an over-reaction in situations where he sees great inequality. This kid's no dummy, Bob. He made all these calls on the fly, and I'm convinced that he did them with as much forethought as the moment would allow."

"You're not going to be popular, Ray," Bob replied. "As a matter of fact, your job has been threatened more than mine today."

"I don't care about my job here, Bob. We have a man inside there, damn it! And he's a bloody good man to boot. Now I reiterate, if they don't kill him, he'll find a way to get to us. It might be a year for all we know, but we better be listening."

"That's if they don't kill him, Ray—that's a big if. So he saved the girl," Bob argued, "she might have been expendable anyway for all we know, and both of them are sitting in a warehouse with air-conditioned heads."

"Certainly a possibility, but if this were a mission, and we placed an agent in that situation with these results, we would be hopeful his survival skills would see him live."

"He's not trained, Ray."

"Well, he doesn't need the special language skills in this scenario, since they know who he is up front—they took him. So they won't think he's a spy. Plus he saved the girl and brought out the plans, so he's not an enemy. It sounds like he played everything right to get inside, if it's possible. If not, Matt Hurst just sacrificed his life for his country."

"Yeah," said Bob, "and gave them who knows what?"

"We don't know what he gave them now, do we, Bob?"

"No, Ray, but this is thin—very thin."

"Maybe, but the people who did this might never be brought to justice. Hurst might have put into play our only hope of one day finding out who they are."

Bob couldn't fight the logic anymore. "Okay, it is what it is, I guess. There's nothing we can do now. Hurst chose this path and we'll have to wait and see how that works out. God help us if he was wrong, Ray."

"God help him, Bob. Either way, he's got balls."

* * *

Kim Sullivan was going over the newest rewrites her staffer was bringing. She had already sent back four. "Look Karen, we go on in thirty minutes, you guys have got to do better than this. He's trying to take a stand here. Stop looking so weak!"

Bob was behind her and spoke her name: "Kim." She turned, surprised.

"Bob, what brings you down here? I thought you would have some pressing things going on."

"We all do, but you and I need to talk."

"Now's not exactly the time. Besides, I think his stand is pretty clear with you."

"He's wrong, Kim."

"I see. Well that puts you in a real tough spot, now, doesn't it?"

That's what he loved about this girl: instant assessment. "Yes it does, but not if you believe, too."

"Okay, look. I like you Bob, you're one of the fair players, but this is a very unpopular opinion around here right now. As a matter of fact, this conversation is blasphemous."

"Take a minute after the press conference and hear me out. If you don't agree, I will never bring it up to you again. I trust you that much, Kim."

Kim Sullivan knew a huge compliment when she heard one. Bob Thompson was a legend, and not known for blowing smoke up peoples' asses.

"Okay Bob," she replied. "I will hear you out off the record. But this is not my norm. Then again, you're not the normal customer either."

* * *

The sun was setting as Pablo looked at the headlights coming down the highway. The only cars that traveled on the quarry road at night were the security cars they employed. Outside security was fairly light, as they had a commercial agency that patrolled the outer fence several times a night. Other than that, they just used good fences and dogs to keep people off the property, since no one knew of the hidden complex. It wouldn't be wise to advertise things by having a visible army stomping around. The entire complex was dug out of the mountain, starting in the giant warehouse that housed all the dump trucks.

Of course, that's where the fortifications started and ended. The entrance was a downward-sloped driveway that hit a series of tank-proof steel passageway doors. Pablo had left it as simple as that, since they were in a mountain, after all. The complex wasn't really built to be defended against ground troops anyway. It was designed to be untouchable.

If someone actually got here, then the game was already over. No, this base could only be removed by nuclear annihilation or a bunker buster. But they would need guidance systems for that, and by now they were starting to figure out what they were up against.

When Vera had told him her back-up plan, he had liked it and bought a couple of properties in key locations on the exit routes near the Mexican border. She had fronted the company and acquired the plane, so all was going according to plan.

Then their time frame had gotten moved up. They had learned that Dr. Cooper's funding was about to be reduced. Vera was the least-senior employee, so she was susceptible to being laid off.

If they had let her go, it would have ruined everything. So even though he'd already set up the strategically placed houses for a potential military attempt, it appeared he wasn't going to be using them. She had never learned to fly the plane. Like so much about this whole thing, he had left things in play on a hunch. Pablo had known her training. She had known the resource existed. He had been pleased to see that Vera had been able to find a way to make it happen.

With all the unknown variables, and struggles to live, she had kept the whole board in view and made the right moves at the right times. Pablo really couldn't have been more proud of her. Now she was coming home.

But according to Felipe, he must brace himself for two things. First, "She won't let the *gringo* go no matter what," and second, "we're bringing the *gringo*."

* * *

Kirk Rogers walked into his subordinate's office and sat down. "What have you got, Greg?"

"Something out of a sci-fi novel," Regional Director Bird answered.

"Come again?"

"First, we found the farm they used," Greg said. "It was rented under a blind that was a dead end, of course. The barn was converted into a silo and had four slide tray launchers. The roof had breakaway slats that the drones exited out of. They had a Mexican family living there for free, and the only rules were, 'never go near the barn, and call a number if anyone ever came around.'"

Kirk asked, "Did we get the number they were left?"

"Yes—another dead end."

"So they were drones, huh?" Kirk said.

"Yes, looks like Colonel Prior was right for not putting any more birds up after what he saw."

"So where's the sci-fi part, Greg? We have this technology now."

"We found no accelerant," Greg explained.

"What do you mean?" Kirk asked.

"We found no accelerant, Kirk. We found battery acid and some kind of coolant. It's a mixture that we've never seen before. Not only that, but the report of the lightning going off prior to the EMP is also a new scientific development, apparently. Our EMP devices do nothing of the sort."

"Batteries?" That sent his head spinning—it had so many avenues that it brought into play. *Maybe overcharging the battery causes it to explode.*

"It gets worse, Assistant Director. The drones were stealthed."

The silence was long, accentuating the gravity of the last statement. "Okay, so we have a lot of evidence we can break down here right? What did the 1100 LC spectrometer tell us? Did we get any info on the drones that brought the Hornets down outside of El Centro?"

It was Greg's turn to pause before answering. "We're working on it," he said, "but there was an explosive detected on the drone that destroyed the Hornet on takeoff, so that might kill your first thought. It was the same compound as the one used at Conceptual. It's octanitrocubane."

"That's hard for me to believe, Greg."

"Sorry, Kirk, but the 1100 LC doesn't lie. We identified it both in ESI and APCI. It's real."

Kirk was almost talking to himself as he muttered, "We haven't perfected that compound ourselves. I even heard we abandoned it for heptanitrocubane, which despite its poor oxygen concentration seemed to carry a higher yield."

Greg added, "Bob Thompson has already requested the info on the compositions as soon as we get them, Assistant Director."

"Give them to him," Kirk said. "LaRue says right now we have to be above reproach in our actions, more than ever. I'm just puzzled, and maybe Bob can shed some light, seeing he's so interested. Let's get him on the line here, Greg."

Two minutes later, with their secretaries' assistance, the three were talking live.

"So Bob," Kirk said, "we have the compounds used on the door at Conceptual and the first bogie that felled the Hornet outside of El Centro. Apparently the EMP drones self-detonate after their burst wave. We can only assume that's to stop us from exacting their weaponry and propulsion methods. We found out that the payload is octanitrocubane."

Bob shot back, "Come again?!"

"We ran it in the Agilent, Bob. At first we were not getting a clear picture, but then we reduced the testing field to eliminate noise, and the results were immediate."

Troubled, appreciative of the honesty, he thanked them and feigned that this was confusing information and he was just as perplexed as them. He thanked them again for their interagency cooperation and ended the phone conference numb.

The body blows just kept coming. He wondered when they would stop. He hit his comm button. "Get me Bill Westinghouse, Carol." He thought about that, and buzzed back, "please."

* * *

Pablo longed to see her, but the trepidation was there. He had heard the concern in Felipe's voice. He knew at the very least, she was in shock.

There were no lights from any cars right now, just the lights over the grounds of the quarry. Lightning shot out of the east, and just like that, it was raining. The water rolled down the glass. Pablo found himself following a single drop's path all the way to the point where it didn't have enough mass to keep going and it trailed off.

Is that what I am doing? Giving it my all until I have no more energy or mass to keep it going? And then what? How many people have succeeded in such a massive undertaking? The few that tried weren't the best examples.

Every now and then, Pablo would see black shadows skirting about down below. He loved dogs, and had decided long ago that a dog army was good enough to protect the front of the compound. Someone might be able to sneak by a dog or two, but not a pack of them traversing their own labyrinth.

He had the TV on in the background tuned into CNN. The press people had a reason to live again. In the past thirty hours, he'd heard more theories than could be believed. "It's the Russians." "It's the Chinese." "It's the Arabs." Finally, today, he had heard that it could be the work of the North Koreans. Perfect.

It was just the response he had wanted. Now that she actually made it out, he would finally have what he was seeking. They would only find out who it really was when it was time. Until then, they would chase their tails.

Just then, the TV announced that the President of the United States was coming on. *This should be good,* Pablo thought. *I wonder what lie the man will tell.*

"Ladies and Gentlemen," President Caulfield began, "citizens of the United States, it is at this time I come to you with a heavy heart. Not only have we suffered loss of life as a country, but we also suffered an attack on American soil that has cost us dearly.

"Whoever has perpetrated this attack on us believes they have come in here and stolen important military secrets, attacked our citizens and our military, and are now going to disappear into the night. But make no mistake about it, they left a god-awful amount of evidence, and we're going to pore over every ounce of it for many weeks and months to come. We'll find out who did this to our great country, and we will respond in kind to these heinous acts. This was an Act of War, and Congress and the Defense Secretary have already expressed that when the perpetrators are known, we will declare war immediately.

"Are we safe? Yes, we are safe. This was, for lack of a better term, an armed robbery. We're still assessing what exactly was stolen. The type of information would only be useful to a select number of countries.

"What I ask of you, the American citizen, is, let's get all the information we can on the suspects we know. Let's get together and figure this out as I have urged all of our agencies to have unprecedented cooperation throughout this investigation.

"This is new territory for us. New technology has brought new challenges for our country to keep its secrets safe. During the Cold War, there were many cases of espionage and several high profile defections, but no one incident has ever done so much, and in such a stalwart and aggressive fashion, as this.

"For that, we must respond with everything we have! We must send a message to those who wish to place terror in our hearts. We've been through this before, and we have shown the world what we're made of.

"Well, it's time to do it again, America. It's time to show how resilient we are as a nation, and how one we are as a people—especially when you threaten the one thing that binds us together as a people more than anything else: our continued freedom.

"So in the coming months, there will be much work to do, and we must get it done together. The thought of an unprovoked attack such as this going unanswered, probably sits as well with you as with me. Thank you, and may God bless us all."

Pablo took a deep breath. It was just as he had envisioned it would be. It was coming together as only he could have made it happen. They would chase their tails, and he would align his pieces for the final push! Really that's all it would be: a simple push of the button, once he was done setting it up.

He saw the lights of the chopper. It was a mile or so out. He felt like a nervous teen on prom night. His hands were sweaty and his heart rate was elevated. *But was it for her or what she has for me?* Regardless, she would be standing next to him after all, his final test fulfilled. Not that he really had any doubt.

* * *

It was late. God only knew how a sixty-eight year old man could run at this level. The odd part was that he felt great. Bob Thompson dozed off on power naps several times a day, and it worked for him. He could run around the clock in that mode for quite a while.

He was shaking his head reading over a report when she walked in—the only other person he knew that had more energy than him. "Kim," he said almost too casually, waving his hand for her to take one of four leather bound chairs.

The chairs sat in a semi-circle that was positioned around the largest, oldest, black walnut desk that she had probably ever seen. As a matter of fact, Kim noticed that his whole office was an ode to large objects. Everything was giant-sized. *I wonder what Freud would have to say on this one?*

"I got some disturbing news after we talked, Kim," Bob said.

"After we talked?" she replied. "That can't be good, because I was pretty sure you weren't bringing me good news in the first place."

"DHS identified the explosive compound used on the door at Conceptual Labs and on the jets in El Centro. It is octanitrocubane."

"I've heard that name. I heard *we* were working on that, I thought?"

"Yes, you always do your homework, Kim. We were looking at it because of its low shock properties, and the fact it has a 30 percent higher yield than HMX."

"So, I feel the gist coming."

"Yes, the gist. Well, the gist here is that we were specifically looking at this compound as an assassination tool. The key word is 'were.' One of the scientists we employed had told us that there was a better substitute; one in the same family, but with more yield and stability. So we went with heptanitrocubane and as far as we know, he still has all the notes on his octanitrocubane testing."

"And who would this scientist be, pray tell?" Kim seemed unimpressed so far.

"His name was James Haberman," Bob said.

"You're kidding me, Bob?!" Kim replied, stunned, jolted out of her indifference. "You guys were using Haberman?! Why wasn't I told about this?"

"It was a need to know basis, Kim. We had no reason to disclose."

"But this opens a whole new door. This means that one of your own has gone expatriate with a grudge and left a calling card. I thought this guy was assured to be a patriot and there was no way he would turn.

This is a nightmare, Bob! This guy knows everything about our most critical defense systems. Plus, he obviously skewed his findings on octanitrocubane. This is devastating news of the highest order! Where's Bill Westinghouse? This is the guy who we need to talk to at some length. It was his personal assurance to the President that this guy was no threat. That assurance led to the soft search we've been conducting."

"I got to Westinghouse immediately, Kim, he was of little help."

"What did he say?"

"He told me to go fuck myself, and if we wanted to paint Haberman as a traitor, we wouldn't be doing it with his sanction. And I quote, 'I don't care if you have a video of him confessing, James Haberman is no traitor!'"

Kim asked a good question, as always. "Is it possible that Haberman is under some kind of mind control, not acting of his own accord?"

"Maybe," Bob nodded, acknowledging the possibility. He added, "It sure would explain how someone so expertly got into a system that was deemed beyond hacking."

"It answers a lot," Kim agreed. "We looked at Conceptual's books and saw that they were about to make budget cuts, cuts that would have affected Nancy Chavez, who was low person on the Totem Pole. She must have found out."

"You think that sped up their time line?"

"I have a gut feeling it did, Bob, and it would explain why she couldn't fly the plane. No time to learn maybe, or hire a pilot?"

Bob pondered. Then he added, "It would seem that this all ties together. What a lucky-ass break our perpetrators got that the President's own order to ground small aircraft led to them capturing a pilot."

Kim tapped her pen after playing with it in her mouth. Bob wished he was 40 years younger—smart definitely was sexy. She half spoke to herself, "James Haberman, a traitor? That is going to take some time to get used to."

"Tell me about it, Kim. I had a personal relationship with him. He was brilliant and a joy to work with. We recruited him after a long vetting, and Westinghouse had no idea. He was just doing his patriotic duty, he wouldn't take our money. He devised a couple of incredible devices that would be hard to detect, the wearer not long for this world. I really liked him and he never set off any of my alarms."

"Well, we both have a lot of bases to cover on this one, Bob. So why did you bring me here in the first place?"

"It's about Matt Hurst."

"I assumed that. But what about him that I don't already know?"

"Well, by your tone, I would say that you don't believe he works for us. By the end of this conversation, I hope to change that opinion."

* * *

As Doug watched the President, he felt that he had just experienced a situation where the government told as much of the truth as he'd ever seen. President Caulfield must have been really endearing himself in Middle America.

He wondered where Matt was, and thought back to their last words together. They had been on the ground with machine guns pushed up against the back of their skulls, faces in the dirt.

Matt had actually smiled at him and said, "My turn comes later." He had not only believed they wouldn't kill them there, but his comment had appeared to be indicating that he wasn't one of them.

But it was the last thing Matt said that has been running through Doug's head ever since. "Shh, don't tell, it's our secret." If he had done what he appeared to have done, then Matt was crazy because he had gotten kidnapped on purpose. All through his debriefing they had been looking for some thread like that. All Doug could think of was that Matt must have had a good reason to say "Shh."

So he had left that part out when talking to Ray Callahan. He hoped one day that Matt would get a chance to explain what he meant. He felt it was the least he could do for the guy that gave him a story that would earn him a lifetime of pussy.

* * *

They came into the hacienda with Felipe in the lead. Vera was right behind, being carried by a larger-than-average white male. Felipe led them to the couch, but the *gringo* holding Vera chose a barstool instead, apparently because it afforded his back some relief. Pablo saw him trying to adjust into a position he could live with while her arms remained wrapped around his neck.

Pablo came down the stairs and approached her, "Vera, Verasita." He reached out for her and she recoiled slightly at his touch. He looked at her *salvador* and asked, "What happened to her?"

* * *

It was a long trip. She never let him go for even a second.

The first part was a car ride with Matt wearing the stifling hood. But soon it was removed, and they were on another small plane, much to Matt's disappointment. Finally, they were on a private jet, her arms still around his neck, but he needed to go to the bathroom badly. He had actually overfilled his bladder and couldn't go at first, and then it was like he couldn't stop. *This has got to be some kind of record.*

If Matt's back could speak, it would be begging him not to exit the bathroom, for the relief from her weight was more than needed. When he exited the bathroom she launched on him like before, trembling, animal-like. His back immediately returned to its painful, spasm-filled nightmare.

Even with all she'd put him through, when she launched on him, he absorbed her aroma, and his mind convinced his back that everything would be okay. Then they were taken to a helicopter, and finally Matt was here. *Wherever here was.* One thing was for sure, there was nothing within miles of here. That much he gathered on the ride in.

The house was huge. On the way to it, he saw that it was attached to what appeared to be a construction site. It was done in an incredible taste that belied the remoteness of the location. Right next to the house was a monolithic warehouse.

A man driving a cart appeared. He was short and had tattoos every-where, even on his bald head, just like Matt's original escort.

They rode the golf cart through the rain, getting slightly wet even though it had a canopy. The cool rain and air were a welcome feeling for Matt after many stifling hours with her wrapped around him. He was starting to get more than a little claustrophobic, and his neck was done.

They made their way to the hacienda. It was beautiful, even in the rain at night. As they entered the giant horseshoe-shaped driveway, the first thing Matt noticed was the overwhelming aroma of flowers. There were flowers of every kind, and his nostrils were on overdrive. The house was a Spanish style of construction, but it had an abundance of large wood beams that reminded him of the Ponderosa Ranch from the TV show *Bonanza*.

Matt noticed off to the left what appeared to be a living quarters of some kind. Many windows were lit, and he saw shadows dance on var-ious curtains. The house front was well-lit to welcome visitors. It was truly one of the finest houses Matt had ever laid eyes on.

They went up the steps to the entryway. The door itself was a marvel of wood and stained glass that was extremely impressive. They were brought through a living room and into what Matt guessed must have been the den. It was amazing, with giant crossbeams of some apparently-indigenous wood, and huge blocks of granite making up the walls.

With Vera still attached to him he sat down, his original escort suddenly arrived back at his side. From upstairs, a man appeared and began to walk down. It was actually more of a boy or a very young man. He came right up to Matt, and his eyes were like magnets. Matt couldn't look away.

Matt had chosen a bar stool to sit on to give his back a little relief. The man said nothing to him, but went around his backside and tried to talk to her. He said her name, and Matt recognized the voice as the man from the phone.

The little tattooed man was off to the side, watching intently. After she wouldn't respond, the voice from the phone came around to look at Matt asking what happened to her?

Matt replied stoically, "She was raped."

The man/boy slunk into the neighboring leather seat. He looked at Matt with the most pleading eyes Matt had ever seen. His eyes showed that he felt this affront to her with every ounce of its horror. It was the first time that Matt realized how difficult this job was going to be.

Matt's monster had just turned out to be a very caring person, who looked nothing like any monster he'd ever seen. Maybe they were brother and sister—but then Vera's words had come back to him. She had said she was with someone, but had permission to be with another man if she chose.

The man/boy got control of his emotions and was able to ask Matt, "When?"

"Right before we were to leave," Matt replied. "She left me behind as she prepped the plane, and two CIA agents showed up. One was left behind, and one went to find us. I dispatched the one left behind. By the time I found her, she was being raped and tortured. I killed her assailant with his partner's pistol."

Pablo's worst nightmare had just unfolded in a few sentences. Then his analytical mind took back over. "Why would you do that? Why wouldn't you just run?"

Matt looked at Pablo straight in the eyes and said, "You mean apart from the threat to my family?"

The two looked at each other at a level eye-to-eye, a feat made possible by Matt's position on the bar stool with Vera draped over him. If he were standing, it would be eye to throat, because he was that much taller than Pablo. Another of Pablo's many gifts was his ability to read people through their eyes. Many people had noticed that Pablo's eyes reflected his analytical mind, and Pablo noticed the same thing looming in Matt's eyes as well. Pablo could see it clearly. That made him a threat.

But there was something else there, too. Pablo held his gaze and could read something else. It was something very troubling, because it made the situation harder to deal with. This man's eyes held an amount of compassion Pablo had never seen before. As a case in point, Matt carried so much compassion that he was currently wearing a near stranger to the point of total exhaustion.

Pablo knew Matt's story. He was a security guard that his government now thought was culpable for this attack. He was a face they could put on this.

Pablo looked into the *gringo's* eyes for the answer he sought. His choices were that he could have Felipe sneak in tonight while Matt was sleeping and put a knife in his heart, or he could he let him live and give him a new country.

Sometimes very large decisions come down to very minor things. Battles have been won and lost on small turning points throughout history. In this case, there was something in the *gringo's* eyes that conveyed he really cared, not just about his own life, but about the lives of others as well.

The fact Matt wore his emotions on his sleeve enabled him to continue existing on this earth. It was apparent to Pablo that there was no ambiguity in him. That fact alone was enough to save his life—at least for now ...

To continue the saga of Matt Hurst and Pablo Manuel, watch for the second book in the Harbinger of Change Series, *And the Meek Shall Inherit*.

Other books from Timothy Jon Reynolds:

And the Meek Shall Inherit

Now, two years after American citizen Matt Hurst was kidnapped and coerced into betraying his family and country in order to save them, his time of waiting for revenge is over. He has bided his time effectively and has now placed himself in a position to achieve his end game of redemption. *And the Meek Shall Inherit* is the continued saga of Matt Hurst and Pablo Manuel. In order to survive the past two years, the American abductee has had to immerse himself in his captor's world, so much so, that now that the time has come for him to act, will he be able to pull out all the stops to avenge his country's and family's honor? Or has the ideology of his captors taken a hold of him so deeply that he is now willing to act against his own country, something he'd already been falsely accused of doing? *And the Meek Shall Inherit* is a rollercoaster ride of international intrigue and military action, coupled with the inner-turmoil of the man who can stop it all—if he has the will to do so. *Available now.*

Without Wrath

Two years has passed since Matt Hurst saved the world from a cyber-attack that would have erased the data banks of almost every institution on the planet, and he has dropped off the face of the earth, at least to the public anyway. Secretly, the President of the United States has permitted Matt to return to society using an alias, allowing him and his family to settle in the Pacific Northwest. Matt turned down an analyst position with the CIA to work for a clandestine group of patriots named TJAC. All was going well, until, using his alias, he befriends a video gaming legend. When that legend names Matt's alias, Tom Holsinger, as the developer of a game Tom helped to invent, all hell breaks loose for Matt and his entire family. Every enemy that Matt Hurst had ever made is now converging on the Seattle area, each of them were looking to settle a score with the man who ruined their plans for world domination. *Without Wrath* is a fast-moving thriller that ends up delivering a real message to a nation that so desperately needs one. *Without Wrath* delivers, but it also leaves the reader pondering the greater real world picture that lies within its pages and beyond. *Available now.*

Chesed

Just past the one-year anniversary of the attacks on America and his family in Seattle, Matt Hurst could no longer duck the public's need to know all the facts about the exploits of his life. Hoping that clearing the air would be the salve he needs to re-obtain autonomy, Matt and his family host a television special that clears all the speculation once and for all. Unfortunately for Matt, destiny has other plans for him, and yet again, he is thrown into a world of international intrigue and suspense. And once again, if he wants to get out alive, he will have to pull out all the stops, as his enemies are far more reaching and powerful than ever. *Chesed* balances action, intrigue, and the ruthlessness of the corporate world, with brotherhood and hope, lifting the reader to believe there really could be so much more for all of us. *Coming September 2016*

Timothy Jon Reynolds formerly worked as a criminal investigator for the Dayton Hudson Corporation. In his tenure there, he literally oversaw hundreds of criminal cases of almost every nature. It was there that started writing in his mind — even if he didn't know it at the time. After leaving that career for a safer one, he began working as a manager in the biomedical industry, eventually moving on to owning his own company. Nowadays he travels the northwest as a Sales Manager for the company that bought his, taking in and absorbing the places and people he visits and meets. All as fuel for his stories. His feeling is that writers, "need fresh faces and stories around them constantly, otherwise they will stagnate and the writing will suffer." When he is not traveling, Tim enjoys being a Northern Nevada resident with his wife and children, complete with all the civil liberties that great state provides.

www.ingramcontent.com/pod-product-compliance
Lightning Source LLC
Chambersburg PA
CBHW060140130626
46556CB00006B/2422